MAN ON TWO PONIES

AN EVANS NOVEL OF THE WEST

DON WORCESTER

MAN ON TWO PONIES

M. EVANS & COMPANY, INC.   NEW YORK

Library of Congress Cataloging-in-Publication Data

Worcester, Donald Emmet, 1915-
Man on two ponies / Don Worcester.
p.   cm.—(An Evans novel of the West)
ISBN 0-87131-668-4 : $16.95
I. Title   II. Series.
PS3573.0688M3   1991
813'.54—dc20   91-41370
CIP

M. Evans and Company, Inc.
216 East 49th Street
New York, New York 10017

Manufactured in the United States of America

9   8   7   6   5   4   3   2   1

To Roger Russell (Nas Naga), who gave me the title.

A Word About Sources

The books that were most helpful in keeping the story historically accurate are: George H. Hyde, *A Sioux Chronicle* (University of Oklahoma Press, 1956), Robert W. Mardock, *The Reformers and the American Indians* (University of Missouri Press, 1975), James Mooney, *The Ghost Dance Religion and the Sioux Outbreak of 1890* (14th Annual Report of the Bureau of American Ethnology, 1896), Luther Standing Bear, *My People the Sioux* (Houghton Mifflin Company, 1925), Rex Allen Smith, *Moon of Popping Trees* (Reader's Digest Press, 1975), Robert M. Utley, *The Last Days of the Sioux Nation* (Yale University Press, 1963), and Stanley Vestal, *Sitting Bull: Champion of the Sioux* (Houghton Mifflin Company, 1932).

Chapter One

Wide-eyed, his heart pounding, ten-year-old Running Elk pressed his face against the cold window—the train was rushing headlong at the full moon, which was sitting on the track ahead. He held his breath, but gasped when the train whistle screamed. The moon defied the whistle and seemed to be growing larger—the train couldn't miss it. Trembling, Running Elk glanced quickly at the other Brulé and Oglala boys—all were tensely staring out the windows as if paralyzed by fright. Then Spotted Tail's eighteen-year-old son Stays-at-Home, who had a scar across the bridge of his nose that turned white when he was angry, sang a brave song to mask his fear. "Enemies tremble at my name," he began, and other boys joined in, but their voices weren't convincing. *They know we'll hit the moon and be killed.* Quivering in anticipation, Running Elk sat back, pulled his blanket around him, and closed his eyes—he didn't want to watch.

His thoughts flew back, as they often did, to that day in the Moon of Thunderstorms three summers ago when his father Pawnee Killer had ridden away. Tall, muscular, with the dignity of a fearless warrior, Pawnee Killer had placed his hands on Running Elk's shoulders, his bear claw necklace clicking softly. He wore moccasins and his powerful legs were encased in fringed leggings of elk skin. On his breast were two scars made by tearing through his own flesh to free himself from the Sun Dance pole. To the Brulés, Oglalas, and other Tetons, or Prairie Sioux, Sun Dance scars

1

were a mark of honor, signifying that Pawnee Killer was among the bravest of the brave.

"My son," he said softly, "We may not meet again. Bluecoat soldiers are marching toward our last hunting ground. We must fight them or become like women." He paused, while Running Elk looked up at him, feeling he would burst with love and admiration.

"Take me with you. I can shoot a rifle."

"No, my son. You have seen only seven summers. Your time will come. Be brave always. Remember that it is better to die fighting your enemies than to run and live to be old and feeble."

Across the tipi from them his mother, Scarlet Robe, sat in buckskin blouse and skirt, her oval face bent over the moccasin she was sewing. Her hands stopped moving as she listened, but she didn't turn her head. Leaving Running Elk, Pawnee Killer leaned over her tenderly. "I go," he said, his voice husky.

Scarlet Robe looked up longingly at his face, which had lost its usual stern expression. "Come back to us safely, my man."

As he followed his father from the tipi to watch the warriors ride away on their spirited war ponies, Running Elk glanced back at his mother. She was bent over the moccasin again, but he saw a tear roll down each cheek. Buffalo robe over his shoulder, and holding his Winchester in his right hand, Pawnee Killer headed north with the others. *I want to be a warrior like my father. Nothing else matters.*

Remembering his father's admonition to be brave always, Running Elk forced the moon from his thoughts. Exhausted by the tiresome train ride from Dakota Territory to Pennsylvania, he fell asleep. He didn't awaken until he felt a hand on his shoulder shaking him. Short, stocky round-faced Whistler, his fourteen-year-old friend, leaned over him, nodding toward the window.

"Look back," he said.

Rubbing his tired eyes, Running Elk fearfully peered out the window—the moon was behind them! They'd passed the edge of the earth where the moon rose and hadn't fallen off! What could that mean? He stared at the moon, unbelieving.

Long Chin, or Charles Tackett, a solemn mixed blood of medium height and scraggly beard who was married to Brulé chief Spotted

Tail's daughter Red Road, entered the car. He'd been hired as interpreter for the boys who were to attend the new Indian school at the former cavalry post of Carlisle Barracks in Pennsylvania. Running Elk knew that his father never trusted any interpreter hired by the government, but Long Chin seldom smiled, so maybe he didn't lie.

"We turned west at Harrisburg," Long Chin told the boys in Lakota, the language of the Teton tribes. "That's why the moon is behind us. In the morning we'll be at Carlisle."

I don't want to be at Carlisle. I want to be back at Rosebud. Running Elk thought of that day not many suns ago when he and others had been running races among the tipis near Rosebud Agency. A twelve-year-old boy named Winter, whose forehead was pockmarked and who had an undying curiosity about the whites, joined them.

"There's a big crowd at the agency," he told them. "Let's go see what's going on." He was off on the run, breechcloth sailing behind him.

They trotted after him to the log buildings and saw many Brulé men and women standing outside the council room. The boys boldly walked up to the windows, shielded their eyes with both hands, and pressed their faces against the glass. Seated at a table were two Wasicuns—white men—one a tall army officer with a big nose. With them was a white woman who smiled at the boys and held out sticks of candy with one hand, motioning for them to come in with the other. The boys squealed and ran off to talk about it.

"I wonder why those Wasicuns are here," Running Elk said. "They never bring good news."

"I don't care why they're here," Plenty Kill replied. "I want some of that candy." His father, the mixed blood Standing Bear, had a little store at the agency. Plenty Kill, a long-faced, bright-eyed boy of twelve, who was always among the first in any adventure, led the way. Running Elk brought up the rear. *I'll probably be sorry if I talk to the Wasicuns, but I'd like some candy.* Long Chin met them at the door of the council room.

"Come in boys," he said in Lakota. "I want to show you something." Thinking he meant the candy, they trooped in, but what he showed them were two short-haired, solemn-faced Indian boys dressed like whites. Long Chin nodded toward the tall officer, who forced a smile. There were some men Running Elk instinctively liked at first sight. Captain Richard Henry Pratt was not one of them.

"Captain Pratt asked me to tell you that if you go east to his new school you can learn to talk like whites and wear clothes like these Santee boys," Long Chin continued. "You'd like that, wouldn't you?" Running Elk looked for the candy, but it had disappeared. *Just like the Wasicuns.*

The boys left the room to talk about it. "I'm going to ask my father to let me go," Plenty Kill said. "I know he'll want me to learn to talk like the Wasicuns."

"Mine won't," Running Elk said. "He hates all Wasicuns. I'm sure my mother won't want me to go either. Or my grandfather." Since Pawnee Killer had ridden away three years earlier and had remained in Canada with Sitting Bull after defeating Long Hair Custer on the Greasy Grass, Running Elk and Scarlet Robe had lived with her father, Two Buck Elk, and his wife.

No Brulé parents were willing to send their children far away to learn to talk like the Wasicuns—only the squawmen and mixed bloods were. Captain Pratt then appealed to Spotted Tail. A large, handsome man, a famous warrior, and head chief of the Brulés, he was known as Speak-with-the-Woman because of his attachment to the opposite sex. He had four wives and was "speaking with," or courting, another. Ever since he had been held at Fort Leavenworth for two years, Spotted Tail had refused to fight the whites. "We must get along with them," he often said. "They are more numerous than the leaves on all the trees. If we fight them we will be destroyed." But Spotted Tail, who was able to manipulate agents, didn't allow them to rush his people into becoming made-over whites.

How it happened Running Elk didn't know, but when Captain Pratt hired Long Chin as interpreter for the boys, Spotted Tail agreed to send four of his sons and a granddaughter to the new Carlisle Indian School. "If they learn to read and write and talk like the whites we won't have to rely on government interpreters," he explained. "They lie to us and change our words."

4

Other chiefs and headmen naturally followed Spotted Tail's lead, among them the wrinkled old warrior Two Buck Elk, whose left ear had been disfigured by an enemy arrow. "Grandson," he said, touching the ear as he spoke, "I want you to go with the others. Be brave and learn to talk like the Wasicuns."

Dismayed, Running Elk went to his mother. "I don't want to go. I want to find my father."

Since Pawnee Killer had failed to return Scarlet Robe seldom smiled, and her eyes seemed perpetually sorrowful. She looked at him sadly. "I don't want you to go either, my son, but if your grandfather says you must, we have no choice. I can't stop it; I'm only a woman."

That night Running Elk tied his pony to a stake near the tipi so he wouldn't have to hunt for it. Before dawn he filled a small buckskin bag with dried meat, hoping it would last until he found other Brulés or Oglalas. Taking his bow and arrows, with his blanket over his shoulder, he mounted his pony and rode north. Pawnee Killer was with Sitting Bull's people in Grandmother's Land, and it might take many suns to find him. But it was better to go hungry searching for his father than to be sent far away to the east.

Because his pony had been tied all night, he stopped to let it graze for a time along a stream. He watched it hungrily cropping the tall grass, feeling elated that in a few moons he'd be with his father again. He heard hoofbeats and looked up to see two riders approaching at a trot. In blue jackets and black hats, at a distance they looked like soldiers. As they approached he felt suddenly weak—they were Indian police. He eyed their unsmiling faces with mounting fear. The police worked for the agent, so all fullbloods resented them. Both had pistols strapped to their waists and Winchesters in their scabbards. They stopped their ponies and looked down at Running Elk, hands on the pommels of their saddles, their faces expressionless.

"You come with us," one said.

"I can't. I'm looking for my father."

"Agent says you go to school. You go."

Back at the agency thirty-four boys and girls, including Running Elk, were loaded in wagons along with their families for the journey to Black Pole on the Missouri. The younger children looked frightened; the older girls appeared resigned. The glum expressions on the faces of the older boys made it clear to Running Elk that they would escape if possible. There was little talking as the wagons rolled along over the hills and prairies. The afternoon of the third day they reached Black Pole, where the families huddled together in silence. Oglala children and their parents soon arrived from Pine Ridge Agency. Sick at heart and dreading what was coming, Running Elk kept his eyes on his moccasins, glancing occasionally at uprooted trees floating down the Missouri.

The sun was near the horizon when Whistler shouted, "It's coming! It's coming!" Running Elk looked at the approaching riverboat, with smoke pouring from its stack, then at his mother, who gasped and placed a hand over her quivering lips. He looked wildly around for some place to hide.

"Remember what your father said," Scarlet Robe whispered. "Be brave, my son." Her voice trembled.

The riverboat docked and men lowered the gangway. Long Chin stepped forward. "Come with me, boys," he said.

Heart pounding, Running Elk followed him along with the others, while Red Road and their interpreter brought the girls. Once on deck they spread out along the rail, all anxiously looking at their families. As the sun dropped below the horizon and the last rays turned the clouds red, the mothers began wailing loudly. The girls and small boys cried piteously for their mothers. The boatmen ignored the clamor and pulled in the gangway; the crying on board and ashore grew louder. When a shrill whistle blew overhead all flinched and looked up at it in fear; then the paddlewheel at the stern of the riverboat started turning. Terrified, Running Elk looked at his mother, who stood forlornly on shore weeping as she faded from sight. Running Elk gripped the rail with both hands, leaning forward and straining his eyes.

The boys rolled up in the blankets they wore and tried to sleep on the floor of a big room, but the motion and noise of the paddlewheel kept them awake. In the morning the riverboat docked and they sleepily followed Long Chin ashore. He led them up some steps into a little Wasicun house with two rows of seats covered with fuzzy red cloth and a window by every seat. The girls went into another little house just like it, and there were many more in a long row, all of them resting on strips of steel that stretched as far as Running Elk could see. He was wondering where the Wasicuns slept, when with a sudden jerk the houses all began to move. He leaped to his feet, ready to run to the door.

"Maza Canku!" Stays-at-Home exclaimed. "Iron Road." Running Elk had heard of the Wasicuns' Iron Road, but he had never seen it. The boys sitting by the windows ducked back every time a big pole flashed by as the train picked up speed. Soon it was racing along faster than the swiftest Brulé buffalo ponies. Running Elk's skin tingled at the thought of hurtling through space like an arrow from a bow.

They had traveled on day after day, seeing town after town, eating the strange foods given them, and trying to sleep in their seats. Running Elk was stiff and his muscles ached. When the train stopped in the morning after they'd seen the full moon, Long Chin entered the car. "This is Carlisle," he told them. "Everybody off." *My father is farther away than ever. How will I ever see him again?*

Wearily they trudged the two miles from the railroad to Carlisle Barracks, a number of two-story brick buildings surrounded by a high brick wall with an iron gate. The untrampled grass around the buildings made it clear they hadn't been lived in for years, and there was an air of lifelessness about them that reminded Running Elk of abandoned cabins he'd seen. Ghost houses! He felt gooseflesh on his arms as he stared at them.

Long Chin led the boys into one of the silent buildings, while the girls followed Red Road and their interpreter into another. Tired and sleepy, the boys ran into the building, eager to lie down on beds like the Wasicuns used. They ran from room to room, upstairs and down, but all were empty. Long Chin left them for a time, then returned and herded them into a big room on the first floor that had a cast-iron stove in the center. Running Elk glanced around the empty room, then at Long Chin.

"This is where you'll sleep," he told them. "I've just learned that none of the supplies Captain Pratt ordered have arrived, not even the food." Murmurs of protest arose.

"We're hungry," the pockmarked Winter said.

Long Chin held out his hands, palms up, and shrugged. "There's nothing I can do about it. I'm hungry too, but we'll just have to get along the best we can."

Running Elk and the others wandered hungrily among the buildings. People came from the town and stared at them like they were strange animals. Some smiled and tried to talk to them, but no one could understand what they said. When a woman offered Running Elk a piece of candy, hungry though he was he ran to the stables and kept out of sight. Stomachs empty, and with only the blankets they wore, they tried to sleep on the floor that night. It was the Moon of Falling Leaves and the air was cold, but there was no fire in the stove.

After a breakfast of bread and water the next morning, again there was nothing for them to do but wander around the old cavalry post. Running Elk thought of his mother, wondering if she still cried for him, and if she'd cut off her hair like the Tetons did when some family member died. *I might as well be dead.*

At midday all of the children gathered around the door of the room where they'd eaten breakfast, sniffing the strange odors that came from the kitchen. When a woman came out and rang a bell, all dashed in, the oldest boys first. They sat at long tables where the food had already been dished out onto plates.

Running Elk stared at the two carrots and small piece of fatty meat on his plate. He picked up the meat and nibbled it, wondering what it might be but certain it wasn't beef. Closing his eyes, he chewed it up and swallowed it. Meat was the main food of the Tetons, and he hungered for more, no matter what it was. He looked left and right to see what others were doing.

With fork in hand, his friend Whistler was chewing on a piece of carrot, and Running Elk knew from his expression that he didn't like it. With his own fork he cut off a piece of carrot and put it in his mouth as cautiously as if it had been a live coal. Not liking the taste, he swallowed it whole, which brought tears to his eyes. Somehow he ate both carrots. Still famished, he looked at the others. All eyes were on the kitchen door. *They're as hungry as I am, and there's nothing more to eat. They intend to starve us to death.* He remembered the times he'd squatted in his mother's tipi, eating his fill of beef or venison that had been roasting on a stake over the fire. His stomach protested.

"Captain Pratt has requested that you be given regular army rations," Long Chin told them when they reluctantly went outside. "He told them you can't be expected to learn on empty stomachs. The food will soon be better."

The afternoon seemed longer than usual, for they had nothing to do but think about food and mourn for their families. When the sun finally neared the horizon, Running Elk felt more homesick than ever. In his mind he pictured the riverboat pulling away from shore while his mother cried for him, and a lump rose in his throat. After dark they rolled up in their blankets in the cheerless room, too unhappy to talk. Then Stays-at-Home and others sang brave songs. In their building the girls heard them and wailed loudly. Running Elk bit his lips to keep from sobbing like a girl.

On the third day Long Chin brought them big sacks with slits in them. "These are your mattresses to sleep on," he told them. Running Elk looked at the thin cloth—it wouldn't be any better than the bare floor. After he had handed them out, Long Chin continued. "Out behind the stables is a haystack. Go there and fill these with hay."

In the morning Long Chin took them to the schoolroom, which had rows of desks and chairs facing a blackboard. A white woman in a long blue dress—Long Chin said she was their teacher—stood in front of the blackboard, smiling nervously at them. Running Elk recognized her and frowned; she was the one who had offered them candy. Finally she turned and made some white marks on the blackboard.

"Those are white men's names," Long Chin told them. "Each one is different. You will choose one, and that will be your name hereafter."

Running Elk glanced at the other boys to see their reactions. All looked as shocked as he was. Having Wasicun names! He couldn't imagine what that might mean. If his old name was dead, would he be someone else? If he had a Wasicun name, when he died he might not be allowed to travel the Spirit Trail that all dead Tetons followed to the Spirit Land. Even worse, he might have to go where the Wasicuns went. *I don't want a Wasicun name.*

When the teacher finished writing the names she faced the class, holding a long pointed stick in one hand. Long Chin beckoned to Running Elk to come forward. Reluctantly, dreading what he might have to do, Running Elk dragged himself up to the teacher, who handed him the stick. He reached for it like it was a sleeping snake, holding it gingerly in his moist right hand, not knowing what to do with it.

"Touch the name you want," Long Chin ordered. Running Elk looked at the other boys, wishing they could tell him if it was right to take a Wasicun name, but they stared at him blankly.

"Hurry up," Long Chin said. "Don't take all day about it." Not knowing what any of the names were, Running Elk touched one of the shorter ones. The teacher wrote the name on a tape, sewed it to the back of his buckskin shirt, then erased the marks so no other boy could choose the same name. Running Elk returned to his seat, wondering if his new name would make him feel and even speak like a Wasicun.

One after another, each boy touched a name without any idea what name he was choosing. When all were back in their seats the teacher held up a piece of paper, said something, lowered it, then looked at them as if expecting a reply.

"She's calling roll," Long Chin told them. "When she calls your name you must stand up and say 'present.' " Since no one knew his name, nobody answered. The teacher walked around the room looking at the names on the shirts, then stopped by Running Elk. "Billy," she said.

"That's your name. You're now Billy Pawnee Killer," Long Chin told him. "Stand up and say 'present.' " This continued until all the names had been called. Stays-at-Home was now William Spotted Tail. The chief's other sons were Talks-with-the-Bear, now Oliver; Bugler, now Max; and Little Scout, now Pollock. The adventuresome Plenty Kills, now Luther Standing Bear, was the only one who seemed to be pleased to have a Wasicun name. It took several days for all to know their new names.

One morning Long Chin brought with him to the schoolroom a large burly man who looked like a mixed blood and who held a short, heavy strap in his hand. "This is your disciplinarian," Long Chin told them. "His name is Campbell, and he will punish anyone who makes trouble. I advise you to do whatever you're told."

Billy and the others looked at the man, hardly believing what they'd heard. Tetons never punished children beyond expressing disapproval. Campbell stared at them unsmiling, his brawny arms folded, the strap dangling from one hand. He looked mean.

After school that afternoon Long Chin and a red-faced man with short gray hair met them outside the building. The man stood stiffly erect, hands by his sides. "This man is a former soldier," Long Chin explained. "He's going to teach you how to march like they do in the army. Line up in two rows."

March like the hated bluecoats after his father had fought them! Billy clamped his jaw shut, clenched his fists, and folded his arms across his chest. This was too much. He took his time getting into one of the lines.

Through Long Chin the old soldier told them which was left and which was right. "When I say 'left,' lift your left foot, then put it down. When I say 'right,' do the same with the right foot. Keep your hands by your sides," he told them.

Defiantly Billy stood with his arms folded, both feet on the ground as the others marched in place. He was so angry he didn't hear Campbell approaching behind him until he was yanked from the line and felt the strap across his back. Then he was flung back into the line, falling to his knees against Julian Whistler. Julian helped him to his feet. "Do as he says," he whispered in Lakota. Soon they were keeping in step and turning and stopping on command. Thereafter they marched to meals and to school, looking as downcast as prisoners of war.

A few days later Long Chin announced their hair would be cut the next day. Cutting hair was a sign of mourning among the Tetons. *I don't want my hair cut, even though we have much reason to mourn.* That evening the older boys held council to discuss it.

"If I'm here to learn to talk like a Wasicun," the slender, square-jawed Oglala Robert American Horse said grimly, holding a braid in each hand, I can do it better like this, with my hair on."

"Hau!" the others said in agreement.

The next morning they saw a man with a long mustache carrying a big chair into a room in the school building. Billy watched nervously as Long Chin led one of the younger boys out of the room. The teacher was writing the alphabet on the blackboard, but he ignored her. Soon the boy returned, eyes lowered in shame, his hair cut off clear to the scalp.

"You're next," Long Chin said. Billy's legs felt numb as he followed Long Chin into the other room. The man with the long mustache stood behind the chair, holding a pair of clippers in his hand. On the floor beside him was a small pile of hair in two little braids. Campbell stood nearby, strap in hand.

"Get in the chair," Long Chin ordered.

"No! I don't want my hair cut!"

"Captain Pratt's orders. There's nothing you can do about it, so get in the chair and keep quiet."

"No!" Billy shouted. At that Campbell grabbed his arms and pinned them behind his back while he struggled to free himself. Angrily Campbell threw him to the floor and lashed him repeatedly. Finally Billy stopped struggling, choking back sobs. Campbell sat him down hard in the chair, while the barber quickly clipped off his hair.

Eyes on the floor, Billy limped back to his seat, the welts on his back throbbing painfully. *If I had a knife I'd kill him.* The others had heard his cries, and all quietly submitted to the indignity of having their long hair cut off. That night Billy slept fitfully, for he kept feeling his scalp. Losing his name had been bad, but losing his hair was worse. *Will there be anything left of me that is still Brulé? Would my father know me now?*

A few days later a wagon arrived with a load of big boxes. "You're going to wear white men's clothes," Long Chin told the boys. "Carry these to the room." The older boys carried the boxes, while the younger ones chattered excitedly, eager to see their new clothes. They crowded around Long Chin while he opened the boxes. Curious, Billy watched out of the corner of his eye, not wanting to appear eager.

Starting with red flannel underwear, Long Chin held up a garment in front of each boy until he had made an approximate fit. The same process was repeated for gray pants, coats, vests, and dark gray shirts. Each boy also received socks, heavy boots, suspenders, and a cap. None of the clothing fitted well, but most of the boys were too excited to notice. The boots squeaked when they walked; some of the younger boys walked around the room after lights out for the pleasure of hearing their boots. Billy wasn't amused. *I'm glad my father can't see me. He'd probably think I'm a Wasicun.*

When they arose next morning, Billy started to dress. "Do the pants button in front or in back?" he asked.

"In front," one boy replied.

"No, in back," said another. Fortunately, a few of the boys had slept in their clothes and showed them where the pants buttoned.

What else can they do to make us forget we're Tetons? We have Wasicun names, our hair has been cut, we march like blue-coats, and now we dress like Wasicuns. The thought of being made over to look like a Wasicun filled Billy with resentment and worry. Like the others, he was painfully homesick, and it seemed that every day the world of the Tetons was farther away. After they learned to say a few simple sentences, Pratt announced that anyone heard speaking Sioux thereafter would be punished. That meant there was little talking if anyone was near, and they were more lonesome than ever. When no one was in sight, Billy spoke quietly to Julian in Lakota. "I don't want to forget how to talk like a Brulé," he said. "What will my father think if I can only talk like a Wasicun?" The round-faced, usually good natured Julian looked sad.

"I wish none of us had come here. Our people will despise us when they see us."

Forty-seven forlorn Pawnee, Kiowa, and Cheyenne children arrived one day. Although the Brulés and Pawnees had been deadly enemies in the old days, Billy almost felt sorry for them.

Eventually each boy had an army cot, a wooden box for clothes, and a chair. Then they were given strange-looking shirts. "These are nightshirts," Long Chin told them. "At bedtime, take off your clothes and wear these to sleep in."

"Why do they give us so many things to look after?" Paul Black Bear grumbled. He was always late getting ready for the inspections Captain Pratt held every Sunday morning. Billy was wondering what his father would say if he saw him dressed like a woman. He'd probably think the Wasicuns had turned his son into a girl.

That night they put on their nightshirts just before lights out at nine o'clock then tiptoed outside to scamper around barefooted on the cold grass. In the loose-fitting garment and with no disciplinarian watching, for a few delightful moments Billy felt almost free. Then they heard Pratt's office door open and dashed inside. Billy was sure Pratt saw them, but he never mentioned it.

"You're all going to work in shops with white craftsmen," Pratt told them one morning in the Moon of Hairless Calves. "This is Carlisle Indian *Industrial* School, and the main reason you're here is to learn a trade. When you leave you'll be able to work and support your families like white men do. The government is tired of feeding you Indians in idleness, so the sooner you learn to do something useful the better. It doesn't matter how much English you know if you can work with your hands."

Told he would learn to make harness for work horses, William Spotted Tail exploded, and the scar across his nose became livid. When Campbell came for him he fought back. "Kill him! Kill him!" Billy shouted in Lakota as the two grappled, but Campbell was too strong. Sullenly Willian went to the harness shop, with Campbell following. Not wanting to taste the strap again, Billy hurried to the carpenter shop with Julian. Robert American Horse was in the smithy, and Luther Standing Bear was put in the tinshop. Others learned bricklaying or tailoring.

Each new thing that happened to them made Billy more desperate. Losing their names and their hair, then having to dress like Wasicuns and march like the hated bluecoats was almost more than he could stand. Now they were being forced to work like Wasicun laborers, something no proud warrior would submit to even to save his life. The shame of it all could never be washed away. *They're trying to kill the Indian in us on purpose, but what will be left? I want to be a Brulé warrior like my father, not a Wasicun carpenter*. Glumly he learned to measure and saw boards squarely, and to drive nails straight.

School continued afternoons, and they learned new words, the numbers, and geography. One day the teacher showed them a round object painted in several colors. "This is a globe," she told them. "It's just like the earth, which makes a complete turn on its axis every day. Like this." She spun the globe. The boys looked at one another and smiled. Everyone knew the earth was flat and had four corners, and it didn't turn. And she thought it was round and spinning all the time. That was amusing. Wasicuns were silly.

"It can't be like she says," Julian said after school. "If the earth turned upside down every night, everyone would fall off and there wouldn't be anybody left. Flies can walk upside down. People aren't flies."

"Hau," the others said. Billy was sure they were right.

In the Moon of Frost on the Tipi, the teacher brought a white-haired man in a dark suit and shiny black shoes to class. "He's an astronomer," she explained. "He studies the stars through a telescope, and he has something to tell you."

The man cleared his throat. "A most interesting celestial phenomenon will transpire next Wednesday night at nine-thirty," he said. Billy and the others stared at him with puzzled expressions. "Excuse me. I forgot you're Indians. What I mean is that the earth will pass between the sun and the moon. The earth's shadow will cover the moon briefly, cutting off its light. It's called a lunar eclipse." The boys smiled. The funny looking Wasicun couldn't know what he was talking about.

The night of the eclipse was clear, and the children stood on the grass outside the buildings after lights out and gazed at the full moon. Billy wondered how long they would have to wait in the cold before they knew nothing would happen. But when the earth's shadow began crossing the moon, he clapped hand to mouth in surprise. All watched awestruck as the moon's light was gradually blotted out. Billy expected the older boys to sing brave songs, but no one made a sound. When the moon began to emerge from the earth's shadow, however, the younger children chattered gleefully and pointed their fingers. The moon had died and come to life again! Billy exhaled deeply. *From now on I'll believe what the teacher tells us. The earth is round, not flat. Somehow people don't fall off.* He couldn't imagine how the astronomer knew there would be an eclipse at exactly the time he said. Either it was magic or white people know a lot of strange things.

In the Moon of Ripe Berries, which the whites called June, the first school year ended, and Pratt planned a big celebration. Spotted Tail, Two Strike, Black Crow, and two other Brulé headmen, dressed in their finest buckskin shirts and leggings, stopped at Carlisle on their way to Washington. From Pine Ridge Agency came Red Cloud and several other Oglala chiefs in their finery to take part in the ceremonies. There were also a number of well-dressed white ladies and a man with a camera. Captain Pratt was the center of attention, and he kept the chiefs around him, giving them no opportunity to talk to their sons. Billy couldn't tell from their solemn faces what they thought of the school.

The chiefs were nearly ready to depart for Washington when Spotted Tail demanded to see his sons. "Can you talk like Wasicuns?" he asked as Billy listened.

"Only a little bit," William answered, rubbing the scar on his nose, "but they've given us all Wasicun names and they make us go to church on Sundays." Spotted Tail frowned.

"If you're not learning to speak, what are you learning?"

"To make harness for horses." Spotted Tail's face turned black, like he was strangling.

"Make what?" He was almost shouting.

"Harness for work horses," William said, hanging his head.

"Why?"

"There's a man they call the disciplinarian. If we don't do what they say, he beats us with a leather strap. We hate it here. Take us home."

His younger brothers echoed his plea. "Yes, yes. Take us home!"

Spotted Tail charged off to where Pratt was standing, the interpreter trotting to keep up with him. The boys followed to hear what Spotted Tail said. Pratt, who was accustomed to bullying helpless Indians and who flew into a rage when anyone opposed him, tried to browbeat the most powerful chief of the Brulés but was shouted down. Red Cloud and the other chiefs came, and all supported Spotted Tail. The white ladies looked shocked. Then, leaving Pratt helplessly fuming, the chiefs departed for Washington.

"I hope your father comes back and takes us all home," Billy said to William later.

"Forget it," Long Chin told him. "You won't see them again. Captain Pratt is asking the Indian Commissioner to send them home by another route. He doesn't want them here again."

Chapter Two

The chiefs did return, and Billy's hopes rose when Spotted Tail demanded a council with everyone present. Pratt objected to including the boys, but Spotted Tail brushed his objections aside. Since the chiefs had to speak through interpreters, the boys knew all that was said.

Pratt sat scowling as the grim-faced Spotted Tail rose to speak. "We sent our sons, the sons of chiefs, to learn to talk like whites," he said, pausing for the interpreter. "Instead you make them work like common Wasicun laborers. You have them beaten—the Tetons do not beat children. You are an evil man!" Red Cloud, American Horse, and Two Strike echoed Spotted Tail. Pratt had lied to them. His school should be destroyed.

When the others had finished speaking, Spotted Tail arose again. "I am taking all of the Brulé children home," he said. He turned to the boys. "All of you get ready." Red Cloud nodded to the Oglala boys—they were also to go home. Thrilled, Billy glanced at Pratt, wondering what he'd say. Pratt's face was white—if all of the Teton children left his school would have to close. Elated, Billy dashed to the room, undressed, and put on the shirt, leggings, and moccasins he'd worn when he arrived. Ignoring Pratt's orders, all were talking and joking in Lakota. Soon they'd be on the train heading for home. Billy felt like singing.

He looked up to see the solemn Long Chin standing in the doorway, and he had the same sinking feeling he'd felt that morning when the two Indian police rode up. Before a word was uttered, he knew that Long Chin brought bad news. The blood seemed to drain out of his body, and his skin felt suddenly cold.

"Get back into your school clothes. You're not going home, at least right now." All looked at him with shocked expressions.

"Why not?" the round-faced Julian asked.

Long Chin explained that a big man in Washington, Secretary of the Interior Carl Schurz, had wired forbidding Spotted Tail and Red Cloud from taking the Teton children. Billy waited anxiously the next few days while telegrams flew back and forth between Pratt and the secretary, whose warnings were relayed to the chiefs. When told that the Secretary of the Interior demanded that they leave their children at Carlisle, all but Spotted Tail backed down.

"My sons are going home with me," he said grimly. "No one is going to stop them. And I will get the rest of them away from here as soon as I can."

Billy watched as Spotted Tail's sons ran to his side, wishing he could join them. The other chiefs and headmen surrounded father and sons like buffalo bulls protecting cows with newborn calves from wolves. Campbell stood nearby, wolflike, ready to grab one of the boys if he could. Before Pratt could order men to guard the gate, Billy slipped through it and ran the two miles to the station as if his life depended on it. The train was on a siding, and three men stood near the engine, but they ignored Billy.

Looking toward the school, Billy saw the chiefs coming in carriages. Still panting hard, he felt a wave of fear when he saw Campbell following them. He dashed into a car and crouched under a seat, trying to make himself small and invisible. His heart was pounding and sweat poured from his face as he prayed to Wakan Tanka, the god of the Tetons. "Help me, Grandfather," he breathed. "Don't let him find me." He heard voices, then heavy steps in the aisle, and knew no Brulé walked that way. He tried to shrink farther under the seat.

A powerful hand jerked him to his feet, and he found himself face to face with a scowling Campbell. Holding Billy's arm with one hand, he raised the strap with the other. Outside the car Spotted Tail and the others prepared to board the train. Campbell lowered the whip and dragged Billy out the door at the other end of the car. "Wait till I get you where they can't hear you squall," he snarled. "I'll teach you to run away." He kept his promise.

After his beating Billy staggered to the stables, the welts on his back throbbing painfully. His shirt seemed to be sticking to his skin, and he wondered if it was from blood. He took it off, and with swollen eyes was trying to see over his shoulder when he heard voices.

"Oh, what he did to your back," a girl's voice said. He turned and saw Mollie Deer-in-Timber, hand over her mouth. She was a dainty girl of ten with small hands, fairly light skin, and wide, expressive eyes. With her was another Brulé girl her age. Embarrassed to have them see him, Billy could only stammer, "Go away and leave me alone."

"I'll get something to put on it," Mollie said. "Don't move. Wait right here." The two ran off. Billy didn't know whether to leave or stay as she'd commanded. He was putting on his shirt, trying to make up his mind, when they returned.

"Take it off," Mollie ordered. He obeyed, wondering why he let a little girl tell him what to do. He still wished they hadn't seen him. He felt her small hands gently rubbing something soothing into the cuts on his back and shoulders. "Does that feel better?" she asked when she finished. He had to admit that it did, but he didn't care to talk about it.

For an exhilarating moment it had seemed that he might escape, but now he might as well be dead. The painful welts on his back were nothing compared to the ache in his heart. *I was so close to escaping, so close.* He imagined himself lashing Campbell to a tree, giving him a taste of his own strap until he screamed, then shooting him full of arrows, but taking care not to kill him too quickly and end his agony. Now only one hope remained, that Spotted Tail would have them all sent home.

A week after the chiefs left, Long Chin and the girls' interpreter met them when they came outside following supper. "Captain Pratt has arranged for most of you boys to work on farms around here for the summer and learn about farming. Men with wagons will be here for you in the morning." The girls' interpreter announced that they would live with families in Carlisle and other towns to learn housekeeping.

"That means we'll be alone among Wasicuns all summer," square-jawed Robert American Horse said. "No one told our fathers we'd have to do that. I don't want to learn farming. It's woman's work. The other things they make us do are bad enough."

Long Chin shrugged. "Captain Pratt's orders. Says it's for your own good." He left before there were other complaints. The boys and girls wandered aimlessly around in the late afternoon sun. Running Elk was thinking about what Long Chin had said when he was suddenly aware that Mollie Deer-in-Timber was by his side. He hoped she wouldn't remind him of his beating. He didn't want to talk to her but he looked at her face and into her large, soft eyes. *They're like a doe's eyes.*

"I'll be with a family in Carlisle," she said, gently steering him toward the shade of an ancient elm. "I hope there'll be girls my age." Billy said nothing. "I'm glad we'll be living with Wasicuns. My mother told me we should learn everything we can from them so we can teach our people to do things the way they do."

"I don't want to learn to do things like a Wasicun. If they had left us alone we could still live in the old way. I don't want to forget I'm a Brulé. I want to be a warrior like my father."

She knelt in the grass. Billy looked at the boys, hoping Julian would signal him to come, but he was talking to others. Since Mollie was looking up expectantly at him, Billy squatted uncomfortably beside her. *She should be a teacher. She knows how to make you do whatever she wants.*

"My mother says there won't be warriors any more, now that we're on the reservation. She says we have to learn to do things the way Wasicuns do. That's why Captain Pratt started this school."

Billy chewed a blade of grass. It was disturbing to hear a Brulé, and a girl at that, saying such things. What was most troubling was the nagging thought that she was probably right, but he didn't want to think about it.

The prospect of living with Wasicuns, away from all Tetons, was disturbing even if, as Mollie said, he could learn useful things from them. Monday morning, thinking about Spotted Tail's sons, he glumly climbed into a wagon with other boys. The girls were watching and waving, Mollie among them. He started to wave back, then saw that none of the other boys were responding, so he pretended to be stretching his arm.

Soon they were on a country road among cornfields and orchards. The driver stopped at one farm after another, checked his list, then escorted a Brulé or Oglala boy to the house. At one farm he beckoned to Billy. "Hop down," he said. "You go here with Henry Purvis." He knocked on the door of a neatly painted farm house. A pleasant-faced woman opened the door, then finished drying her hands on her apron.

"Here's yer Injun, ma'am," the driver said. "Name of Billy Pawnee Killer."

"Henry," the woman called over her shoulder, "Billy is here." She held the door open while he slowly entered. He was still envying Spotted Tail's sons, and the corners of his mouth were turned down. He didn't know enough English to carry on much of a conversation if he'd felt like talking. He wanted only to be left alone, but there was no hope of that. "I'm glad to see you, Billy," the woman said. "We've been looking forward to meeting you."

Henry was a stocky man of middle height with graying hair and a brown beard. His skin was weathered, his muscles hardened by daily work, his expression placid. Mild and good-natured, he was frugal as well as hard-working, neither extravagant nor tight-fisted. He held out his hand like all Wasicuns did, so Billy limply extended his own.

Mrs. Purvis was a kindly woman whose graying hair was tied in a ball at the back of her head. Like his own mother, she was never idle, always cooking or sewing. Billy never saw her without her apron except on Sundays, when they went to church in the morning and sat in rocking chairs on the porch in the afternoon.

Louise, their blue-eyed daughter who stayed with them summers when not teaching, wore her blonde hair in two braids. She always put on a sunbonnet when she went outside to shield her white skin form the rays of the sun. She reminded Billy a little of his teacher at Carlisle, but he didn't want to be reminded of that.

Billy found he couldn't dislike any of them, but he still didn't want to be there—he wanted to be at Rosebud. He felt lonely, all by himself among Wasicuns. He wondered if his mother still remembered him, and if his father had returned from Canada. *Will I ever see them again?*

The first chore Billy learned was to harness the huge horses and hitch them to the wagon. Then Henry taught him to drive the team along the winrows while he pitched hay onto the wagon. It was exciting driving the big team, but it was still Wasicun work, and Billy tried not to feel proud.

"Billy catches on fast," Henry said as they ate ham, sweet corn, string beans, and mashed potatoes at supper time. Mrs. Purvis placed a glass of milk by Billy's plate. He looked at her questioningly. "Haven't you ever drunk milk?" He shook his head. "Drink it. It's good for you and I know you'll like it." He drank a little and had to agree that she was right. He had second helpings of everything. All of this was followed by a slice of apple pie with a piece of cheese on it. Billy had to admit that farmers ate well even though they had to work hard.

After supper, while Henry read and his wife sewed, Louise showed Billy one of her school books. "You know the alphabet, of course." He recited it. "Let's see what words you know." She pointed to a list, and he read the ones he recognized, wondering why he didn't pretend he knew nothing. Soon she had him learning new words and reading sentences. "You learn quickly," she told him. "By the time you go back to Carlisle I bet you'll be way ahead of the others."

Reminding him of Carlisle was a mistake. "I don't want to go back there ever," he said, scowling. "They beat us and make us work like Wasicuns. I hate it. I'd rather be dead." As he thought of Campbell his face contorted, and his fingers opened and closed like he was grasping for something. Louise quickly changed the subject.

"Let me read you a story about Hansel and Gretel," she said.

Soon he was worrying about their troubles and momentarily forgot his own. *Learning to read may not be a bad thing.* By the end of the summer he felt at home with the Purvis family, and under Louise's guidance he actually enjoyed reading. That frightened him a little. *I'm getting to be like a Wasicun.* He wondered what Mollie Deer-in-Timber would think of that.

"You're welcome to come back every summer," Mrs. Purvis told him in the Moon of Yellow Leaves when he had to return to Carlisle. "Henry and I never had a son of our own before." He felt embarrassed but also warm inside when she gave him a farewell hug.

Louise patted his shoulder. "Keep on with your reading, Billy. It's the road to knowledge." He promised he would.

Earlier he'd hated the idea of returning to Carlisle, but when he thought of Mollie Deer-in-Timber he forgot about it. When he saw her she looked even prettier than he remembered. "I can read much better now," he told her the first time they had an opportunity to talk. "I like to read. Do you think I'm getting too much like a Wasicun? What did you learn?"

She ignored the first question. "I can follow recipes and bake pies and cakes," she said proudly. "Some day I'll bake a cake for you."

The second year the boys in the tailor shop made uniforms for all. They were blue with two thin red stripes down the outside seams of the pants. Some of the boys were proud to wear them, but they reminded Billy of the bluecoat soldiers who had forced the Tetons to live on the Great Sioux Reserve. *It's just one more Wasicun trick to make us forget who we are.*

The year passed uneventfully. Billy recalled Spotted Tail's promise to get them all away, and waited for word that he had succeeded. Sunday afternoons he walked around the post with Mollie or sat under the elms, happy to be with her even though they might sit in silence. He spent a second summer on the Purvis farm; his reading and speaking improved considerably and Louise got him into the habit of reading newspapers. In the Moon of Ripe Plums, a few months over a year after the chiefs' visit, Long Chin received a letter from the Brulé agent.

"My God!" he exclaimed. "Crow Dog murdered Spotted Tail! I'll have to tell Red Road her father's dead." Long Chin learned later that Crow Dog and White Thunder hoped to replace Spotted Tail as head chief, and so Crow Dog shot him. *There goes our only hope of getting away from here. That means two more years.* Billy remembered Pratt's promise to the families that he'd send their children home after four years.

The third year Pratt sent men to the agencies to recruit more Sioux children, but because of Spotted Tail's action and the fact that several children had died at Carlisle, no family responded. Billy was shocked one day in October to see about fifty unhappy Teton children being herded to the school by two men and a woman. Inside the gate the men left the children and headed for Pratt's office.

"Why did your parents let you come?" Billy asked White Crow, a sad-looking Brulé boy he had known. "Don't they know about this place?" White Crow looked around desperately, as if wanting to hide.

"They know, and they refused to allow us to come. But the agent had the police waylay us. When our fathers protested he threatened to cut off their rations and let them starve."

One morning in November Billy saw Pratt leaving in a hurry and looking grim. "Is someone in his family sick?" he asked Long Chin.

"Not quite, but he's about as upset. Some people heard about the disciplinarian beating children and they got Congress to introduce a bill doing away with disciplinarians at all Indian schools." Billy had steered clear of Campbell after the first year, but others hadn't been so fortunate.

"That's good news."

"Not to Captain Pratt, it ain't. He's on his way to Washington to tell them if the bill passes it will mean the end of schools like Carlisle. They won't want to cause that, so they'll likely drop it. Too bad. I don't hold with beatings." He was right; the bill was withdrawn.

In March Long Chin received another letter from the Brulé agent. "Got news for you," he told Billy. "The Brulés and Oglalas who've been with Sitting Bull in Canada and at Standing Rock Agency are now back at Rosebud and Pine Ridge. Pawnee Killer is among 'em.''

One more year and I'll be with my father. I hope he won't be ashamed of me. I know that every day I'm getting more like a Wasicun. I don't want to—I can't help it.

In May of the fourth year Billy was counting the days until the school term ended, thrilled that at last he'd be going home. *I wish I could grow long hair before my father sees me, but I can't wait for that.* Finally in June the day came, and Pratt assembled the first group of Teton students.

"I promised your parents to send you home after four years," he said. "The four years are up, and tomorrow you can go. We've taught you enough to hold jobs and earn your living, but if any of you want to stay longer, you're welcome to remain two more years."

That night after supper the boys talked gleefully of going home. The adventuresome Luther Standing Bear was silent. "Aren't you glad to be leaving?" Billy asked him.

"I'm not going. A man named Wanamaker who has a big store in Philadelphia wants one or two of us to come work for him. Captain Pratt recommended me." He seemed pleased.

Robert American Horse, who had also been silent, now spoke. "My father sent word he wants me to stay." His father, the Oglala chief American Horse, was considered the greatest orator of all the Tetons. "He wants me to be able to talk in Wasicun like he does in Lakota. I must do as he wishes."

Clarence Three Stars, another Oglala, admitted that he also intended to stay. "It's not bad here once you get used to it," he explained. That was true, Billy had to admit, for he'd gotten accustomed to the school routine, and keeping busy had made him forget to be unhappy. Seeing Mollie Deer-in-Timber every day helped him even more.

"The reason I'm staying," Clarence confessed, "is that Maggie Stands-Looking wants to become a teacher. If she stays, I stay."

Billy pondered that. He'd never thought he'd consider for a moment staying one day longer than necessary, but he understood

Clarence's predicament. *Would I stay if Mollie Deer-in-Timber stayed?* He shook his head, glad he didn't have to make that decision.

With hands trembling from joy, Billy bundled up his possessions after breakfast the next morning. He'd waited for this moment longer than he cared to remember. Now it had come! Soon he'd put Carlisle out of his mind, and with his father's help become a Brulé warrior. It seemed too good to be true. He felt a sudden chill on the back of his neck and looked around. Campbell stood in the doorway, frowning down at Billy.

"You can unpack," he said gruffly. "The agent wrote that your father stays with other hostiles and is considered a trouble-maker. Captain Pratt says you're not to go back to him and waste all the good training he's given you. You're to remain two more years." He turned and left.

Billy's numb fingers dropped his bundle. He couldn't believe it. Two more years! By then it will be too late. He thought of the two boys who had died at Carlisle and almost envied them. He considered hiding on the train, then remembered the beating he'd gotten the first time he tried that. Feeling sick, he hid in the stables, not wanting to see the others leave. He heard Mollie and Julian both calling his name, but he didn't reply.

Once the others were gone, Billy resigned himself to remaining two more years. People in the community had given books to the school library, and he spent most of his free time reading books like Cooper's *The Last of the Mohicans* and Scott's *Ivanhoe*. He soon discovered that reading helped make the time pass quickly.

Most of all he missed seeing Mollie Deer-in-Timber. *I should have said goodbye to her instead of acting crazy. Tomorrow I'll write her and tell her I miss her.* "Dear Mollie," he wrote, "I wish you were still here." *No, I wish I was at Rosebud.* He scratched out the line and tried again. Finally he crumpled up the paper and gave up.

He was in the library reading as usual when Long Chin looked in. "Always got your nose in a book, don't you? You're more of a Wasicun than I am,'' Long Chin told him. ''You could probably teach at one of the reservation schools if you wanted to.''

Shocked, Billy thought about that, and realized that what Long Chin said was true. Wearing Wasicun clothes, having his hair short, and reading regularly now seemed natural to him. He'd even forgotten the Brulé way of doing things. He knew the Wasicun words for the days and months, but he had trouble recalling the Teton names of the moons. It had happened so gradually he hadn't been fully aware of the change in him. Now it was too late. Even though he longed to be a real Brulé, he was comfortable living like a Wasicun.

At sixteen Billy was a few inches under six feet, but not heavy-set like many Brulés. His face was handsome, but after the years at Carlisle the corners of his mouth were usually turned down, giving him a slightly sullen look. He could speak and read English as well as most interpreters, but he'd forgotten many Lakota words. It had been nine years since he'd watched his father ride away; he still remembered that day vividly, but most memories of Rosebud had become hazy.

With his clothes in the cheap suitcase he'd been given, and the carpenter's tool box he'd made that contained a saw, hammer, ruler, and a few chisels the carpenter had donated, he set out on the long train ride to Valentine, Nebraska, thirty miles from the Rosebud Agency. On the way he thought of the day two years earlier when the others had been sent home. *If I'd returned then, I might still be a Brulé.* Now I'm more Wasicun than Indian. I wonder if my father even knows I'm alive.

When the train puffed to a stop in Valentine, he picked up his suitcase and toolbox, left the car, and walked toward the little station. *This is what I've wanted for years. I should be excited and eager to get to Rosebud, but I'm not.*

Waiting for him was Joe Smith, a slow-talking mixed blood with a broken front tooth, who he remembered as an agency employee. ''Agent sent me to meet you,'' he said leading the way to a buckboard with a pair of Indian ponies hitched to it. Billy put his gear in the back of the wagon, then climbed up and sat by Smith.

In a way it reminded him of the wagon trip to the Missouri six years before. Then they'd all been scared witless, not knowing what awaited them. Now he was going among Brulés looking like a Wasicun, knowing what to expect, and he dreaded that as much as he had earlier feared the unknown.

"You don't look like no Brulé to me," Smith said, "especially you don't look like no son of ole Pawnee Killer. He's what they call irreconcilable, and I reckon he always will be. Stays with others like him and avoids all whites. They still consider him a likely trouble-maker."

Most of the way they rode in silence, while the ponies trotted and the buckboard bumped along over the rough road. Billy gazed at the distant hills and the open stretches of prairie grass on every side. His pulse quickened when he caught sight of a buck antelope flashing its white rump in warning to others, then saw a dozen of them scamper away. The land seemed much vaster and the sky bluer than he remembered. *I should never have left this land. Once I belonged here too, like the antelope. But it's no place for an imitation Wasicun with the skin and heart of a Brulé. But where do I belong? Nowhere?* The thought troubled him.

As they traveled, Billy thought of his father. Pawnee Killer had been one of the most respected Brulé warriors, for he had led many successful raids and counted many coups. It didn't matter what the whites thought of him; Billy wanted only to be with him again, so he could forget everything about Carlisle. Otherwise . . . Smith interrupted his thoughts.

"You won't know the place. It's some changed since Wright took over as agent in '83. He got lots of families to build cabins and grow some corn. Of course they ain't farmers by a whole lot, and most still sleep in tipis, but more are tryin' to farm. At least their wives are. Sure ain't like the old days." He paused. "Glad you're finally comin' home?"

Billy looked down at his worn boots. "Now that I'm here I don't know if I'm glad or not. It's what I've wanted every day for six years, but now I'm not sure I belong here any more. I'm all mixed up. I don't even know what I am."

"I'll tell you," Smith said slowly. "You're kinda like us breeds.

Whites hate you 'cause you're too much Indian. Indians hate you 'cause you're too much white. You're a man on two ponies, that's what you are.''

Chapter Three

They reached Rosebud after dark, and Billy spent an uncomfortable night on a thin mat in Smith's cabin, wishing for a cot like the one he had at Carlisle. *Wasicun!* He forced the thought from his mind. In the morning Smith fed him a breakfast of greasy pan fried bread, fried salt pork, and bitter coffee. He forced himself to eat it, trying not to think of the ham and eggs, biscuits and honey, and coffee with cream that Mrs. Purvis had served.

"Reckon you should let the agent know you're back so he can put you on the ration roll. You don't want to miss gettin' all this good grub." Smith grinned, showing his broken tooth while wiping his greasy hands on his pants. Billy nodded, then went outside to see Rosebud by daylight.

The setting was as he remembered it. Bathed in early morning sunlight under a cloudless sky, the agency's brown log buildings were nestled in a bowl of hills dotted with dark green pines against a background of yellowing grass. Just seeing it and breathing the pine-scented breeze made him proud to be a Brulé. In the old days it had been a favorite camping place of his people. That was why Spotted Tail had insisted on locating the agency there, that and the fact little land near it was suitable for farming. Although he knew the old life was gone, Spotted Tail had resisted the government's efforts to force the Brulés to take up farming.

Now, however, most of the tipi camps that had clustered around the agency in all directions when Billy had last seen it were gone. The tipis that remained were of white canvas, not those of mellowed buffalo hide with paintings of warriors and soldiers on them. Somehow Agent James Wright had persuaded the families to move to areas where they could plant an acre or two of corn and build cabins. There were now many cabin settlements scattered over the land, some of them thirty miles or more from the agency.

Later, not knowing what to expect, Billy set out for the agent's office next to the council room, carrying suitcase and toolbox. Some of the Brulé men he saw wore government issue shirts and pants along with moccasins. A few had cut the seats out of their pants and wore what was left as leggings; they also wore breechcloths and had trade blankets or worn buffalo robes over their bare shoulders. *Even the ones who dress like whites still keep their hair long. But it's clear some have changed and some have not.*

Feeling self-conscious in his outgrown blue uniform, Billy knocked on Wright's door and was told to come in. The office contained only a few chairs, a deerskin on the floor, a filing cabinet with a buffalo skull on it, and a scarred oak table Wright was using as a desk. A stocky, broad-shouldered man with a brown beard, Wright reminded him of Henry Purvis, and he felt at ease.

"I'm Billy Pawnee Killer, just back from Carlisle."

"Been expectin' you, Billy," Wright said, holding out a gnarled hand. "Tackett wrote you'd be coming." He glanced at the toolbox. "I see they trained you to be a carpenter."

Billy nodded. "Summers I worked on a farm."

"Good. I'm a farmer, you know. There isn't likely to be much carpenter work here, outside what the staff does, but when you're eighteen we'll set you up on a farm. What will you do in the meantime?"

"I haven't seen my mother for six years, my father for longer than that, and I'm anxious to get acquainted with them again." Wright stroked his beard.

"I think you should know that few of those men who were with Sitting Bull or Crazy Horse have adjusted to reservation life, and some of them likely never will. They're like caged tigers torn from the jungle. They camp as far from here as they can and still draw rations every ten days. They hate white men and avoid them, but they hate even worse any Sioux who looks or acts like a white.

I doubt that they'd let you, with your short hair and uniform, even spend a night in their camp.''

Billy frowned. "But surely, if my father wants me there...?"

"You should let him know you're back, of course, but it would be better for me to send him word and see what he says." Billy's frown deepened.

"I want to see him. I must see him."

"Well, in that case, don't expect him to ask you to stay. You'll take some gettin' used to, Billy. Not only by the others, but by your own parents, especially your father. There are some pretty wild warriors in that camp, and if they didn't run you off, they'd make life miserable for you. I don't even send the police to those camps if I can help it."

"They couldn't make it much worse than it was when I went away. I must see my father. Seeing him again is what I've lived for." Billy shuffled his feet. Wright stroked his beard again.

"I understand," he said softly, leaning forward on his elbows. "I hope it works out for you." He pointed to a map of the reservation tacked to the log wall, and circled his stubby finger. "They're usually somewhere in this area, but they move whenever they need fresh grass for their ponies. The trader, John Culver, can find out where they are through his wife's kinfolk. She's Brulé.''

On his way to the trading post Billy saw a familiar-looking youth approaching, but at first he didn't recognize him. Then he knew it was his friend Julian Whistler. He'd let his hair grow into two short, pathetic-looking braids that dangled to just below his ears on each side of his round face, and he wore a red and white striped blanket uncomfortably over his bare shoulder. His expression was solemn, but he still didn't look like a typical young Brulé fullblood. Even with blanket and braids he appeared different, like a Wasicun trying to pass for an Indian.

"Billy!" Julian exclaimed. "You're back. Pratt must have run out of excuses for keeping you."

"You were lucky, my friend. You left after four years."

"Four were too many. Nobody here has any use for us now, and if we do anything different, like shaking hands or sleeping in cabins, they jeer and call us Wasicuns. Even our own families,'' he said, curling his lip. "They act like we changed because we wanted to become make-believe Wasicuns, not because we were forced to. Pratt always bragged that he'd kill the Indian in us and leave the man. He should have killed both instead of sending us home the misfits he made us."

"Have you done any carpenter work?"

Julian laughed bitterly, toeing the dirt with his moccasin, the short braids skipping back and forth on each side of his unhappy face. "Not one of us has worked a single day at what they made us learn. Either there's nothing for us to do or the Wasicuns say we're trying to take their jobs. 'We don't need Injun carpenters,' they say. Those years were wasted—worse than wasted." He waved his arms violently, and the blanket slipped from his shoulder. "Where will you live?" he asked, pulling the blanket around his waist with both hands.

"I want to live with my father, but the agent thinks he'll throw me away when he sees how I look."

"Even if he doesn't, you'd be going straight from Carlisle to one of the wildest camps on the Reserve." Julian shook his head, and his braids flew. "You've been away so long you can't have any idea what that would be like. I know I couldn't stand it, and I doubt that you could for long. After living like we did and being busy all the time, the hardest part is having nothing to do but feel sorry for yourself and wish you were dead. I'd gladly work as a carpenter just to have something to do."

"Living with my father is the only way I can become a Brulé again. I've got to, if he'll let me."

"Hah! Look at me! Too late for that, my friend. I don't know which is worse, an imitation Wasicun or an imitation Brulé, but those are your choices." Shaking his head again, with his ridiculous braids gyrating, he turned to go.

"Where does Mollie live?"

"Deer-in-Timber? Her family has a cabin down the creek a couple miles. She helps the teacher at the school there, though I hear she'll get married before long."

Billy picked up his suitcase and tool box and continued on his way. *Mollie Deer-in-Timber getting married! I never thought of that happening. I should have talked to her before she left.*

I should have written and not let her forget me.

John Culver, the trader, was a tall, round-shouldered man with twinkling blue eyes and a sandy colored mustache that hid his mouth. He was smoking a pipe, and like most whites and Indians at Rosebud he wore khaki shirt and pants and Brulé moccasins. Billy introduced himself and shook hands. "Mr. Wright said you probably can tell me where my father is camped," he said. "But first I must see my grandfather, Two Buck Elk, and borrow a pony."

"You're fresh back from Carlisle, I see," Culver said. "I went to college in Pennsylvania for a couple of years before I got the wanderlust and headed west. Now I'm a squawman with a couple of mixed-blood sons. Come a long way, ain't I?" He smiled. "You know, if I had it to do over I wouldn't change a thing." Billy knew he'd like Culver.

"Your father is Pawnee Killer, you say?" Billy nodded. "Not figurin' on stayin' with him, are you?" Wishing he hadn't been asked that, Billy nodded again.

"I must see him, and I don't have anywhere else to go. I'll stay with him if he wants me." Culver's mustache twitched.

"If it doesn't work out like you want, come see me when you get back." He took Billy outside and pointed out the trail to Two Buck Elk's camp, about ten miles away.

Leaving suitcase and tool box at the trading post, Billy set out on foot for the camp. When he was almost halfway there a family of Brulés in a buckboard drawn by a team of trotting ponies approached, going in the same direction and leaving a cloud of dust behind. Billy stopped, expecting them to offer him a ride. The driver was dressed like a white man, but his hair was long. He glanced at Billy, frowned, and drove on without slowing down. The woman looked straight ahead, but the two children in the back of the wagon turned their heads owl-like to stare at Billy through the dust.

When he reached the little settlement Billy saw that a white canvas tipi stood by every cabin, and near each was a buckboard. In the distance he saw small patches of knee-high corn. His grandmother, in a long calico dress, was entering a cabin, and he knew that Two Buck Elk was probably in the nearby tipi. Remembering the Teton custom just in time, he struck the tipi with his hand to announce a visitor, then raised the flap and peered in. His grandfather was sitting crosslegged on a green and white blanket, leaning against a willow backrest and smoking his pipe. He wore pants and moccasins, but no shirt. The flesh hung loosely on his arms.

Two Buck Elk looked up at Billy with an expression of surprise, then of sorrow on his wrinkled face. With his left hand he touched his disfigured ear.

"Grandfather, they finally let me come home," Billy said, entering the tipi.

Two Buck Elk looked him over sadly. "What have they done to you, grandson?" he asked hoarsely. Arising, he walked around Billy, inspecting him from all sides. "You're as tall as I am," he said. "But your hair! They promised to teach you to talk like a Wasicun, not to make you look like one. They lied."

"Do you think my father will know me?"

Two Buck Elk started to answer twice, but checked himself each time. He knocked the ashes from his red stone pipe and returned it to its beaded buckskin case before replying. His reluctance to speak was ominous. Billy stared at him, holding his breath, wanting him to say what he hoped to hear.

"Grandson," Two Buck Elk said softly, "there are many things that may be hard for you to understand. I don't understand some of them myself. We can't fight the Wasicuns any more—they are too many. If we can't fight them, we can only live in peace with them and do what we must, what they tell us. If we can't fight them it is senseless to hate them." He paused and drew a deep breath as if gathering strength to continue.

"Your father and the other warriors who fought with Sitting Bull and Crazy Horse live on hatred of the Wasicuns, and they want only a chance to die fighting them. When your father heard that I had sent you away to learn to talk like a Wasicun he was furious. 'You destroyed my only son,' he said. 'My son is no more! I should kill you!' Perhaps I deserved to be killed. If he felt that way about you learning to talk like a Wasicun, how will he feel to see you looking like one, even walking like one? It would be wise not to let him see you, at least until your hair is long again."

They stood for a time in silence, while Billy's thoughts went back to his father's affectionate farewell. *Down deep inside he must still love the son he knew. Surely he'll want me to become that son again.* "I've been waiting nine years just to see him. I can't wait for my hair to grow long. That will take years."

Two Buck Elk remained silent, but Billy was sure he knew what the old warrior was thinking, as he tugged at his left ear. It would be better for his father to go on believing he was dead and never have to see what had happened to his son. *But I must see him!* He left the tipi and entered the open door of the cabin, where his grandmother was stirring something in a big pot on the stove. When she saw him she gave a little cry. "Grandson!" she exclaimed.

"How is my mother?" he asked.

"She mourns for you yet. She has never forgotten you, grandson. But you look so different without your hair." Billy frowned.

They spoke little after that. Billy slept on a mat of grass his grandmother prepared for him. In the morning Two Buck Elk caught a spirited bay pony and saddled it. "He's yours to keep, grandson," he said, handing Billy the reins. "We always ride in the wagon. He's a good pony—in the old days he might have been a buffalo runner," he said sadly.

Billy mounted, feeling a bit nervous, for he hadn't ridden in years. His grandmother handed him a small canvas bag filled with dried meat. "Grandson," Two Buck Elk said, "you are welcome to share our tipi if you wish." *He's sure my father won't want me to stay, but he's got to be wrong. He must be.*

The lively bay traveled at a distance-covering jog trot. On either side of the trail Billy saw cattle grazing, and once passed two Brulé cowboys. By mid-afternoon the big camp loomed up ahead. At last, after waiting so long, he would finally be face to face with his father. He tried to visualize Pawnee Killer, wondering if he'd look exactly as he had that morning he rode away or if he'd appear older.

The tattered buffalo-hide tipis were strung out on high ground along a creek, while on his left three boys watched the grazing pony herd. Billy rode up to them; they stared at him wide-eyed. *They think I'm one of the police, and they know the police mean trouble.* "Which is Pawnee Killer's lodge?" he asked the nearest boy in Lakota. The boy hesitated, then pointed to one of the tipis.

As he rode to it, Billy saw a few men and women at a distance, but they ignored him. A feeling of apprehension swept over him as he dismounted and with trembling hands tied the pony to a stake. Holding his breath, he struck the tipi, raised the flap, and entered to see his father at last. Pawnee Killer wasn't there.

Scarlet Robe gasped and clapped a hand to her mouth. "My son! You're back at last! It's been so many summers. But..."

"Where is my father? I want to see him."

"He's hunting antelope." She paused and lowered her head. "My son, I hate to tell you this, but you must not be here when he returns."

Billy looked shocked. "Doesn't he want to see his own son?" She looked at him sadly, then lowered her eyes.

"It's so hard to tell you. Your father...I mean you've been among the Wasicuns so long your father has convinced himself that you died when they took you away. He believes that, well, because he couldn't bear to think you were becoming a Wasicun. To see you as you are would be a knife in his heart. He still loves the son he once knew, and he always will. But to him that son is only a memory, not flesh and blood. When your hair is long perhaps you can see him, even be his son again. But not now!" Her voice trembled and broke. "For his sake and mine, he must not see what they have done to you." She looked at him appealingly, head tilted to one side, her eyes filled with tears.

Billy's heart was on the ground. Everything he'd waited for, lived for, had exploded in his face. First his grandfather, then his mother, opposed him seeing his father. *It isn't fair. Don't I mean something to them? I may look different, but I'm still the son of Pawnee Killer.* He stared coldly at his mother, the corners of his mouth down.

"Forgive me, my son. Don't think me cruel, or that I don't love you. I've never stopped thinking about you or longing for your return. It's only that seeing you as you are would destroy your father. You can't want to do that to him. Maybe later, when your hair is long...." Billy didn't wait for her to finish.

Blindly he untied the pony and mounted, oblivious to the scowls of men and women who were watching. As he rode out of camp he saw two warriors wearing breechcloths and leggings approaching, each with an antelope across his pony's shoulders. Billy stared at them. There could be no doubt—one was the proud figure of Pawnee Killer! *Maybe he'll know me and tell me to stay.* His heart was pounding and his mouth felt dry as he breathlessly watched his father. The two riders would pass within fifty yards of him. He slowed the bay, ready to turn and follow them.

The warrior with Pawnee Killer saw Billy's short hair and uniform and glowered at him, but Pawnee Killer didn't even look in his direction. It was as if he'd sensed that the rider was dressed like a Wasicun and didn't merit even a glance. Billy opened his mouth to speak, but no words came. The two warriors rode on without looking back. Billy exhaled deeply, feeling weak. He loosened his rein and let the bay pony pick its way.

At the trading post next day Billy numbly tied the pony to the hitching rack and stiffly entered, his leg muscles aching from the long ride. Culver was talking to three Brulé men; they wore the usual pants and shirts, and their hair was long. Billy stared enviously at their hair as they walked past him to the door. Culver leaned against the plank counter, feet crossed, arms folded, looking at Billy's somber face. *He doesn't need to ask. He knows.*

"I saw him but he didn't see me. I can't let him see me till my hair is long and I look like a Brulé again." Culver nodded sympathetically. "And what kept me alive, especially those first years, was the thought of being with him again."

Culver was silent for a moment. "What will you do now?"

Billy didn't answer right away. "I don't know. My grandfather said I can live with them. There'd be nothing to do but sit and watch my hair grow. I'd go crazy doing that."

His mustache twitching, Culver walked around the counter and placed both hands on it. "I can use a clerk and handyman who knows both Lakota and English. Pay is five dollars a month. There's a cabin with a cot in it out back where you can sleep, and you can draw your rations and eat with the other hands." Billy's head was lowered; he looked up at Culver without raising it. "I know it's not what you had in mind, but it would be something to do for a few years. You could save your pay and buy cattle. That's all this country's good for. Think about it."

"I will, but I've forgotten a lot of Lakota words."

"They'll come back quick enough," Culver said.

Billy rode aimlessly around the agency. Most of the Brulés he'd seen, except his father and those at his camp and a few near the agency, dressed like whites but kept their hair long. *If my hair was long I'd look just like them, no matter what Julian says. It's not the clothes that matter, it's the hair. But that will take years.*

Then he recalled something else Julian had said. After being at Carlisle, the hardest part was not having anything to do. Even working like a Wasicun was better than watching the sun rise and waiting idly all day for it to set.

Back at the trading post, Billy tied his pony and entered. "What will I do with my pony?" he asked. Culver smiled.

"You can put him in with my bunch. A boy turns them out to graze mornings and pens them at night. Now let's get you out of that uniform and into clothes that fit."

Chapter Four

The trading post was one big room with storage compartments at the back. Behind the plank counter were shelves containing canned goods, boxes of rifle cartridges, knives, rolls of calico, and other brightly colored cloth, and other items. Hanging from pegs in the wall were a few saddles, bridles, and lariats, and the smell of new leather filled the air around them. A rack held a row of Winchesters. From the ceiling were suspended cooking pots, pails, and baskets. "It'll take a while to get to know where everything is," Culver told him, "but I guess you've got lots of time." Billy winced.

"You'll find the Brulés, like the Oglalas and the rest, are divided between what the government calls progressives and nonprogressives," Culver said as he pulled a pair of khaki pants from a stack. "Try these." Billy held them to his waist while Culver lit his pipe. They looked about right.

"I've seen both kinds. It's easy to tell which are nonprogressives."

"At first the progressives were mostly squawmen and mixed bloods, but not any more," Culver continued, searching through a stack of shirts. "A growing number of fullbloods are following the agent's advice and making an effort to adapt. For nomadic hunters who once claimed this whole country, settling down on one little corner of it is pretty hard, but some now admit the old days are gone and are trying to forget them. Even so, most of them move their cabins every few years."

"Why?"

Culver laughed. "For a good reason. The first year or two after the sod is turned they can grow corn. After that the weeds take over. It's a lot easier to have the agency farmer plow a new place than battle those weeds. Of course the women do most of the planting, but the men like to move, too."

"What about the nonprogressives?" Billy asked, buttoning the new shirt.

"They refuse to build cabins or plant corn or let their children attend the schools Wright had built at the cabin settlements. They don't do much but draw their rations and clothing and talk about raids and buffalo hunts they remember. They figure the whites took their hunting grounds and killed off the buffalo, so it's up to the government to feed them. They're right about that, but it's slow death for them. You'd think they'd be glad to become cowboys and work with the Brulé cattle, but few will even do that. The government would like to wring their necks for refusing to become imitation whites, but I feel sorry for them. They're pining for something they'll never see again. It's pathetic." He knocked the ash out of his pipe.

"Do they come here?"

"Whenever they need anything and have antelope or deer skins to swap."

"My father?"

"Once or twice a year, maybe. He avoids whites, mixed bloods, and even fullblood progressives." He paused, then leaned forward, looking Billy in the face. "I know it won't be easy for you, but you'd be better off to forget him. You're not the son he once knew, and he's not the father you remember. You need to get on with your own life and not, like the nonprogressives, spend your time mourning for something you've lost. That's a hard thing to say, Billy, but I know it's what's best for you."

After thinking about it, Billy shook his head. "I've waited nine years to be with him again. I may have to wait nine more, but there's one thing I want above all, and that's to hear him call me his son. Once I hear that I won't care what happens, but until he does I'll never know who I am." Culver's mustache twitched like his lips were moving, but no words came out.

Billy settled into the routine of the trading post, glad he had something to occupy his time. He built new shelves for the post and storerooms. "You're a pretty good hand with a hammer and saw," Culver told him, as he inspected his work. *I never thought I'd be pleased to hear anyone say that.*

One day Billy looked up and felt a sudden thrill to see Mollie Deer-in-Timber and her mother enter the post. At fifteen Mollie was taller and prettier than ever in the dress she'd made, which was tight enough to show that she was becoming a woman. Her eyes opened wide for a moment when she saw Billy. She walked toward him, looking pleased but not quite smiling.

"Billy, it's good that you're finally back," she said, offering her hand like a Wasicun. Her mother eyed Billy suspiciously.

"Julian told me you're helping the teacher." She nodded. "You never baked a cake for me like you promised." She smiled. "Julian also said you'll be married soon." The smile faded and she lowered her eyes.

"It's not that I put you out of my mind as soon as I got back, Billy. I kept hoping you'd write me." She looked embarrassed to admit that. "When you didn't I was sad for a while, for I knew you'd forgotten me and that I must forget you. It wasn't easy."

"I meant to write," Billy stammered. "Really I did. I tried to, but it sounded so stupid I tore it up." She looked a little sad.

"My father wants me to marry a white man. He says I'm too much Wasicun to live like an Indian. There's a man... He's a bit older, but I think he'll be a good husband. He wants to wait a year or two, till I'm older."

As she left with her mother, she said, "I hope I'll see you the next time we come." Billy weakly tried to smile. He felt empty inside, and could think of nothing to say. *I never knew how much I wanted her. Now it's too late.*

Culver regularly received newspapers from Dakota Territory and Nebraska, and Billy got in the habit of scanning them when no one was in the post. In November he read that the Friends of the Indian had met with Secretary of the Interior L. Q. C. Lamar to give him their views on what his Indian policy should be.

The Friends of the Indian held their annual meeting at A. K. Smiley's plush hotel at Lake Mohonk in October 1885 to decide for the government what it should do about the Indians. The time has come, they agreed, to give each Indian family a farm, sell the surplus land, cut off free rations, and force the Indians to support themselves. We must educate the Indians and make them citizens whether they want these things or not. A few expressed concern over pushing the Indians too rapidly, but the majority favored all possible speed in stamping out the Indianness in all Indians by one great stroke.

Captain Pratt, who had been invited to attend because of his humanitarian work with Indian children, recommended turning the Indians out into the white population to sink or swim. When someone worried that the Indians weren't prepared to cope with that and would surely sink, Pratt cheerfully agreed. "A few, those who deserve to, will survive," he said, and dismissed the rest with a shrug. The well-fed brethren now spoke of starving the Indians into submission by cutting off their rations in the same breath they talked of educating them. As St. Paul said, "He who will not work shall not eat," they intoned.

Their course set, in November they sent a delegation to Washington with the distasteful task of making their views known to new Secretary of the Interior Lamar. Not only was he a Democrat— even worse, he was a former rebel slave owner. Hoping he would be as amenable as the Republican secretaries they preferred to deal with, they presented their plan for scrapping all treaties, allotting land to families, cutting off rations, dissolving the reservation system, and making all Indians citizens.

Lamar listened politely, then told them bluntly that he would have no part in uprooting the Indians and casting them, unprepared, into the position of tax-paying citizen land owners. "No hard and fast policy can be applied to all the tribes," he explained, "and making them suddenly citizens and land owners is nearly as cruel as a war of extermination. Those that are ready I will push on; those that are not I will protect." The brethren withdrew to regroup and plan their attack.

"Who are the Friends of the Indian?" Billy asked Culver. "I didn't know Indians had any white friends."

"There are some wealthy Republicans in the East who like to

champion causes, and after the slaves were freed they forgot them and discovered the Indians. The brethren are sincere and well-meaning folk who do what they decide is right, but they insist on having their own way even when wrong. None of them has ever seen an Indian, but no matter. They've made their fortunes, so what they think and say must be right—the arrogance of wealth, someone called it. Occasionally they may do something good, like blocking the Edmunds land grab, but they're dangerous friends because they're so self-righteous.''

"The Edmunds land grab?"

"A couple of years ago, when you were in school, a commission under Newton Edmunds of Dakota Territory was sent to ask if the Sioux would sell some of their land. On his own, Edmunds drew up what he called an agreement that was intended to swindle the Sioux out of more than half their land, then claimed the Sioux had approved it. The brethren heard about his methods and blocked it, not that they object to the Sioux selling land. Then Edmunds said that the government had broken a treaty when it took the Black Hills, which set a precedent for doing it again. That didn't fly either—at the time the brethren said treaties are sacred, and of course Congress backed off. Now it sounds like their attitude toward treaties has changed, thanks to Captain Pratt.''

Ration day was visiting time, the chance to see friends and relatives from distant camps. Every family collected the stringy beef, salt pork, coarse flour, brown sugar, and cheap coffee that had to last them for ten days. Then they made pan bread, cooked beef and salt pork in a big pot, and gorged themselves. "That's how it was in the old days,'' Culver observed, chewing on his pipe. "They'd go hungry until they had a successful hunt, then everyone ate all he could hold. Most of these families run out of food and go hungry for a day or two before drawing rations.''

When all were sitting around with full stomachs, Wright came and talked to them through a mixed blood interpreter. "Like I've said many times, all I ask is that you build a cabin and tend an acre or two of corn. We'll help with the cabin and supply a door, windows, and a cookstove for it.'' The interpreter called the stove a kettle on legs, the Lakota expression for it. "If you plant an acre or two of corn, the government will also give you a wagon and harness for a team, and a sewing machine for your wife.''

Each time, Billy noticed, four or five families accepted the agent's offer, while other nonprogressives glared at them. Their wives enviously watched the gleeful women receive their sewing machines, then scowled at their husbands. At later ration days Billy saw some of these same nonprogressives agree to build cabins and plant corn, while their wives stood by smiling. Wright's methods were successful, but they aroused the resentment of the die-hard nonprogressives.

Billy watched for Mollie Deer-in-Timber on ration days but seldom saw her, and she rarely accompanied her mother to the trading post. Whenever he thought of her marrying a Wasicun he felt sick. Then he realized that what hurt wasn't that the man was a Wasicun, but that she was marrying someone else.

In March 1886 Senator Henry L. Dawes of Massachusetts introduced a bill for alloting Indian reservations, giving each family 160 acres. Dawes told reporters that in the bill he tried to safeguard the tribes in every way, but it had been changed over his protest. The provision requiring the majority of men in any tribe to approve of allotment before it could be applied to them had been dropped.

''If my land in severalty bill should become law,'' Dawes added, ''it will depend entirely on the character of the government agents who execute its provisions whether it is a success or failure. If it is entrusted to men of unflinching honesty and broad views, the Indians will be secure in the possession of the best lands of the reservations, but if it is entrusted to dishonest men the Indians will be cheated out of their lands.'' *That means we'll be cheated, just like that candy they promised us.*

Under the bill, when the President decided to have a reservation surveyed, allotments could be made only to Indians who voluntarily applied for them. But after four years, those who had not applied could be forced to accept allotments. ''If that bill ever becomes law and is actually put into effect,'' Culver said, ''it will be absolute disaster for most tribes. Let's hope it fails.''

The nonprogressives watched with growing ire as others were rewarded with wagons and sewing machines. The wife of Wooden Knife, a crusty old nonprogressive with a missing front tooth, grumbled about wanting a sewing machine so loudly she finally stirred him to action. That provided a little excitement and broke the monotony of reservation life for a few days. Wooden Knife came to the trading post one day and lisped to Culver, who turned to Billy.

"He needs to talk to the agent and wants an interpreter who won't twist his words. Go with him and see if you can help him."

In the agent's office Billy translated Wooden Knife's request, while the old warrior stood like a statue, with arms folded and head high. "He says that you should give his wife a sewing machine like other women have."

"Tell him that if he wants her to have one, he must agree to build a cabin and plant corn like the others have done," Wright replied, stroking his beard. "When he does that she can have one, not before. That's the rule. Tell him it's up to him."

When Billy relayed this, Wooden Knife was furious. "We'll get them our own way," he growled as he stalked out. Billy didn't translate that remark.

On the next issue day, when most of the Brulés were at the agency as usual, Wooden Knife and his friends rode up.

"Everything in the warehouse belongs to us!" he shouted. "It's ours for the lands the Wasicuns stole! They can't make us work for what is ours."

Those with him shouted "Hau!"

"You interpret for me," Wooden Knife told Billy. His friends crowded into the agent's office behind the two. Billy sympathized with Wooden Knife—what he said made sense—but the habit of obedience to white officials drilled into him at Carlisle made him regard the old warrior as wrong and likely to be punished for defying the agent.

Shouting threats, Wooden Knife and his friends backed Wright into a corner while Billy did his best to translate their noisy demands. Wright shook his head. "No!" he thundered.

Yelling "Kill him! Kill him!" Wooden Knife and the others ran out, loudly complaining to anyone within hearing about the bad treatment they'd received from the agent. Crow Dog, the killer of Spotted Tail, took them to his cabin. Billy remained at the agency and didn't hear what Crow Dog told them, but when they returned late in the afternoon they were still angry.

In the meantime, Wright had summoned the Indian police, and after seeing them and shouting more threats, the troublemakers withdrew. They soon reappeared, this time waving their Winchesters and singing war songs. Realizing they were in a mood for killing, Billy and others ran out of their way. *They must have lost their heads—willing to fight over sewing machines. What has happened to the Brulés?*

The council hall was soon jammed, with Wooden Knife and his excited warriors on one side, the police and friends of the agent on the other, howling into one another's faces. Several police elbowed their way through the crowd to the door of the agent's office. Wright opened it and held up his hand for silence. Finally the shouting ceased, while Wooden Knife bared his remaining teeth and his friends glowered at the agent, menacingly fingering their weapons.

"If anyone wants to speak as a friend," Wright told them through Billy, "I will listen to him."

Wooden Knife pounded on the floor with his war club. He shouted that the Great Father had told them if their agent didn't treat them right they should throw him out, and that was what they had come to do. While Billy translated, a fierce-looking warrior named Eagle Pipe grabbed the agent by one arm and pulled. The police held fast to the other, and Billy feared they would tear Wright apart. Many were shouting "Kill him!" but they waited for someone else to do it. More police struggled to the agent's side and pushed him through the door into his office and out another door into the yard, with the angry crowd close behind. The police finally escorted Wright to safety. He appeared flustered but not fearful.

The aroused warriors circled the agency, still shouting threats. Finally the chiefs arrived with a band of former Akicita, or tribal soldiers, who were armed with whips and whose authority was still respected. Most of the shouting died down for the moment. Then the crowd broke up into small groups and began quarrelling furiously, all trying to talk at once. A few crowded around the Indian police, shoving and threatening them.

This kept up until sunset, when the warehouse clerk happened by on the way to his cabin. Three of Wooden Knife's warriors grabbed the frightened clerk and took his keys to the warehouse. Then all rushed to the building, unlocked the door, and in the dark helped themselves to whatever they found. Wooden Knife emerged triumphantly bearing a sewing machine, when the chiefs and the Akicita returned and ordered the crowd to leave. Taking their loot, Wooden Knife and his friends happily departed.

The Brulés called this the "night issue," for it was the only time that items in the warehouse were ever distributed after dark. Wright treated it as a small matter and made no attempt to recover any of the stolen goods. He merely demanded that Wooden Knife apologize, which he willingly did. To the Tetons at every agency the night issue was a great event, and after tempers cooled, the Brulés also loved to talk about it. They had manhandled the Great Father's agent, nearly tearing him to pieces, and they hadn't been punished. Whenever anyone mentioned the night issue, all roared with laughter. And in the winter count showing the major events of 1886, the bearded agent was depicted as being pulled out of his office.

A few days after the affair Wright came to the trading post, and Billy heard him ask Culver what he thought about it.

"It tells me that although the Brulés appear to be settling down and farming, under the surface they're seething, ready to explode. If one shot had been fired they might not have stopped until a bunch of whites and Indian police had been killed. Should the government do anything else they consider unjust, like taking their land, there's likely to be big trouble." Wright stroked his beard but said nothing. That same year his term ended, and he turned the agency over to George Spencer. Wright's son George remained as clerk for the new agent.

As the months passed, Billy's hair grew long enough to tie at the back of his head with a piece of cord. Julian visited him occasionally, but he seemed uncomfortable with anyone whose presence would remind others he had been to Carlisle. Billy tried to convince himself that Julian looked more and more like other Brulés, and that the same transformation must be happening to him. At least Julian's braids now reached his shoulders and didn't look so ridiculous. Mollie Deer-in-Timber seldom came to the trading post, but when she did she wasn't talkative, and Billy felt tongue-tied.

The Dawes bill finally passed, and in February 1887 President Cleveland signed it into law. Nothing more was heard of it for a long time, for no attempt was made to put it into effect among the Sioux.

"Will I ever look enough like a Brulé to satisfy my father?" Billy asked, touching the hair at the back of his neck. "I still don't feel like a real Brulé, and I wonder if I ever will. The fullbloods ignore me unless they need an interpreter or someone to write a letter. I doubt if anything will change when my hair reaches my waist."

Culver removed his pipe from his mouth. "I wish I knew, Billy. Only time will tell. Even though there's no carpenter work for you, it would be a shame to throw away all you learned and go back to being a blanket Indian. You're helping by what you do for them, and when you're older you should be able to do even more. They'll come to appreciate you for what you know."

There had been a drouth the previous summer, and the winter had been more severe than any that the oldest warriors could remember. Cattle died by the thousands all over the northern plains, and hundreds of white ranchers were ruined. The Sioux cowboys worked hard to save their cattle and held their losses to thirty percent, less than half the average white losses.

Billy turned eighteen in 1887, and at the agent's urging chose a place for a cabin near a creek a few miles from the agency. White workmen helped him build a snug one-room cabin of squared pine logs, with door, windows, and cookstove the government supplied. An assistant of the agency farmer plowed an acre of land to be planted with corn. Billy couldn't look at the cabin without thinking of sharing it with Mollie Deer-in-Timber.

In late spring Billy planted the corn in neat rows, then watched almost eagerly as the green shoots pushed up through the dark earth. A fat progressive named Bull Bear rode by the cornfield one Sunday afternoon while Billy was hoeing weeds between the rows. Bull Bear, who had married two sisters, stopped his pony and looked at Billy with an expression of disapproval on his chubby face.

"It isn't right for a man to work like a woman. If you were a real Brulé you'd have a wife to do your planting," he said, then rode on.

Billy leaned on the hoe and stared after Bull Bear. *He's right, of course. I'm still too much Wasicun, and I don't even realize it.* He thought of the rich fields and orchards around Carlisle and remembered the roasting ears he'd eaten in the summers. They'd be a welcome change from the ration issue; he looked forward to harvest time. Every day he gazed up at the cloudless sky hoping for rain.

In mid-July he rode out to check on his corn. His heart sank, for from a distance he saw nothing green. He stopped his pony at the edge of the plot and dismounted. His stunted corn had given up the struggle. He'd blistered his hands keeping down the weeds, and now this. Sick at heart, he glumly walked among the shriveled stalks that rustled pitifully in the hot wind, kicking at the brick-like clods. He wanted to strike out violently, but there was no visible, tangible enemy. *Only grass and weeds will grow here. The Wasicuns are making fools of us, telling us to plant corn.* That some month Mollie Deer-in-Timber married her white man, an agency employee.

In the fall Billy read that Dawes had introduced a new Sioux land purchase bill. *Why doesn't he leave us alone? We have troubles enough already.* Under the new bill each tribe would have its own reservation and the rest of the Great Sioux Reserve would be declared surplus and sold to whites. When a reporter questioned Dawes about his Sioux bill, he replied, "There's so much pressure in Dakota Territory for Indian land I'm afraid that twenty-five thousand Sioux can't hold out much longer against five hundred thousand whites. I would rather see them part with enough land to satisfy the Dakotans than to risk losing all." Billy felt a chill when he read that. *Will the Wasicuns ever be satisfied? Or will they keep on until our land is gone and we are no more?*

The new Dawes' bill became law on April 30, 1888. Under it the educational provisions of the 1868 treaty were extended. Each family would be given a wagon, a yoke of oxen, two cows, farm tools and seed, and twenty dollars in cash. Everyone but Dr. Theodore Bland was certain the Sioux would be delighted with such a generous offer. Of all the Indian reformers, Bland was the only one who visited the agencies to learn what the Sioux wanted and needed. The Friends of the Indian ignored him because he disagreed with them, so he had founded the Indian Defense Association and published *The Council Fire*.

As Billy learned, the trickery of the Edmunds commission, as well as broken treaty promises, had united the Sioux in bitter opposition to any land sale. The squawmen of each band read the papers and alerted the chiefs to the new threat. They worried about the progressives and others who might be persuaded or cajoled into signing the new agreement. "The whites promised rations and clothing when they took our land before," old Two Strike said. "We don't need another agreement. And who cares about schools? If they didn't use the police to round up our children there'd be no schools here."

When the Brulé chiefs learned that the bill had become law, old Two Strike came to the trading post. "You can write like the Wasicuns?" he asked Billy.

"Yes."

"Write to Grass at Standing Rock and Big Foot at Cheyenne River for me. Tell them to bring the chiefs and headmen here to decide what we must do to keep our lands." Billy wrote the letters, and before long delegations from other agencies began arriving at Rosebud. The Brulés were so excited at the coming of famous chiefs and warriors from other Teton tribes they abandoned their farms and hung around Rosebud to watch and listen. The chiefs held council to decide on the steps all should take to block the commission. Agent Spencer repeatedly urged them to return to their farms, and finally sent the police to break up the council. The chiefs simply rode off to distant camps and continued their talks.

"What can I do to make them get back to work?" Spencer asked Culver, stamping his foot in frustration.

"The word I get is that there's great excitement at all the agencies," Culver replied, puffing on his pipe. "No one else is doing any farming, so don't worry about it. There's nothing you can do anyway. They've been expecting another land grab attempt, and now that it's on the way they're naturally up in arms about it. My advice is to leave them alone."

The chiefs agreed they would simply say no to the land sale and refuse to discuss it, then they returned to their agencies. "I've never seen the Sioux so determined," Culver said. "I wonder if they can hang together."

"I hope so," Billy said. "We'll soon know, I guess."

"Look at this," Billy said a few weeks later, tapping the paper he was reading. "The Friends of the Indian say that Captain Pratt is the ideal man to head the commission to persuade his friends the Sioux to sign the agreement. His friends the Sioux!" Billy's voice was almost shrill. "And he's actually been appointed. Wait till they see how many friends he has here." He put down the paper. "What do you think will happen?" he asked, looking worried.

"United the Sioux can hold out a while longer, maybe a few more years at most. If the government would ever admit that they can support themselves only by raising cattle, it would be clear they need most of the Reserve for range. But if it ignores that and sets aside just enough land to provide a farm for each family, it will feel justified in taking the rest, one way or another, like it took the Black Hills."

Thinking of the thousands of whites in the East, Billy knew the Sioux were helpless. *There's no hope for us. The Wasicuns are determined to take our land and destroy us. I'll never see my father.*

Chapter Five

Snaggle-toothed Joe Smith brought Culver a note one day. He read it, then beckoned to Billy. "It's from Spencer. He says there'll be a flock of reporters at Standing Rock, which is the commission's first stop, and they want to hire the best interpreters from each agency. He wants you to go if I can spare you. I can, and it's a chance for you to earn a little extra money, depending on how long it goes on. You can also see Captain Pratt in action, and tell me all about it. Will you go?"

Billy felt the ends of his hair tied together by a string at the back of his neck, wondering if he would look even sillier with short braids like Julian's. He thought of watching Pratt browbeating the Hunkpapas into selling their land and then gloating about it, and shook his head. "I couldn't stand seeing him make them do what he wants. I saw enough of that." He put his hand on his stomach. "Just the thought of it makes my stomach churn."

Culver drew on his pipe. "If the Hunkpapas hang together and follow Grass that's not likely to happen even if Pratt harangues them for a month. You saw Grass when he was here. He's the Hunkpapas' leading progressive, and he's plenty smart, not one who can be stampeded by loud talk. I'd bet on him over Pratt."

Billy wasn't entirely convinced. "If you think so, I'll take the chance. I wouldn't want to miss seeing them turn Pratt down."

When the time came, he and three mixed bloods who'd been to school in Nebraska traveled by train from Valentine to the Missouri, then boarded a riverboat for Standing Rock Agency upriver. Billy's thoughts went back to the time they had sailed from Black Pole, while everybody wailed. A dozen reporters were also on their way to cover what they called the Great Sioux Land Cession. They were of all shapes and sizes, and they prattled on incessantly. One of them, a freckle-faced redhead who was chewing on the stub of a cigar, saw Billy and stopped him.

"You look like an honest to God Indian," he said, removing the cigar with tobacco stained fingers. "Can you speak English?"

"Yes. I'm one of the interpreters."

"Where'd you learn it?"

"Six years at Carlisle." The redhead's face brightened and his freckles seemed to dance.

"Carlisle! Then you must know Captain Pratt." Billy glumly nodded.

"I wish I'd never heard of him."

The freckled reporter slapped his thigh. "You can't mean he ain't the great humanitarian, the friend of the Sioux, like they say? That's funny. I've had my doubts about that turkey all along, just from what I've heard about the way he runs his school. Kinda like a prisoner of war center, I hear. Fill me in on him." Billy did.

When he finished the redhead introduced himself. "I'm Bud Jones of the *Epigraph*. I need an interpreter, and you're the man for me. The paper'll pay you two dollars a day. Agreed?"

Pleased, Billy shook hands with him.

Captain Pratt, looking more important than ever, arrived with the commission and several aides a few days later. Billy recognized the Reverend William J. Cleveland, the mild-mannered Episcopalian missionary at Rosebud who was well-acquainted with the Brulés and fluent in Lakota. The third commissioner was James V. Wright.

"He's a treaty maker for the Indian Service," Jones explained. "Knows treaties but not Indians. This looks to be Pratt's show. I think I'm goin' to enjoy it."

"I hope we both do." Billy was still worried.

Agent James McLaughlin, a heavyset, white-haired man who was acknowledged the most experienced and ablest Sioux agent, didn't conceal the fact that he opposed the sale. "But my orders are to assist the commission," he told the reporters. He assembled the Hunkpapas the following day, and they set up canvas tipis in a big area near the agency. Then they squatted in a half-circle facing a table set up for the commissioners in front of agency headquarters. Billy saw chief Grass sitting on a stump and looking solemn. Sitting Bull, whose camp was forty miles away, had refused to come.

Before the talks started, Pratt, exuding confidence, had copies of the sale agreement distributed among the Hunkpapas, but they refused to touch them. Pratt smiled grimly, then began talking through his interpreter.

"First," he said, trying to make his voice sound pleasant, "I want to assure you that no character of threat, menace, or force will be used to influence your votes." He paused for the interpreter. "It is a matter that will be left entirely to your free will," he added, still smiling. Then the smile faded and his face darkened. "Of course I should warn you that failure to approve the agreement will make further action which will be taken in regard to the reservation problematical." Then he straightened up to full height and looked down at the faces of the Hunkpapa men seated on the ground in front of him.

Jones snorted and wrote something on his notepad. "If that's not a threat I don't know what is. He's trying to intimidate them right off." He lit a match with his thumbnail and lighted his cigar.

The Reverend Cleveland, in his squeaky preacher's voice, slowly translated the agreement, explaining the meaning paragraph by paragraph. The Hunkpapas listened in icy silence, moving only to brush flies from their faces. Grass sat with arms folded, his face like carved granite.

When Cleveland finished, Pratt asked if there were any questions. No one responded. Frowning, Pratt dismissed them for the day to talk it over among themselves.

"Who do the Hunkpapas listen to?" Jones asked.

"Chief Grass. The whites call him John Grass."

"Let's talk to him." They caught up with Grass as he was heading for his tipi.

"This man would like to ask you a few questions," Billy told him in Lakota. Grass looked at Billy, then at Jones, who held notepad in one hand, cigar in the other, and apparently decided the reporter was friendly.

"First," Jones asked, "how do you and your people feel about selling your surplus land?"

"We don't have any land that our descendants won't need in the future. Our land is not for sale. It was promised to us forever. All Tetons have agreed not even to discuss selling it with these men."

"Thanks, you've answered all my questions."

Although the Tetons had agreed not to take part in the talks, the Hunkpapas finally decided that Grass should reply to Pratt. Speaking with great dignity, he brought up the Treaty of 1868, going over its provisions point by point, while Pratt glared at him. Then Grass went over the government's unfulfilled promises one by one. "In every treaty we have made with the Great Father we have had to give up more land," he said. "Now we have no more land than we and our children will need. Half of our land is unfit for farming anyway, and whites wouldn't buy it." He paused, while Pratt glowered at him.

"I think it is wrong for the government to offer us only fifty cents an acre," he continued, "when it plans to sell it for $1.25. Go back to Washington and tell the Great Father that the government should fulfill its promises in the old treaty. After that we may be willing to talk, not before. If the government hasn't kept its old promises, why should we expect it to keep its new ones?"

The Reverend Cleveland looked shocked. "Bless my soul!" he said.

"I know nothing about old treaties," Pratt said testily. "We're here to make a new agreement, not waste time talking about what's over and done. Stick to the subject." The stony faced Hunkpapas gave no sign of being persuaded.

Red-faced, Pratt leaned forward, both hands on the table. "You had better talk about this some more, until you come to your senses," he said. "You can be making serious trouble for yourselves." Then he picked up the agreement and stalked away. Billy looked out over the Hunkpapas, fearful he'd see signs that they were weakening. He saw none, and exhaled deeply.

The same process was repeated day after day for two weeks, with the Hunkpapas listening to Cleveland explaining the terms of the agreement and Pratt assuring them that it was favorable to the Sioux and hinting that dire things would happen to them if they failed to approve it. Cleveland was getting hoarse, while Pratt appeared increasingly impatient.

Jones and other reporters had quickly realized that they were unlikely to write about the Great Sioux Land Cession after all and they began calling Pratt a bungler and worse. The man from the New York *Tribune* called his methods "bulldozing." Jones described Pratt as heavy-handed, incompetent, conceited, and tyrannical. Toward the end of the second week someone sent Pratt a clipping of Jones' remarks.

Clutching it in his hand, Pratt charged up to McLaughlin, his face livid, his oversize nose red. "I demand that you have the Indian police eject this man from the reservation," he almost shouted, shoving the clippings in McLaughlin's face. The agent shrugged.

An Indian policeman rowed Jones across the Missouri, off the reservation, where he set up his tent. "Don't miss a word he says," he told Billy. "When they finish for the day, come over and tell me. If that SOB thinks he can silence me, he's in for a surprise."

Finally Pratt could stand no more. "Unless you're simple-minded," he said, "all of you understand this agreement and its advantages. It has been explained often enough. The time has come to vote. This ballot means in favor." He held up a paper that was printed in red ink. *That was Cleveland's idea. He knows red means life and happiness.* Pratt held up a ballot printed in black ink. "This one means against." Black was a bad color. "Come forward and choose one or the other."

Chief Grass sat with arms folded, his face expressionless, his eyes fixed on Pratt. All of the Hunkpapas silently watched Grass, to see what he would do.

"Come forward and vote!" Pratt repeated hoarsly. "Now!" No one stirred, while Pratt's face turned crimson. "You will vote, and you will vote right!" His voice was shrill.

At that twenty-two squawmen and mixed bloods arose and walked to the table. There they chose ballots in favor of the agreement, while the Hunkpapas frowned at them. Pratt glared at the silent men, looking like he wanted to kill them. When Grass finally arose, Pratt smiled nervously and mopped his red face with his handkerchief.

But Grass didn't come forward. "We have listened to your talk long enough," he said. "We are going home to tend to our farms." He turned and walked majestically away, the others following. Pratt made a strangling sound while the Reverend Cleveland looked like he had been caught worshipping false idols.

Elated, Billy glanced at Agent McLaughlin and saw him put his hand over his white handlebar mustache to conceal his smile. The Hunkpapas had remained united, and Pratt had been humiliated. It was enough to make Billy feel like singing and dancing. Now, if the others followed the Hunkpapas' lead, the land agreement was dead. He watched the Hunkpapa women strike the tipis and load the wagons. Pratt remained seated at the table, face in hands, but Billy couldn't feel sorry for him. When McLaughlin approached Pratt, Billy sidled closer to hear what was said, wondering if Pratt had recognized him. If he had, he'd given no sign.

"I hear that the Indians at all the big agencies are also united against selling any land," McLaughlin told Pratt. "That means there's no use going to Cheyenne River, Rosebud, or Pine Ridge." Pratt looked at him blankly, as if he hadn't heard or understood.

"My friends at Crow Creek and Lower Brulé tell me they're not opposed," the Reverend Cleveland said timidly.

"You're sure?" Pratt asked, clearing his throat.

Cleveland nodded, but his face didn't reflect confidence. "That's what they told me," he hedged.

"We'll go there then."

Billy hurried to tell Jones. "We'll just tag along," the freckle-faced Jones said, throwing away a soggy cigar butt. "Pratt doesn't know for sure who I am, and he's got no right to stop me anyway." When the riverboat paddled south the next day, he was with the other reporters. Pratt stayed in his room, out of sight.

At Crow Creek, which was east of the Missouri, Billy talked to some of the fullbloods and quickly learned that most were opposed to the land sale and fearful over the possibility of losing their farms. The agent assembled the Indians, and before Pratt had a chance to talk Chiefs White Ghost and Drifting Goose informed him that they wanted him to send word to Washington for them. "Tell the Great Father," they said, "that we want to see him and tell him about our problems." Pratt brushed them aside.

"We're here to talk about a land agreement," he told them, "not to waste time talking about going to Washington. The Great Father wants you to approve this paper he sends you. If you don't, no telling what Congress might do about your rations."

Cleveland wearily explained the agreement yet another time, then told them to discuss it and return in the morning to vote.

When the votes were counted the next day, 120 squawmen, mixed bloods, and progressive fullbloods voted in favor, while 282 said no. The Reverend Cleveland's friends had been mistaken.

Jaw set, Pratt took his commission to Lower Brulé, which was across the Missouri. When he learned that the Lower Brulés were also opposed, he changed his tactics but not his brusque manner.

"Pratt sent word to Iron Nation that if the vote on the agreement is favorable, he'll ask the Indian Commissioner to order all the chiefs here for a council," Billy told Jones. "That will be a great honor for these people, so don't be surprised if they say yes." Jones chewed on his cigar and wrote on his notepad.

"That's strange," he said. "The Commissioner has always been dead set against letting the Sioux get together to discuss anything. It's easier to deal with them separately, so they can't know how the rest think." The vote was 244 in favor, 62 opposed. Jones chuckled. "You figured that one right," he said.

A week later the delegates began arriving from other agencies in wagons and setting up tipis. Billy saw Agent Spencer with old Two Strike, Crow Dog, and other Brulé headmen. When all had arrived, the commission and chiefs sat under a canvas awning in front of agency headquarters, while the rest crowded around them. Cleveland explained the agreement again. "He could probably recite it backwards by now," Jones said, knocking the ash from his cigar.

Pratt was next to speak. "You have been brought here to take steps to end the bad conditions under which your people live, and to bring them up to the level of whites," he told them. "You must not stand in their way." His tone was harsh.

"Some of you have asked to be taken to Washington to see the Great Father," he continued. "He doesn't want to see any of you until this land matter is settled and settled to his satisfaction." His voice had a metallic tone. "He considers you chiefs bad leaders. You have failed to get your people to support themselves by farming. The Great Father has asked you many times to do these things. His patience with the Sioux is nearly exhausted. He has only to raise his hand, and bad things can happen to you. Don't forget that." He looked at them coldly, letting his words sink in.

"The government has tried for years to destroy the influence of the chiefs," Billy told Jones. "It hasn't let us have a head chief since Spotted Tail was killed. Now Pratt's blaming the chiefs for everything that's gone wrong." Jones chewed on his cigar and wrote on his pad.

J. V. Wright, the treaty maker, who had done nothing but yawn frequently for days now spoke. "The Great Father has given you this opportunity to sell some land you don't need," he told them, "but all you do is talk about going to Washington to see him. He knows what's best for you. Why don't you behave yourselves and do as he asks?"

"Why didn't he just call them bad boys and threaten to spank them?" Jones asked, scribbling away.

Pratt arose again. "The time has come," he said. "The Great Father has asked you to sign this agreement"—he tapped the paper lying on the table—"then to go home and tell your people to sign it." He held up a quill pen. "Who'll be first to do what the Great Father asks?" Not a single Indian came forward. Pratt turned on his heel and stamped away, muttering to himself.

The canvas tipis soon came down as the delegates prepared to return to their agencies. Billy collected his pay then shook hands with Jones, whose face was more freckled than when he arrived.

"Thanks for your help," he said. "If I ever need an interpreter again I'll call on you."

Billy rode back to Rosebud in one of the agency's wagons, smiling inwardly the whole way, eager to tell Culver what had happened. The government had sent Pratt to bully the Tetons into selling half their land, but he'd succeeded only in making them more united than before. He felt proud of the Hunkpapas for standing up to Pratt. *Now maybe they'll realize the Tetons won't sell any land and leave us alone.*

Captain Pratt wrote a short, bitter report in which he recommended that the government ignore treaties and seize the Sioux lands without further discussion. The editor of the *Word Carrier*, a little mission paper, learned what was in the report. He noted that because Pratt had failed he was recommending breaking the Treaty of 1868 and taking Sioux land by force, if necessary. In his anger he vengefully even urged the government to issue bacon to the Sioux instead of fresh beef. The *Word Carrier* quoted a former Sioux agent: "The ill effects of a salt pork diet on the health of the Indians is notorious," he said. "It would be far more humane for the government to issue them arsenic instead of bacon and get the poisoning process over quickly." Of Pratt's methods of dealing with the Sioux, the editor said that "few were good, some were criminal, and most were impractical."

The Dakota Territory papers continued to blast Pratt for bungling the land agreement. Dakotans, they said, want half of the Great Sioux Reserve and they want it *now*. The government should send real men to deal with stubborn Indians, not blustering nonentities like Captain Pratt. The Friends of the Indian, for reasons of their own, also urged the government to reduce the Great Sioux Reserve by half.

Although the government had denied again and again that chiefs had any authority, it now invited the leaders of each Teton tribe to Washington in an effort to salvage the land deal. Because so many newspapers had covered the Pratt commission's dealings with the Sioux, many now sent reporters to cover the Washington council in detail. Over the years the Sioux had learned much in their dealings with white officials, and they did most of the talking. The Indian Bureau officials listened patiently, trying occasionally to steer the talk to the land sale. The chiefs ignored them, jumping from complaint to demand while carefully avoiding any mention of the land agreement. They rambled on endlessly, while the glum officials squirmed in their seats, crossed and recrossed their legs, stifled yawns, and peeked at their watches in disbelief.

The Oglalas, as they had at every opportunity, brought up the old matter of payment for the ponies General Sheridan's troops had taken from them in 1876. The officials looked at one another. Then, hoping that a conciliatory gesture might get the talks onto the right track, they promised to ask Congress to make a generous settlement. The Oglalas smiled.

At that the Tetons from the Missouri River agencies recalled that General Terry had taken hundreds of their ponies the same year. The money from the sale of those animals had been used to buy them 600 head of stocker cattle, but the officials were unaware of that, so they agreed to tend to the matter. These concessions, far from getting the chiefs to talk about the land sale, opened the floodgates to a torrent of demands based on promises of long ago as well as new things the Sioux wanted, such as a red farm wagon for every family and rice and dried apples added to their rations. And they didn't want money from land sales wasted on schools and farm tools—they wanted to spend it themselves in the trading posts.

At the mention of land sales, the weary officials pricked up their ears. They suggested that the chiefs return home and persuade their people to sign the agreement. The chiefs were indignant. The officials threw up their hands in surrender, and the chiefs were sent back to their agencies.

Billy was elated that the chiefs had remained united and unyielding. The Great Sioux Reserve was still intact. In late October, Two Strike and the others arrived back at Rosebud.

"This is only round three," Culver cautioned. "It's way too soon to celebrate. The presidential election is almost on us, and much depends on how it turns out." Billy still felt jubilant—first the Pratt commission had been roundly defeated, then the chiefs had stood their ground under pressure from big men in Washington.

In the election in November, Benjamin Harrison won the presidency. "Nothing will happen until he takes office in March," Culver said, knocking the ash from his pipe. "Then we'll see."

That winter of 1888-1889, measles struck at all the agencies and hundreds of children died. The widespread grief made the Brulés appear despondent, resigned to a life of sorrow. *Disease is something else the Wasicuns brought us.*

Billy read in late February that Harrison planned to appoint Baptist minister Thomas J. Morgan as Indian Commissioner, and had instructed him to base his policy on the views of the Friends of the Indian. Morgan promptly attended one of their meetings. "I place myself in your hands," he told them.

"The brethren must be rejoicing," Culver said grimly, chewing on his pipestem. "For the Sioux this is the worst news I've heard in a while."

When Morgan announced what his Indian policy would be, he declared that it had been his "long established conviction that the reservation system is an anomaly that cannot be permitted to continue." The Indians must be absorbed into the white population as quickly as possible.

"Poppycock," Culver said. "He's just parroting what the brethren poured in his ear. God help the Indians." Billy thought of Pratt's defeat and the stand the chiefs had taken. *What can they do to us now?*

Another day Culver handed him a paper. "Read this," he said, tapping a column with his pipestem. "General Crook has been in Boston making speeches about Indians. You'll like what he has to say." Billy had heard of Crook, the stern officer who had helped defeat the Teton hostiles and force them onto the reservation.

"The Indian is a human being," Crook began. "One question today on whose settlement depends the honor of the United States is, 'How can we preserve him?' " Billy eagerly read on. If the Tetons have a powerful ally like General Crook, that should help them fight off any land sale. "We must not try to force them to take civilization immediately in its complete form," Crook continued. "If they are treated justly, the Indian question, a source of dishonor to our country and of shame to true patriots, will soon be a thing of the past."

It was hard to believe, but here was an army officer who had fought and defeated the Tetons, who admitted that Indians are human beings. He wanted them treated justly, and not pushed too fast, while those who called themselves Friends of the Indian treated them like ignorant children and would force them to change rapidly even if it meant starving them into submission. Billy read on.

"I wish to say most emphatically that the American Indian is the intellectual equal of most, if not all, the various nationalities we have assimilated," Crook continued. "He is fully able to protect himself, if the ballot be given, and the courts of law not closed to him."

"I never thought I'd hear a white man say anything like that,"

Billy said. "And one who used to fight us. I can't believe he really said that, after hearing what the rest want to do to us. Why don't they listen to him?"

"Crook knows Indians as well as any man, and he says what he knows is true. The brethren are dead wrong, and they listen only to those who agree with them."

Two mixed bloods and their Brulé wives entered the store. One of the men nodded toward the shelves behind the counter. "Cloth," he said. "Two yards."

Billy watched the women to see which of the brightly colored rolls caught their eyes then set both rolls on the counter. He measured and cut the cloth while the two men looked at the Winchesters and Culver refilled and lighted his pipe. The men paid for the cloth and followed their giggling wives to the door.

"What Crook said applied to you," Culver said, making a jabbing motion with his pipe. "You have a responsibility to him to keep on learning so you can help others adjust, and to prove that Crook and men who agree with him are right about Indians. If you were to forget what you've learned and go back to being a blanket Indian like most of the Carlisle boys have done, you'd help prove him wrong. Those who say that Indians can't or won't learn to live like whites and do the things whites do unless they're driven to it would like that. Think about it."

Billy touched the short braids that fell to the back of his neck. He'd tied them together so they wouldn't flop around like Julian's had done. "I guess you're right," he admitted. "I've thought about it a lot, but I'm still mixed up. It hasn't gotten any better. Joe Smith was right when he said I'm a man on two ponies. I thought I wanted to go all the way back to the blanket and forget I'd ever been away, but I wanted that mainly to please my father, and I was too late. I still hope to hear him call me his son, but I know my chances are pretty slim. I might as well cut my hair, and when I've given up all hope I will. But I haven't yet. Something could happen to change things, though I don't know what."

In February 1889 the Omnibus Bill passed in Congress. Dakota Territory would become the states of North and South Dakota and enter the union along with Washington and Montana in November.

Congress also passed a new Sioux Act to remove the Indians' objections to the earlier one and end opposition to the land sale. President Cleveland signed it on March 2, just before leaving office.

Not long after President Harrison was inaugurated, the Democrats on the agency staff began to be replaced by Republicans. The Friends of the Indian had been ardent supporters of the Civil Service system and had protested loudly when Cleveland had replaced Republicans in the Indian Service. Now, when there were wholesale dismissals of Democrats, they were strangely silent.

"The brethren can't bring themselves to criticize their own administration," Culver said, shaking his head, "especially after it handed them what they've wanted most—a free hand to meddle with its Indian policy."

The Friends of the Indian were too busy making plans for the Sioux to care about Civil Service. Our first goal, they announced, is to cut down the Great Sioux Reserve by nine million acres and force every family to settle on a farm. Raising cattle won't do. It lets them keep roaming around, and that's bad because they enjoy it. The brethren even protested that when in Washington in October the chiefs had promised to promte the land agreement, and that most Sioux now favored it. No one but they believed that.

The new Sioux Act set the price for land to be ceded at $1.25 an acre for the first three years, seventy-five cents for the next two, and fifty cents an acre thereafter. Funds from the sales would be held for the Sioux at five percent interest to be used for education. Because the Sioux had worried about allotment, the act specified that the program could not be introduced at any agency until a majority of the men approved it. At that time each family would receive 320 acres instead of 160. The act also allocated $28,500 to compensate the Oglalas for the ponies seized in 1876, at $40 per pony. But the Sioux must accept or reject the agreement, not abstain from voting.

"The chiefs did a good job in Washington," Culver remarked as he read the agreement's provisions, "better than any of us realized." He tapped the article with his index finger. "I've never seen Congress in such a generous mood. This time the Sioux had better accept before Congress has second thoughts about it. They'll never be so free handed again—they leaned over backwards to make it attractive. If it's rejected, Congress will be miffed, and they'll figure a way to take the land without adequate compensation. Believe me.''

Billy frowned. Why do we have to give up our land? If they get half of it now, how long will it be before they take the other half? He only hoped that the government would send another bungler like Pratt, and that the Tetons would remain as united as before.

Chapter Six

When Congress authorized President Harrison to send a new commission to negotiate with the Sioux under the terms of the new act, he quickly responded. This time the commissioners would not be what the Tetons considered small men. Harrison named Charles Foster, ex-governor of Ohio, as chairman, then added William Warner, head of the Veterans' Administration. Neither had been involved in negotiations with Indians, but the third member was expected to do the persuading. General George Crook, Three Stars to the Tetons, had years of experience in dealing with Indians, and he had campaigned against the Sioux hostiles in 1876.

The announcement of his appointment stated that Crook had been named to the commission because he was an old friend of the Sioux. Culver snorted when he read that. "An old friend of the Sioux! Most of them will be surprised to hear that. They fear him for good reason, but they respect and trust him as a big chief who has never lied to them. I don't know any who call him friend."

"From what he said, he must be a friend of all Indians. At least he said that Indians should be treated fairly. I can't believe he'd try to force us to sell our land," Billy said, fingering the braids at the back of his neck.

Culver scratched a match on his pants leg and lit his pipe. "Crook being on the commission is goin' to make a lot of Tetons think twice about opposing the sale. Just seeing him will bring back the sound of bugles and the rattle of sabers. Putting him on the commission is a pointed reminder that the bluecoats are somewhere in the background. And it was just a year ago that Pratt recommended taking the land by force.''

''Three Stars wouldn't want to do that.''

''He's a good soldier, and soldiers do what they're ordered whether they like it or not.''

The commission, it was announced, had been given $25,000 for ordinary and ''unusual'' expenses. ''That means Congress doesn't intend for them to fail this time. It gave them plenty of money to hire or bribe mixed bloods and maybe even a few fullblood progressives to do the arguing for them,'' Culver observed. ''That will make their work a lot easier. I'm not sure how it will turn out, but once they're here, it's not likely they'll leave until they have what they came for.''

''But if we stick together and refuse to sell . . . ?'' Billy thought of the Hunkpapas, and how they'd stayed with Grass through all of Pratt's threats. ''Pratt couldn't force the Hunkpapas to sell.''

''Crook's not Captain Pratt.''

Dr. Bland and the Indian Defense Association also had a war chest, and they printed warnings to the Sioux not to sell and distributed them at Pine Ridge. Joe Smith brought one of the sheets to show Billy. ''I been over to Pine Ridge and got this,'' he said, showing his broken tooth. ''I hear tell that Red Cloud and the other chiefs got letters telling them to stand pat. They really got their backs up about it.''

After he left, Culver laid his pipe on the counter. ''The lines are drawn,'' he said, ''and except for Dr. Bland's folks it's the U.S. against the Sioux Nation. That's so one-sided the Tetons likely can't hold out this time, but it's in their interest to accept anyway. It would be best if it could be managed without generating hard feelings, but that isn't likely to happen.''

Billy thought some more about General Crook. If Three Stars doesn't actually like Indians, at least he respects them as humans and wants them treated fairly. When he finds they don't want to sell, that should settle it.

In the East, the Friends of the Indian waited, ready to rejoice over news that the Sioux had given up half of the Reserve. The Dakotans, whose demands had led to the Sioux Act, had suffered so severely from the prolonged drouth that they were no longer concerned over Sioux lands, at least for the moment. With statehood approaching, they were involved in political maneuvering over the location of the state capital, and ignored the land commission.

One afternoon in late May, Agent Spencer came to see Culver. "The commission is coming here first," he said, flourishing a letter. "They arrive next week, and I'm supposed to have all of the Indians camped around the agency until they settle the land question. I've been after them to get their corn planted, and now this." He waved the letter again. "If it drags on they'll miss planting time, and there goes any farming this year. After pushing farming here more than at any other agency, it has to take a back seat to talking the Indians out of their land." He paused, watching Culver light his pipe. "The Commissioners said to bring all of them in," Spencer continued. "Some of the old hostiles probably won't come in unless I send the police. And if they do come, they're likely to disrupt the talks if any of the others want to sell. I'll be damned if do and damned if I don't. What would you do?"

Culver blew smoke at a fly buzzing around his face. "Those ex-hostiles will never vote one way or the other, but they won't let anyone else vote if they can help it. You'll come out better if you don't even tell them about it. If enough of the others vote in favor, the commission can still get the required three-fourths approval.

"Good. I was thinking along that line, and you've confirmed it."

Billy watched as one group after another set up canvas tipis on the open land around the agency. The men seemed puzzled. Farming had seemed almost sacred to the agents, but now, when their women were ready to plant corn, the police had ordered them to come to the agency to talk about selling land they were determined not to sell. The agent had warned the chiefs that no family could leave until the commission was through with its work.

Late in the afternoon the commissioners and their staff arrived in wagons from Valentine. Billy joined the crowd that gathered to watch, eager to see Three Stars. He wore a brown corduroy suit; his beard was full and bushy, and his hair was short. Chairman Foster had a goatee. Warner was clean-shaven except for a carefully trimmed mustache. The large crowd of Brulés watched as the commissioners' aides set up tents near the agency headquarters.

The commissioners appeared to be on a friendly visit, with nothing in mind but leisurely talks with the Brulés. They immediately bought fifteen fat steers and had them butchered and roasted over fires, then invited everyone for a feast. For the Brulés it was like a successful hunt in the old days, when every family was roasting hump ribs, and men and women wandered around visiting and gorging themselves until they could eat no more.

But in the old days, when they celebrated, they danced. Then the missionaries had persuaded the Indian Bureau to ban all dancing as heathenish. Old Two Strike beckoned to Billy. "Tell Three Stars we want to dance," he said.

Feeling awed and unsure of his voice, Billy cautiously approached Crook, who was wiping the grease from his flowing beard. "Two Strike asked me to tell you they want to dance," he said nervously, fingering the braids at the back of his neck. "The agent doesn't allow dancing."

"Come with me," Crook said, and set off to find Spencer, walking with the measured tread of a veteran infantryman. "They want to dance," Crook told Spencer. "I see nothing wrong with it, and it'll put them in a good humor." The agent frowned.

"It was the Commissioner who ordered us agents to stop the dances," he said. "But he also ordered me to cooperate with your commission in every way. This is one of the ways. They can put on the Omaha Dance if they want to."

Billy relayed the good news to Two Strike, and when the feasting ended, the dance began. The Brulés enjoyed it enormously, while Three Stars looked on and smiled. Only the Reverend Cleveland looked unhappy, and he quickly left.

"I saw Louis Richards and other mixed bloods visiting Three

Stars in his tent after the feast," Billy told Culver next day.

"Some of them were here this morning early," Culver said, "and they all had money to spend. I'm sure it was some of that $25,000 Congress provided for 'unusual' expenses."

That same afternoon, when he went to the agency for the mail, Billy saw old Swift Bear of the Corn Band talking to Three Stars. Of all the chiefs, Swift Bear was the only one who was always eager to please white officials and who could never say no to them. He must have forgotten that all Tetons had agreed not to discuss the land sale, for on June 4 he asked Three Stars to call a council. Crook was happy to oblige him. The Brulés had formed a big circle with their wagons, and it served as the council ground. In the center was a canvas shade for the commissioners, the chiefs, and the interpreters, who sat on wagon seats.

The council opened with the goateed chairman Foster reading the agreement, pausing after each sentence for the interpreter. Then Three Stars spoke.

"The white men in the East are like birds," he told them. "They are hatching out of their eggs every year, and there isn't enough room for them in the East. They must go elsewhere, as you have seen them coming for the last few years. They are still coming, and they will come until they overrun all of this country. You can't prevent it, nor can the President prevent it. Everything is decided in Washington by the majority, and these people come out West and see the Indians have a big body of land that they aren't using, and they say, 'we want the land.' " He paused, then his face became solemn.

"Last year when you refused to accept the bill, Congress came very near opening the reservation anyway. I'm certain that you will never get better terms than are offered in this bill, and the chances are you won't get so good. It strikes me that instead of complaining about the past you had better provide for the future." When he finished speaking, he told them to talk about it among themselves and to return in the morning. The Brulés broke up into groups, and Billy saw that in each the mixed bloods were doing most of the talking. *The Brulés don't want to sell their land. Those men can't possibly make them change their minds.*

The next morning Crook explained the agreement's benefits for the Tetons. "I have no personal interest in this matter," he told them. "It's up to you. Think about it and talk it over for a few days, then decide. We have other work to do and can't stay much longer. If you don't sign the agreement soon we'll assume that you don't intend to sign it, and go on our way."

Billy felt relieved to hear that—it was what he'd expected of Three Stars. "All we have to do is hang on for a few more days," he told Culver. "Then the commission will leave and we'll still have our land. At least he isn't trying to bully us into selling."

"Don't bet on it. A lot of that was just so it won't appear that the commission is being heavy handed. He knows this is the best offer the Tetons will ever receive and that they must accept it. He's not likely to leave until they do, and there's been a lot of money changing hands." Billy said nothing, hoping Culver was wrong.

At the next council old Swift Bear invited squawman Charles Jordan to speak, while the fullbloods narrowed their eyes. Jordan had lived among the Tetons for many years, and his wife was Oglala, but that didn't give him the right to speak. "I am convinced we should sell the land they want," he said. "The men who oppose selling it just want to sit around forever, eating free rations and neglecting their families." Billy sensed a wave of anger sweeping over the fullbloods, who scowled at Jordan. Squawmen and mixed bloods, their inferiors, were boldly speaking up in councils and acting important only because they knew more about the whites. They'd have it out with them right now, Billy thought as he looked at their angry faces, but they're afraid of Three Stars. Crook had praised these men as the most forward-looking element, the hope of the Sioux, but to the fullbloods they were traitors.

After the commissioners left the council ground, the Brulés all tried to talk at once. "Three Stars is right!" Louis Richards shouted. "It's to our advantage to sell now, not later."

"We don't want to sell!" White Crow roared. "If we do they'll cut our rations!"

"No! They'll cut them if we don't," Richards replied.

They argued heatedly for half an hour. Billy noticed that some fullblood progressives were silent, and he felt fear. They're weakening, he thought, and he remembered seeing some of them talking to Three Stars. It appeared that all who spoke privately with Crook came away agreeing with him. Only a month earlier all had sworn to remain united, to stand fast against the land sale. Now that unity was drifting away before their eyes, vanishing like the smoke of a campfire. Billy's shoulders sagged. He felt helpless. As they were leaving, Hollow-Horn-Bear walked up to Richards. "Don't tell Three Stars about this talk," he said. The mixed blood nephew of Swift Bear didn't reply. *Three Stars pays him, so he'll tell him.*

"The Brulés have many worries," Culver observed when Billy told him about the quarrelling. "Some are real, some are imaginary. For one thing, they're sure that any government proposal is a bag of snakes; the sweeter the offer, the more deadly the bite. The Edmunds crowd confirmed their suspicions. They look for deception in every sentence; they're especially nervous when they can't find it, for they're sure it's there. They know what they have now, but they don't know what they'll have if they agree. They've been burned so many times they're sure it will happen again if they say yes. That's unfortunate, for this is a good offer, and one they should accept. But however it turns out, it will leave bad feelings that won't go away soon. That's also unfortunate."

J.T. Lea, a white man that the Indian Bureau had sent several weeks earlier to take a census of the Brulés, entered the trading post to buy a hunting knife. "How's your work coming?" Culver asked.

"They sure hate to be counted, but I'm getting it done."

After Lea left, Culver shook his head while sparks flew from his pipe. "This is the worst time for making a head count, while the commission is trying to negotiate a sale."

"Why did they choose this time?"

"Someone in the Indian Bureau figures there may not be as many men as are on the rolls. To help the commission, they want to reduce the number and make it a lot easier to muster a three-fourths vote. But nothing arouses the Sioux more than being counted. They know nothing good ever comes of it, and it worries them."

"Should it?"

"It should worry them more than they realize. Right now that count is to help the commission, but it can also affect their rations. Sioux rations have been reduced each year since '85 to way below what the treaty guaranteed. When Congress wants to save money, it thinks first of the Indians—they don't vote. The Brulés have kept from starving only by not reporting deaths and by claiming more children than they have. There are a lot fewer people than are listed on the rolls, and some will avoid being counted if they can. This head count may help get the land, but it could mean disaster for the Tetons." Billy remembered the Friends of the Indians' talk about starving the Sioux into submission and shuddered.

"Another thing they fear is that this agreement will cancel the 1868 treaty, and they don't like the pricing system. All of them are smart enough to see that if settlers wait five years they can have the best land for fifty cents an acre."

"All of this land was once ours. It's up to us to hang on to what's left."

"I know, and I don't blame the Sioux for not wanting to part with any more. They've heard, too, that tribes whose reservations have been broken up into individual allotments are in worse shape than before, worse off even than the Sioux. And allotment is likely to follow the land sale, sooner or later. The old chiefs know very well that allotment will break up the tribe and end what influence they still have. In spite of all this, I agree with Crook that this is the best offer they'll ever receive and they should take it while they can."

At the next council, White Bird asked the question most often on the lips of the Brulés: "What about our rations? As soon as you get our land, the government will cut our rations."

"I assure you that there is no connection between the land sale and your rations," Crook answered wearily. Like the others, White Bird didn't appear convinced. Being confined to a reservation was bad enough, but having to see their families go hungry was a frightening specter. Again and again the commissioners had insisted that the land sale had nothing to do with rations, but the question refused to die.

As he listened to the talk after the council ended, Billy was appalled to see that many fullblood progressives were wavering. What held them back was worry over what Pratt and the Friends of the Indian had said about scrapping treaties and ending rations. They needed positive, unequivocal assurance from Three Stars himself.

"We have told you repeatedly that what you fear won't happen," Crook told them gruffly in the morning. "I have now written our promises to you on this paper and signed it. I will leave it with you." A murmur of approval rose from the Brulés. Three Stars had won over many fullbloods, that was clear. Soon some of them were arguing in favor of the agreement, and that made Billy feel queasy.

When they met on June 7, Hollow-Horn-Bear, who still opposed the sale, spoke. "The Brulés," he said, "have chosen twelve men to represent them, and those men have asked me to speak for the tribe. The Brulés don't want to talk to the commission. They want a big council of all the Teton chiefs to deal with it. If four men have to decide, and two are here and two far away, they will decide differently. Only by having all the chiefs together can we reach a decision fair to all. That is all the Brulés have to say."

Crook thanked him, then invited any man who wanted to speak to come forward. Billy was shocked. The Brulés had chosen Hollow-Horn-Bear to speak for them. No one else had the right to talk. Three Stars must know that.

"He's trying to get around the chiefs and the tribal council by appealing to individuals," Culver said quietly, as he and Billy stood at the edge of the crowd.

"He talked about being fair. What he's doing is unfair. The Brulés chose Hollow-Horn-Bear to speak for them."

After a long silence, Louis Richards, Swift Bear's mixed blood nephew, arose. "Every man has a right to his own opinion," he said. "The tribal council has no right to decide for all. Many of us have studied this agreement, and it has lots of advantages for us." He looked over the crowd. "The commissioners would like to see you men who are against it."

Old Two Strike, who was not ashamed to be called nonprogressive or to admit that he opposed the land sale, immediately replied. "The tribal council has always had the right to choose who will speak for the tribe, as you know very well." He scowled at Richards. "It has chosen Hollow-Horn-Bear to speak for all," he said, then sat down.

Good Voice leaped to his feet. "I am a man who works hard," he said, "and I am as good a progressive as you." He glared at Richards. "When Hollow-Horn-Bear spoke for the tribe he spoke for me. You try to make it sound like the tribal council is fighting Three Stars, when it asked only for all Teton chiefs to be brought together to talk to the commission."

Crook slowly arose. "The Great Father didn't call a general council," he said, holding the lapels of his corduroy jacket, "because that would make too many Sioux neglect their farms during the planting season." Yet planting time would soon be past for the Brulés, and it appeared that they would remain at the agency until the commission released them. When several men told Spencer they wouldn't sign the agreement and wanted to look after their cattle, the agent threatened to arrest them if they left.

"When I was here before," Crook continued, "I expected much good of you, and now after eleven years I come back and find that you have done very little toward civilization. You have been content to sit and eat rations the government gives you, thinking it is always going to support you in idleness. When I was here before I was proud of you. You were full of manhood, and any decision that was required of you, you gave it right away."

After Crook finished, Standing Bear spoke for the progressives in his band. "We want to sign the agreement," he said. "We haven't done so because no one is sure we will continue to receive rations."

Crook, who had addressed this fear again and again, slowly arose and discarded his friendly pose. "I have assured you that rations will not be cut," he said sharply, his face flushed. The tone of his voice gave Billy visions of bluecoat soldiers. At that a group of mixed bloods started to push through the crowd toward the table where the copy of the agreement lay, along with an inkpot and quill pens.

The fullbloods leaped to their feet. Hollow-Horn-Bear shouted for all who stood by the tribe to leave at once. Most of the Brulés rushed away like the cavalry was after them, but they soon stopped and looked back like a bunch of startled but curious antelopes. Billy watched, hoping they wouldn't return. Old Swift Bear, who had never said no to a white official, rushed to the table and grabbed a pen, shouting for someone to write his name. At his elbow was Crow Dog. Crook and the other commissioners looked on, unsmiling.

All of the Brulés who had stopped to watch now began shrieking, while chiefs and headmen tried to herd the others away before they could be stampeded into signing. Agent Spencer sent the Indian police to stop the chiefs from driving the waverers away.

Many of those who had rushed away began drifting back. Hollow-Horn-Bear hurried to Crook. Through the interpreter he begged Three Stars to let them return to their farms.

Unruffled, Crook replied, "Why not stay until tomorrow and have another talk? It's not good to quit when you're mad, and I can see you're hopping mad."

"I'm not mad!" Hollow-Horn-Bear roared. In the meantime the police had stopped Yellow Hair and White Horse from trying to make the others leave.

Billy realized that nearly three hundred had already signed, mostly mixed-bloods and squawmen, but also the fullblood members of the Loafer and Corn bands. Louis Richards and other mixed bloods now went among those who remained away from the table. "You're disloyal," Billy heard Richards say, "and you know what happens to disloyal men." No Teton wanted to be accused of disloyalty, and the hint that disloyal men would suffer later troubled them.

The councils continued. Those who remained opposed loudly protested their loyalty while more and more men touched the pen as their names were written. As he watched, Billy had a sinking feeling. Crook had broken their resistance. On June 12 he announced that more than the necessary three-fourths of Brulé men had signed. The commission's work at Rosebud was successfully concluded.

Episcopalian Bishop W. P. Hare, who had observed the councils, remarked to Culver that the commission, "convinced that the bill was essential, carried persuasion to the verge of intimidation. I don't blame them if they sometimes did. The wit and patience of an angel would fail often in such a task." Charles Hyde, who had also been watching, called the commission's actions a "shakedown."

Billy had been appalled at the growing number of signers, remembering how the Hunkpapas had taken their cues from Grass and refused to let Pratt stampede them into signing. But among the Brulés, once the signing had started, the resistance of one group after another had collapsed out of fear of punishment, or at the least of losing a share of the benefits. And none wanted to be considered disloyal.

"Three weeks ago we were united against it," he said. "I'm still opposed, but most signed, whether or not they were in favor. What happened to us?"

Culver lit his pipe and blew smoke toward the ceiling. "Crook is convinced that the well-being of the Sioux depends on accepting this agreement. He knows that if they refuse they'll lose their land anyway and likely have little to show for it. So he had the agent corral everyone here where he could keep them under pressure until enough realized that it was a good agreement or their resistance broke down. To accomplish it Crook had to make many promises, and some of them will require action by Congress. He took that chance because he felt it was in the interest of the Sioux and necessary, but now his honor depends on Congress fulfilling his promises. I don't envy him being in that position. It's no place for an honorable man, and you have to admit he is that."

I still can't believe it happened. Everyone was solidly against it, yet somehow three-fourths signed. And Three Stars was the one who did it.

The signing had bitterly divided the Brulés and they quarreled violently. The non-signers said loudly that once the government got their land it would reduce rations, no matter what Three Stars and the others said. The signers hotly denied that would happen. "Which is right?" Billy asked Culver. He knocked the ash of his pipe and shook his head.

"I don't know what will happen when Lea turns in his census report. Right now the rations are barely enough to keep people from starving. A cut is too awful to think about, but everything depends on appropriations. Congress, not the commission controls them. All we can do is hope.''

Chapter Seven

"I offered my buckboard to carry some of the commission's staff to Pine Ridge," Culver said that evening. "I agreed you'd drive the team. You can stay and see what the Oglalas do if you want." Billy looked glum, still bewildered by the collapse of Brulé unity.

"My bet is that Crook will find Red Cloud and his people harder to break down, like the Brulés would have been if they still had Spotted Tail," Culver continued. "Dr. Bland has bombarded the Oglalas with warnings not to sell. Crook versus Red Cloud—that should be a show worth watching."

The four wagons set out early on June 13 and reached Pine Ridge mid-morning of the third day. Billy had seen scouts watching them from a distance, and when the wagons approached Pine Ridge, several hundred mounted warriors in a long line moved toward them at a walk. All held Winchesters and were painted as for war. The sight of those stern warriors, with their feathers fluttering in the breeze, gave Billy a momentary chill. He glanced at the menacing line and then at Three Stars, who was feeling ill. He sat stiffly on the wagon seat, frowning. The warriors stopped a hundred yards away while the chiefs solemnly rode forward to greet the commission. If they were a welcoming committee, that wasn't obvious.

"I don't like this," Crook curtly told the chiefs through his interpreter. "We came to talk to the Oglalas as individuals, not as a tribe controlled by warriors." The chiefs gave signals and the warriors wheeled their ponies and loped away, the ribbons in the ponies' tails trailing behind them. *Maybe Culver is right. The Oglalas look ready to fight.*

That afternoon they met in council, with a huge crowd of Oglalas seated in a big circle. In the center, Foster and Warner sat with Red Cloud, American Horse, Little Wound, and Young-Man-Afraid-of-His-Horses. While Crook remained in his tent, Warner read the agreement to the Oglalas, who listened with expressionless faces. When the interpreter finished translating the last sentence, the chiefs gave signals and a large body of mounted warriors began driving the other Oglalas away.

"See here, what in thunder are you doing?" Foster asked sharply, snapping his fingers.

"The tribal council has ordered that no one be allowed to talk about selling land," Red Cloud replied, unawed by the commissioners, "for the Oglalas have already rejected the sale. There is nothing to discuss. It is time for you to leave." *Culver is right. Even the progressives refuse to sell. It won't be easy for Crook to change that.* He watched Foster and Warner. They showed no sign of being ready to leave. Then he glanced at Crook's tent and saw several mixed bloods leaving it. *He's not too sick to try the same things that worked at Rosebud.*

Crook apparently felt better the next morning, and when he summoned the Oglalas for another council, they reluctantly assembled. Smiling and conciliatory, Foster explained the agreement's advantages for the Oglalas.

"We are here to enable the Sioux to become men again," Foster continued, "and to free themselves from their present slavery. I want to see the day when the son of Red Cloud or your other chiefs shall occupy a seat in the great council of this state. Then instead of having a white man speak for the Indians, the Indians will be able to speak for themselves. In the meantime, it's important for the Sioux to sell some of their land while they can get such favorable terms." *That's what Culver keeps saying. But why should we sell any of it? They said it was ours forever. Let the Wasicuns go somewhere else.*

Foster went on to say that South Dakota would soon become a state, and its people wouldn't tolerate having it divided by the Great Sioux Reserve, which was like a wall between the eastern and western parts. "It doesn't take much sense to see that the whites will break down that wall. It is our duty as friends to advise you of the situation. Unless this act is accepted, and I don't say this as a threat—I say it as a friend, the Senators and Representatives from South Dakota will influence Congress to get it through there somehow. There's no way to stop them. Your choice is to accept a good price for your land now, or risk losing it, and receiving nothing."

Red Cloud spoke next. First he wanted to be sure that white men married into the tribe would have the same rights as fullbloods. Then he rambled on for a time before coming to the point. "My friend General Crook knows something about this last treaty of 1876. My friends, when a man owes ten cents or fifty cents up here at these stores these storekeepers want that paid before he gets any more. Now you come here and ask for more land. You want to buy more land, and I looked around to see if you brought any boxes of money. I couldn't see any, and now I think this is sugar talk again."

Progressive chiefs Little Wound and Young-Man-Afraid-of-His-Horses spoke briefly, and they also dwelt on the past, especially unkept promises. Irritated, Crook had Red Cloud send for his copy of the 1868 treaty, then showed him that all the commitments except the clothing issue had expired.

American Horse said that he knew very well what the land agreement would do to the Tetons. "Today it takes half of our land. Tomorrow a tax man will come and tie ropes to every bit of land we have left. Then, when we have no money to pay the tax man, he will pull on the ropes and drag the land out from under our feet. It has happened to other tribes." The commissioners frowned, for what he said was true at the few reservations that had already been allotted.

White Cow Man agreed with American Horse. "I think that if I spread my blanket right here and you piled money upon it that high," he said, holding his hand palm downward at knee level, "I don't think I could keep it two days. Whenever I get ten dollars, I put it in my blanket and go to the trader's store, and before the day is out I spend it all. I am an Indian and I don't know how to take care of money. Over there at the boarding school I have a son who has been there four years. This young one at the school,

I think he is the one to take a land allotment when the time comes.''

"My friends," Warner said, with a trace of irritation in his voice, "we are talking of a land agreement, not of allotment. That is a totally different matter." He paused to see if they appeared to understand. "That you may have been wronged in the past I do not question, but that the Great Father has watched over you as you would watch over your children, there is no doubt. And yet you come here today and slap the Great Father in the face. It's time to forget the past and to think of the future."

Crook spoke next. "If whites have violated the 1868 treaty," he said, "the Sioux have also violated it." He cleared his throat. "The old days are gone forever. It's time to put them out of your minds and start looking after yourselves. Before we leave we want every man eighteen or older to say for himself if he will or will not sign."

It was clear to Billy that Crook was again maneuvering to get around the chiefs and the tribal council by appealing to individuals. But fearing that no Oglala could win an argument with the commissioners, especially with Three Stars, the tribal council had ordered all to remain silent. The fullbloods obeyed, but that gave the mixed bloods a wide opportunity. As those at Rosebud had done, the mixed bloods argued in favor of the sale and took influential fullbloods to talk to Crook in his tent. Billy could see that a few seemed to have been won over, but none of them did any talking.

Finally Crook called on the Oglalas to come forward and sign the agreement. Squawmen, mixedbloods, and about eighty Northern Cheyennes who had lived with the Oglalas since their flight from Indian Territory, headed for the table. The Oglalas who opposed the sale called on American Horse to talk for the tribe.

American Horse, a sharp-faced man of medium stature, was the greatest orator of all the Tetons, and when he started talking the signers returned to their seats. Billy saw Crook look at Foster and shrug. The commissioners had pretended that they had come only for leisurely talks with their friends the Oglalas, so they had no choice but to listen. American Horse was, after all, a leading progressive chief, but his talk against the sale meant that the commissioners could no longer pretend that only hard-headed non-progressives opposed it.

American Horse talked steadily the rest of the day, pointing to the earth, the sky, and distant hills to emphasize his remarks. At times he was witty, at others solemn. He brought up anything that entered his mind, from visits to Washington to his travels with a Wild West Show. The commissioners glumly listened, but they didn't interrupt him. They looked relieved when the time came to quit for the day. "I hope he's as tired as I am," Billy heard Foster say.

When the Oglalas assembled the next morning, American Horse asked if he could speak about the land agreement, a request the commissioners couldn't refuse. But he talked about the poor quality of the rations issued the Tetons, then turned to the reservation boundaries, spending two hours describing each stream and other landmark in detail. He rambled on about the queer customs and manners of whites, mimicking them as he spoke, to the delight of the Oglalas. Indian police were poorly paid, he said. Ten dollars a month was not enough.

By the time American Horse finished, the day was spent. In the morning he was ready to go again, and he still hadn't exhausted his supply of irrelevant topics to discuss. He complained of the trickery of some Indian traders, and of agents who had stolen their annuities and sold them. He mentioned the evil ways of past land commissioners who had lied to the Tetons. Then he went to great lengths to make it clear that he didn't mean the honorable gentlemen on the present commission. They were all big chiefs, he said, and they spoke with only one tongue. Crook smiled a bit grimly at that.

Billy listened, spellbound, aware that American Horse could talk forever without once mentioning the land sale. As the commissioners stiffly walked away that afternoon, he heard Crook wryly admit, "That rascal is a much better speaker than any of us."

On the third afternoon of American Horse's harangue, Warner reached the breaking point and interrupted the Oglala chief. "I have heard of men being talked to death," he said, "but I had never put much faith in it. Now I know it's possible, and I hope our friend American Horse will not persist in trying to kill us with words." When the interpreter translated this, the Oglalas laughed and hooted. American Horse smiled and resumed his talk.

At the end of the second week, Crook was obviously impatient.

"I must warn you for the last time," he said, his bushy beard waving in the afternoon breeze, "not to listen to chiefs who obstruct progress, who still live in the past. We are giving you another chance to sign this agreement before it's too late."

At that American Horse came forward, followed by Bear Nose, who had talked to Crook a few days earlier. The commissioners looked startled to see American Horse, fearing he'd start another endless speech. Instead, he picked up the quill pen and held it toward Three Stars. "I will sign this, knowing I have done what you tell us is best for our people," he said. Crook quickly recovered his composure and wrote American Horse's name on the paper while the Oglala chief touched the pen. Bear Nose signed next followed by all the men of American Horse's small True Oglala Band. Billy watched unbelieving. By talking so long it appeared that American Horse had discouraged the commissioners into giving up at Pine Ridge without the required number of signatures. Then he surrendered. It was incredible.

When American Horse signed, Little Wound hurried to Captain Pollock, who was acting agent. "Allow the people to return to their homes," he asked. "They need to tend their crops and to hunt for their cattle." Knowing the commission had given up on winning over the Oglalas, Pollock agreed.

While the commissioners walked to their tents, Little Wound confronted American Horse. "Why did you do that?" he asked angrily. American Horse rubbed his sharp nose and looked embarrassed.

"Last night Bear Nose took me to talk to Three Stars," he admitted. "He told me that we can sign this paper and sell part of our land, or we can refuse to sign and lose all of it. I don't want that to happen. The talks made me so dizzy I didn't know what I was doing."

Except for American Horse's True Oglala Band and some of the young men, few fullbloods had signed. Of the older chiefs, only No Flesh had touched the pen. Convinced he was dying, he decided to make a last gesture of friendship to the whites. Most of the signers were squawmen, mixed bloods, and Northern Cheyennes. Less than half of the men at Pine Ridge had approved the sale.

After two weeks among the stubborn Oglalas, the commission called its last council, but only a few hundred Indians came. Warner brusquely told them that half of them had signed; those who refused, he said, had turned their backs on civilization. That didn't appear to hurt their feelings or make them repent.

Crook arose to make his last pitch. "You have shown little loyalty to the government," he said wearily. "Many chiefs promised me they wouldn't talk against the sale, but that isn't enough. They should demonstrate their loyalty by signing to show their people what they should do." No chief came forward. The commissioners shook their heads and headed for their tents. They left a copy of the agreement with Captian Pollock along with money for putting on feasts for chiefs and their bands whenever they agreed to sign.

Since the agreement required a three-fourths vote for approval, the Oglalas had rejected the sale. Billy was elated. When they learned what the Oglalas had done, other Teton tribes would surely follow their example, he was sure. While the commissioners headed for Lower Brulé and Crow Creek agencies, he returned to Rosebud, feeling more hopeful than before.

To keep up with the commission's progress, Culver wrote to traders at the other agencies, and they described what happened. Lower Brulé and Crow Creek, small agencies on the Missouri, were under intense pressure from Dakotans who wanted their fertile land. When Crook promised Iron Nation that if the Lower Brulés lost their land they could move to Rosebud, they quickly accepted. This was a promise he was unable to keep, for when the Lower Brulés lost their land the Rosebud Brulés refused to share their reservation with them. Warner went to Crow Creek Agency, while Foster and Crook headed north.

At Cheyenne River the Indians were solidly against the sale, and so they remained through feasts and dances. Miniconju chief Hump had defied the agent by refusing to disband the Akicita, or tribal soldiers, and he used them to preserve his power. The agent, hoping to gain a measure of control over him, named Hump chief of the Indian police, but that only increased his influence and made him even more independent.

With great difficulty, Crook obtained the signatures of squawmen and mixed bloods, for Hump's tribal soldiers and Indian police broke up several councils to prevent anyone else from signing. Crook sent to nearby Fort Bennett for Major George M. Randall of the 23rd Infantry. The Miniconjus had reason to remember and fear Randall, and his presence in uniform made them cautious and prevented Hump from going too far.

Ordering the Indians to remain at the agency until enough had signed, and leaving Randall and the agent to collect more signatures, Crook and Foster went on to Standing Rock on July 26. In two weeks of heavy pressure, Randall and the agent secured the necessary signatures.

At Standing Rock, Grass immediately informed the commission that the Hunkpapas were all opposed to selling any land. There was plenty of land for whites east of the Missouri, he said. Let them settle there. The commission was acting unfairly, he added, by leaving a copy of the agreement with each agent and telling him to get more signatures after the commission had gone on. He had heard that at the other agencies white men and mixed bloods were paid for every signer they brought in. If that was fair, then the commissioners didn't need to come at all. They could send copies to each agent and say, "Get it signed." The Hunkpapas hooted at this. He knew the commissioners were honorable men, Grass concluded, but it was not right to leave copies of the agreement with men the Tetons didn't trust. Crook looked embarrassed.

This time Agent McLaughlin favored the agreement and used his influence to promote it. The commission, employing its usual methods, soon had mixed bloods promoting the sale. To frighten the fullbloods, Foster announced that the commission already had the necessary three-fourths vote from other agencies, so it didn't matter what the Hunkpapas did. That wasn't true, but it convinced many fullbloods that if the agreement was approved and their names weren't on it, they would be denied the benefits that signers would receive. Then McLaughlin privately told Grass that if he and his people failed to sign they would lose their land without compensation. He had no authority to say that, but it probably would have proved true. Grass, who trusted McLaughlin, surrendered.

On August 3, just as the commission was preparing for the Hunkpapas to come forward and sign, Sitting Bull arrived with a large number of warriors and demanded to be allowed to speak. McLaughlin took Grass by the arm and led him to the table to start the signing.

Whooping and shrieking war cries, Sitting Bull's men pushed through the crowd toward the table. McLaughlin grabbed the agreement to prevent them from destroying it. The police and others pushed Sitting Bull's men back, while they howled and brandished Winchesters. The signing continued amid pandemonium.

The commission departed a few days later, and soon announced that it had 130 more Sioux votes than required. Few whites questioned its figures or its methods of obtaining the signatures. Only Dr. Bland condemned the commission, charging it with misconduct, fraud, bribery, and intimidation, but no one in the East listened. The Friends of the Indian congratulated the commission on its good work in behalf of the Sioux and the nation. Washington officials were greatly relieved that the Sioux had heeded the advice of their old friend General Crook.

The land agreement negotiations left all of the Tetons dazed and angry, wondering how their united opposition to the sale had been manipulated into a large majority in favor. When they recovered from the shock, non-signers called signers traitors, insisting that as soon as the sale was confirmed their rations would be cut. The signers hotly denied that, pointing to Three Stars' assurances.

About the time the commission announced that the agreement had been approved, what the Sioux had feared most occurred. Agent Spencer came to Culver, clutching a letter in his hand and looking agitated. "It's from Commissioner Morgan," he said in a voice that broke. "He says he has discovered some hocus pocus at all the agencies. He says the Sioux have been cheating the government, and he's going to reduce the beef ration here by two million pounds a year. Immediately."

Culver put down his pipe. "My God," he said. "They'll starve to death."

"There's nothing I can do about it," Spencer said, wringing his hands. "I've got to follow orders."

"Hollow-Horn-Bear and a lot of others told us this would happen as soon as they got the land," Billy said. "They could barely wait until the commission got off the Reserve. Three Stars' promises didn't mean much after all."

"Don't blame Crook for this. It's certainly not his doing. Let's give him a chance to straighten it out."

Billy shook his head, while Spencer looked from one to the other, his mouth opening and closing. "After what Crook said about Indians, I thought he was our friend," Billy said. "Then he tricked us out of our land, and now they've cut our rations. Some friend!"

"You'd better explain to the Commissioner in the strongest language that these people don't have enough to eat now," Culver told Spencer. "Beef is their mainstay, poor as it is. Starve 'em and any kind of illness will be fatal." Spencer left, slapping the letter against his left hand. *He has good reason to be upset.* Spencer didn't have to worry for long; on the commission's recommendation, George Wright replaced him as agent that same week.

At the next ration day the Brulés looked shocked at the small amount of beef they received. "Where's the rest?" they wanted to know.

"That's all there is," Wright told them. "I'm sorry. Commissioner's orders."

The Brulés were outraged at the signers, at the commission, but especially at Crook. "You are fools and dupes," the non-signers shouted at those who had approved the sale. "They're paying you like they always have when we've been foolish enough to do what they want." The land sale had split the Brulés into hostile camps. The ration cut brought them to the verge of bloodshed. *No matter what they promise, no matter what Crook said about treating us fairly, the whites want to destroy us. There's no hope for us. Soon they'll be back for the rest of our land.*

One afternoon a few days later Short Bull came to the trading post with a letter in his hand. He was a small, sharp-faced man who had been a famous warrior; at forty-five he was a medicine man and a leader of the nonprogressives. Known for his generosity, he was respected and popular. Like other nonprogressives, he'd always ignored Billy. Now he showed him the letter. "You can read it for me?"

Billy took the letter, which had been written by a white man or mixed blood for a Shoshoni named Blue Horse, who lived on the Wind River Reservation in Wyoming.

"Brother, there is good news," he read. "A God or Messiah has come to earth far to the west of us, in the land of The-People-Who-Wear-Rabbitskin-Blankets or beyond. I have not seen him, but they say he is the Messiah of the Indians and has come to earth to save all Indians from whites. He has promised to bring back the buffalo, so we can hunt again. I wanted you, my friend, to know of this good news.''

Short Bull eyed Billy suspiciously. ''You're not making it up? He really said that? That an Indian Messiah has come to save us?''

Billy translated the letter again for him. ''That's exactly what it says. It's too bad it can't possibly be true.''

Chapter Eight

"It didn't matter after all that they kept us from planting," Billy said one day in July, as hot winds seared the withered grass under a cloudless Dakota sky. He shaded his eyes and stared at distant hills dancing in heat waves. "The corn wouldn't have lasted this long. The Oglalas' corn was coming up good, only Three Stars kept them at the agency so long their cattle ate it. But it would have died by now anyway."

Culver wiped the sweat from his face with a red bandanna and squinted at the sun. "You're right about that. Two Strike says this is the driest summer he remembers, and he's one of the oldest. I hear that homesteaders are leaving the Dakotas in droves, most of them skin and bones."

"Like us, only they don't have to stay here. We're prisoners."

As he watched the Brulés at issue time, Billy knew from their sunken eyes and air of resignation that they had nearly lost hope. They had been hungry much of the time for several years before the drastic cut in the beef ration, but now real hunger was chronic. Bishop Hare and others estimated that their rations were sufficient for only two-thirds of the ten days for which they were issued. Billy knew only too well that was true.

Having no tangible enemy to attack, the Brulés quarreled bitterly among themselves. Tribal leaders continued to condemn the squaw-men, mixed bloods, and Christian fullbloods who had signed the agreement—everyone still blamed the land sale for all of their troubles. "You have betrayed your own people by helping the

Wasicuns," Two Strike said. "You are traitors." Others said much the same things or worse.

Billy observed all of this with mounting concern. The whites have us in a big trap, and there's no way we can ever escape. Little by little they're starving us to death, making our people mad enough to kill each other and save them the trouble. It was all so confusing and hard to understand. The Sioux commissioners claimed that the Great Father watched over them like they watched over their children. They lied. People who called themselves Friends of the Indian were willing to make the Sioux go hungry if they refused to do their bidding. The Grandfather, the Wakan Tanka, had thrown his children away. Then the troubling thought arose—perhaps he is dead, killed by the white men's God.

In early August, Chasing Crane returned from a visit to the Crows and stopped at the trader's store for tobacco. "The Crows have heard about a god who has come to earth," he told several Brulés who were there. "He has been grieved by parents crying for their dead children, and he has promised to let the sky fall down on the whites and to destroy the disobedient." The Brulés looked at him skeptically. What he said reminded Billy of Short Bull's recent letter from his Shoshoni friend. Others also appeared to have recalled it.

"We heard that before, but who believes it?" Lame Deer asked. "It sounds like a Wasicun promise. They say sign this, believe what we tell you, and you'll have everything you want. What you get is nothing." The Brulés talked about it some.

"It sounds like a big lie," Gray Eagle said to Chasing Crane. "Who would help Indians? And how do we know you're telling the truth?"

"I tell you what the Crows told me," Chasing Crane growled. "They believe it's true. That's all I know."

It's silly to expect the impossible, Billy thought. But unless something happens, all of the Tetons are doomed to die of starvation or disease. Biblical stories he'd heard Sundays at Carlisle kept running through his mind. Could it be possible that a new Messiah was actually coming to save the Indians? He shook his head. It was foolish to think that was possible, so he put it out of his mind.

Talk of the Messiah spread among the Brulés and Oglalas, who desperately embraced any phantom of hope. Finally, Red Cloud,

Young-Man-Afraid-of-His-Horses, Little Wound, and American Horse agreed they should hold a secret council to discuss what to do. They sent letters to Short Bull at Rosebud and Kicking Bear at Cheyenne River, inviting the Brulés and Miniconjus to send representatives. After Billy read the letter to him, Short Bull and two other Brulés slipped away and rode to Pine Ridge without informing the agent.

Because the land commission had made so many promises to the Sioux that were not part of the land agreement, Foster got permission to invite a delegation of chiefs to Washington in early December. Crook went over all of the promises with them, so there could be no misunderstanding, for he was determined to see that every promise made was fulfilled. He was particularly concerned over restoration of the beef ration, for he knew the cut must have caused widespread hunger.

He protested to Indian Commissioner Morgan that beef is the mainstay of the Sioux diet. They were already suffering from hunger, he said, and the cut meant severe hardship, even starvation. He had, furthermore, assured them that if they signed the agreement their rations would not be reduced. Both their survival and his honor were at stake. The Sioux had been talked out of half their land and were being forced to work hard to support themselves. Starving them at the outset was not the way to make the program successful, he said.

Morgan airily dismissed Crook's protests. The Indians had cheated the government, he said. Congress had cut the Sioux appropriation and only Congress could restore the beef ration. The chiefs returned to their agencies with Crook's promise to urge Congress to restore the beef issue, but with little else. They knew that the commission's report stated that the Sioux had signed only because they trusted the commission to secure a number of additional benefits not incorporated in the land agreement.

Some of the benefits, such as employing Indians at the agencies whenever possible and permitting them to hold certain dances, required only the approval of Secretary of the Interior John W. Noble, and he agreed to most of them. Others, especially an appropriation of $100,000 to restore the beef ration to the amount promised in treaties, required action by Congress. Knowing that Three Stars was an honorable man, the chiefs were confident that this time, at least, the promises would be fulfilled.

When they arrived back at their agencies in mid-December, the chiefs found many adults dying of influenza, while children succumbed to measles and whooping cough at an alarming rate. The Brulés were sunk in depression.

Hunger was nothing new, but in the fall and winter of 1889 it was worse than ever. Commissioner Morgan denied that any of the Sioux were hungry, and he quoted figures to prove it. The beef contract called for buying fat northern ranch cattle, but to save a little money, he had allowed the beef contractors to buy Texas trail cattle that arrived in the fall in poor condition. On the parched range these animals continued to lose weight; steers that weighed 1200 pounds when fat were down to half that weight after a few months of poor grass and cold weather. They became so pitifully thin that the embarrassed agent stopped having them weighed on issue days.

It was customary to provide one steer to sustain thirty people for ten days, which was adequate only if the animal was large and fat. The practice continued even when the animals were half-starved. The severe loss of weight the steers suffered during the winter months reduced the already shrunken beef rations by another fifty percent or more. *It's part of their plan to destroy us. We are starving and children are dying, but no one in Washington cares.* Only Bishop Hare expressed concern. The Sioux, he said, were so weakened by hunger that when they became ill of any disease it often proved fatal.

None of the papers Billy saw even mentioned that the Sioux were dying of hunger and disease, although as many as thirty a month, mostly children, succumbed at Rosebud, and even more at Pine Ridge. Then he read the plans of the Friends of the Indian.

"We will make the Sioux self-supporting farmers during the coming year," they cheerfully announced. "The whole Sioux tribe must perforce be jostled from the apathy and sluggishness of its old condition and be thrust into one that must, of necessity, compel a struggle in which all will be tested and many saved."

We are being tested right now, Billy thought, but few are likely to be saved, and many have already given up hope. Our children are dying, they said; we may as well die too.

A few days after the chiefs returned from Washington in the Moon of Frost on the Tipi, the Brulés who had gone to Pine Ridge for the secret council brought word that the Oglalas had decided to send men to the Shoshonis to learn what they knew about the Messiah. They invited the Brulés and Miniconjus to send some of their people to accompany them.

The Brulés held a secret council away from the agency to consider the offer. Some of the progressives, who had been too young to remember the old days, called the Messiah story nonsense. Older men, especially former hostiles, insisted that they must learn more before dismissing the story as false. Finally all agreed that several men should accompany the Oglalas to hear what the Shoshonis had to say.

Billy watched Short Bull and two others ride off to the west toward Pine Ridge, wondering what they might learn. *I wish they'd discover that it's true, but it's probably just a cruel trick to get our hopes up for nothing.* He wanted to put it out of his mind and forget it, but it refused to be banished.

A few weeks later, early in the Tree Popping Moon, Short Bull and the others returned, and everyone gathered around them to hear what they had learned. "It is true what we have heard," Short Bull said. "There is a Messiah come to earth who lives in the land of The-People-Who-Wear-Rabbitskin-Blankets. He promised to save the Indians from the Wasicuns."

The Brulés pondered this news, some of them eagerly, others suspiciously. "The Oglalas are sending men across the mountains to seek the Messiah," Short Bull continued. "We must send men at once to accompany them."

"Across the mountains in mid-winter?" White Bear said. "Who would go?"

"I, for one," Short Bull replied. Flat Iron, Yellow Breast, and Mash-the-Kettle also volunteered.

The council approved and the four men set out at once for Pine Ridge. Billy watched them disappear over the hills, this time with a feeling of rising hope, although he told himself to forget them.

A month after Short Bull and the others had departed, Billy read that on February 10, President Harrison had announced that the Sioux land agreement had been approved. The ceded land, he said, was now open to settlement. He did that, Billy thought, even before a single promise made to us has been carried out. There had been no survey to establish the reservation boundaries, nor was there any provision for allotments for the Sioux families living in the area opened to whites. The beef ration had not been restored. *Where is Three Stars?*

On the same day the President also sent the commission's report to Congress along with a draft of a bill containing all of Crook's promises to the Sioux. Billy felt better when he read that the President had urged Congress to pass the bill quickly. *If the Great Father asks them, like us they must do as he says.* He watched the papers for news of action on the bill in Congress.

The long-awaited land rush to the ceded area failed to materialize, although a few families did buy farmsites. Because of the prolonged drouth, however, there was more movement away from the Dakotas than toward them. "They took our land against our wishes," Billy said. "Now that they have it they no longer want it."

"That's the way it looks right now," Culver admitted, flicking tobacco off his lip. "And if the drouth doesn't end pretty soon, in a few years they can buy the best land for seventy-five or fifty cents an acre."

"That's what some men said they'd do. They probably intended to do that all along."

"No, it wasn't any deep-laid plot. It's just one more example of Sioux bad luck. It seems that ever since they settled on the reservation they've been under a curse. It's been all downhill, straight for perdition. And now if the best land goes cheap it'll be a huge swindle, even though that wasn't intended."

Late in March the downcast Sioux learned that General Crook had died suddenly of heart failure. Billy felt sick. Congress will never carry out his promises now, he thought. Others reached the same conclusion. "With him dies our last hope," wrinkled old Two Strike said gloomily. "They made us many promises, more than I can remember, but they kept only one—they promised to take our land, and they took it."

The Oglalas had the same reaction. "General Crook came," Red

Cloud said, "At least he never lied to us. His words gave the people hope. He died. Then hope died again. Despair came again."

The Word Carrier quoted a Protestant missionary on the condition of the Sioux following news of Crook's death. Their state of mind, he said, is "one of uncertainty, almost consternation, like men on a vast ice floe that is about to break up." He's right, Billy thought. We trusted Three Stars. Now he's gone, and there's no one else who might help us. We're lost. At this point, when all of the Tetons were plunged deep in gloom, Short Bull and the others returned to Rosebud. The expressions on their faces contrasted sharply with the despairing countenances of the Brulés who greeted them. It's clear, Billy concluded, they bring good news, but it's too late. The half-starved Brulés had given up hope. The death of Three Stars was the final blow, and they were stoically waiting their turns to travel the Spirit Trail. But the chiefs called a council for the following afternoon, then sent riders to the nearest camps with the news so they could spread it to others, and many could attend.

All morning the next day a stream of families arrived at the meeting place, a few miles from the agency, in wagons and on ponies, wrapped in their blankets against the cold. All were lean, the skin on their faces hanging loosely over the shrunken flesh. They spoke little, waiting mutely to hear what the wayfarers had to say, but with no sign of expectation in their dull eyes. Finally, when all were squatting in a big circle, Short Bull rose to speak.

Billy noticed at once that Short Bull had changed as a result of his journey west. Earlier he had seemed reserved and soft-spoken, as if hesitant to voice his opinions. Now he stood before them exuding confidence; he reminded Billy of American Horse when he spoke at the council in Pine Ridge. Short Bull's sharp face turned slowly as his keen eyes swept over the circle of somber faces.

"My brothers," he began, "our search was successful, but first let me tell you about our journey. At Pine Ridge we joined Good Thunder, Cloud Horse, Yellow Knife, and five other Oglalas. As we left, Kicking Bear arrived in time to accompany us." The Oglala Kicking Bear, Billy knew, was married to a Miniconju woman and lived with her people at the Cheyenne River Agency on the Missouri.

"When we reached the Shoshonis we found five of them and three Northern Cheyennes and an Arapaho ready to start out, so we all rode together. At Salt Lake City we came to a railroad, where a train of empty cattle cars was stopped. Some cowboys invited us to ride the train with them, and helped us load our ponies in the cattle cars. We got off the train in the land of the Paiutes—Nevada, the cowboys called it. The Paiutes took us to their reservation at Walker Lake, where we met the Messiah. His name is Wovoka." A murmur of expectation rose from the crowd.

"Wovoka told us that on the day the sun died, a year ago in the Tree Popping Moon, he also died and went to heaven. He saw God and all the people who had lived long ago. God gave him a new religion and sent him back to earth as the Messiah of the Indian people. Many tribes have heard about him and sent men to see him while we were there. He taught all of us the Ghost Dance and some of the Ghost Songs God gave him." Billy leaned forward, eager to hear more. He glanced at the faces of the others. They were also listening intently, but the expressions on a few faces made it clear they were skeptical.

"Wovoka told us that a new world is coming for the Indian race," Short Bull continued. "It is coming from the west, and it will arrive when the grass turns green in the spring. When it comes the earth will tremble. That is the signal for all of the believers to tie the sacred eagle feathers in their hair. With these feathers we will soar aloft while the new earth buries the old. The new earth will bury the Wasicuns or push them before it, clear across the great water to the land they came from. Then we will come down from the sky and find all of the Indians who ever lived. Everyone will live forever. The buffalo will return and we will hunt again."

He went on to say that they had followed Wovoka's instructions to fast for a day, perform the Ghost Dance, and sing the Ghost Songs; they had died and traveled to the Spirit Land. "There I saw Chasing Hawk and his wife, who told me they would soon be coming. Good Thunder talked to his son, who was killed on a raid many summers ago." Exclamations rose from the listeners, who clapped hands over their mouths in astonishment.

"He gave us these orders. We must obey them exactly so that the new world will surely come. They are: 'Do no harm to anyone.

You must not fight. Do not tell lies. When your friends die, you must not cry, for they will soon return. Do right always.' " Another murmur rose from the throng of Brulés, and Billy found himself holding his breath. It seemed incredible, but it was obvious that Short Bull and his companions believed it without a trace of doubt. When the murmuring stopped, Short Bull resumed his strange tale.

"When we left Wovoka, he said, 'On your way home, if you kill a buffalo, cut off the head, tail, and all four feet and leave them. The buffalo will come to life again.' We thought there were no buffalo left, but we saw several and killed one. We did as Wovoka ordered, and as we rode away we saw the buffalo reappear and trot after the others." The crowd buzzed with excitement, while Mash-the-Kettle, Flat Iron, and Yellow Breast nodded their heads vigorously in agreement. Up to that point Billy had found Short Bull's wonderful tale believable, but a dead buffalo coming back to life was harder to swallow. That raised doubts in his mind about the rest of the story. Still . . . .

Wovoka had given them some cakes of his sacred paint to mix with their own for painting their faces before they danced, Short Bull added. "When you get home, he told us, you must fast for a day and a night, have a sweat bath, then paint your faces before you dance. You must dance for five days at a time, and on the last night you must continue dancing until the sun rises. Then all must bathe in a river before going home. Dance every six weeks, and make a feast at the dance. You must keep this up until the earth trembles." Short Bull paused to catch his breath.

"He also gave us these orders. 'Do not refuse to work for the Wasicuns, and do not make trouble for them. Do not tell them about this.' He also said that the dead are alive again, and when the time comes there will be no more sickness and everyone will be young. When the earth trembles, don't be afraid. If you are a believer, you will not be hurt."

That ended the council, but few left. Little groups gathered to talk about Short Bull's strange but wonderful tale, while Billy listened. "Why would a Messiah come to save the Indians?" a young progressive asked. "Who cares what happens to us?" No one answered. Billy walked to the group that surrounded Short Bull.

"We must do what Wovoka ordered," he was saying, his sharp

face animated. "We must believe in the Messiah and follow his instructions exactly. It is our only hope." Billy left, not knowing what to think. He wanted badly to believe, but everything he'd learned at Carlisle told him that was foolish. Wovoka had ordered them to say nothing to the whites about the Ghost Dance. What should he tell Culver?

Fortunately, Culver didn't ask him about it, although he knew Billy had gone to the secret council. "I just received a letter from the trader at Walker Lake on the Paiute Reservation in Nevada," he said. "He told me that Indians from all over are coming to see a medicine man called Wovoka. He said that some Sioux were there recently, maybe some of our people. It seems that on January 1 a year ago Wovoka was down with a fever when there was a total eclipse of the sun. Apparently he had a vision, and during it came up with a new religion, a peaceful one."

Billy said nothing, but that explained what Short Bull meant when he said that on the day the sun died Wovoka had also died. Could that mean his vision was untrue? He wanted to ask Culver about it, but refrained.

Kicking Bear and his followers at Cheyenne River got fullbloods who'd been to school to write letters for them to friends at all of the agencies. They invited the Tetons to send men for a big council at Cheyenne River, where they would be taught the Ghost Dance along with the songs and rituals to be observed. Billy was called on to translate the letters to Brulés, for they didn't want any white men to see them.

At Pine Ridge the mixed blood postmaster William Selwyn, who had earlier translated letters from the Shoshonis to Oglalas, now translated the messages from Kicking Bear and his friends. At first Selwyn thought the affair not worth mentioning, but now he became alarmed at the growing excitement. He informed the agent that something mysterious and possibly dangerous was going on among the Oglalas, and that Good Thunder, Cloud Horse, and Yellow Knife seemed to be responsible. Agent Gallagher had the Indian police bring the three to his office for questioning. But even though he kept them in the guard-house for two days, they refused to answer his questions. He ordered them to stop whatever they were doing that upset the Oglalas, then released them. They obeyed his orders.

Census-taker Lea finished his work at Rosebud in May, and his figures showed 2000 fewer Brulés than there had been in 1880. Even though much of the decline had been caused by epidemics made more deadly by weakness from hunger, Lea's count meant yet another cut in rations. By this time it was painfully clear that Congress had no intention of keeping the promises Crook and the other commissioners had made or of restoring the beef ration to comply with treaty guarantees.

Chapter Nine

Heavy spring rains gave the Brulés hope that the drouth had finally ended and a much larger number than ever planted corn. Earlier they had planted merely to please the agent and to acquire farm wagons. Now they were so desperate for food that men helped women with the planting and hoeing weeds, something few Tetons had ever done before.

When Short Bull and Mash-the-Kettle began preaching the new religion at a camp on Iron Creek, about eight miles west of the agency, they attracted only a small number of Brulés. But as word spread of the dancers dying and seeing dead relatives before coming to life again, more and more came to join them. They fasted, painted their faces, sang the sacred songs, and danced. At first they danced only on Sundays. Many fell into trances and traveled to the Spirit Land, and afterward described their dead relatives and their clothing and ornaments so vividly that those who remembered the individuals recognized the descriptions as accurate.

News of the arrest of Good Thunder and the others at Pine Ridge caused Kicking Bear to abandon his plans for a big gathering of Tetons at Cheyenne River. Instead, he left for a visit to the Northern Arapahos, and on his return stopped at Pine Ridge to see Good Thunder. The Arapahos are holding Ghost Dances, he said. Some of the dancers fall dead and visit dead friends, and when they come to life again they tell what they have seen. "The Arapahos," Kicking Bear said, "are absolutely convinced of the truth of Wovoka's teaching. Why are the Oglalas idle?"

The Oglalas now ignored Gallagher's orders and held secret councils away from the agency. Red Cloud, who earlier had been converted by a Catholic priest, stated that he believed in the Indian Messiah, and that the Oglalas should begin the Ghost Dance. Progressive chief Little Wound agreed.

"My friends," he said, "if this is a good thing we should have it; if it is not it will fall to the earth itself. You had better learn this dance, so if the Messiah does come he will not pass us by, but will help us get back our hunting grounds and buffalo." Other chiefs concurred, and at camps away from the agency, Good Thunder and his companions began teaching the Ghost Dance songs and rituals. Many excited Oglalas enthusiastically joined in the dancing.

Brulé agent George Wright came to see Culver one day in late June. He had a puzzled expression. "I just received a letter from the Indian Commissioner," he said. "It seems that an Oglala or mixed blood who is attending college in Pierre heard from his parents that they expect an uprising among the Oglalas, or at least something big. He told Charles Hyde about it, and Hyde wrote the Secretary of the Interior. No one paid any attention to it until the Secretary of War reported that there is great excitement among the Crows over the preaching of an Indian Messiah west of the Rockies. The Commissioner ordered all agents to report on it. Do you know anything about it?"

Culver's mustache twitched. "I've picked up bits and pieces about it, but I don't think there's any reason to worry. What I learned from the Paiute trader is that it's a peaceful religion the Messiah preaches, and if they follow it they'll be the better for it. He orders them to tell the truth and do no harm to anyone."

"I see. Then what are they doing that causes excitement?"

"Short Bull and Mash-the-the Kettle have a Ghost Dance camp on Iron Creek, and I hear they've attracted quite a following. The dances are to prepare for the Messiah's coming, when the whites will disappear and the Indians and the buffalo will return. There'll be an earthquake or flood, something like that." Wright frowned.

"They're neglecting their farms, no doubt."

"You've got to remember," Culver continued, "that these people are desperate, and it's quite understandable that they'll grasp at any straw. If left alone to continue their dancing, when the Messiah fails to appear it will die out by itself. Unfortunately, that will leave them even more discouraged than they are now. If you could restore the beef ration and feed them well, the whole thing would disappear. The Ghost Dance is the child of hunger and despair.''

"I wish I could restore it, believe me. I hate to see them hungry, especially when it's not their fault and there's no earthly reason for it. But the President asked Congress to act promptly on the commission's recommendations way back in February. Although the Senate passed the bill in late April, there's still no sign of action by the House. It hasn't even passed the regular Sioux Appropriation bill, either. I can't understand it.''

They talked some more, while Billy listened but offered no suggestions. "To play it safe, I think I'd better send for Short Bull and Mash-the-Kettle and have a talk with them," Wright said, "even though what they're doing seems harmless.''

"Be careful. The wrong kind of action could change that.''

Billy's thoughts turned to the growing numbers of Brulés said to be flocking to Short Bull's Ghost Dance camp. There's something about what they do that changes them. You can look at a bunch and by their faces pick out the ones who have danced. They're still hungry, but they don't look like they're ready to die. They appear downright confident, like they know something good will happen. I wonder if I'd feel that way if I danced with them?

He soon learned that Wright had sent the Indian police to the camp on Iron Creek to bring Short Bull and Mash-the-Kettle to his office. "The Great Father isn't pleased to hear about your new dancing," he told them. "It is causing people to neglect their farms and not send their children to school. I think you had better stop it." Short Bull and his companion apparently agreed without protest, and Wright went back to his plans for the first Sioux agricultural fair. Billy heard that the two Ghost Dance leaders had abandoned the camp on Iron Creek and set up another farther from the agency. He felt relieved that they hadn't stopped the dancing, for if what Wovoka told them was actually true, they must keep it up until the earth began to tremble.

Many Brulés ignored the Ghost Dance to care for their crops. The corn was nearly waist high, the tallest it had been in years, when lack of rain and the searing winds of late July and early August dashed all hope for any harvest at all. For the third summer in a row, all crops withered and died. This time it struck the Brulés much harder than before because they desperately needed corn to survive. Gaunt-limbed men and sad-faced mothers mourning the most recent deaths of their children looked like they had lost the will to live. At that crucial moment the Indian commissioner ordered yet another cut in the beef ration, blaming it on the lack of funds and the failure of Congress to pass the annual Sioux Appropriation Bill.

Rosebud had been quiet since Wright had ordered an end to the dances, but now even the mildest and most obedient progressives were outraged and vocal about the new cut. As he listened to their protests, Billy sensed that the Brulés were ready to explode. On the next ration day some refused to accept the reduced rations until Wright pleaded with them.

Because the 500 restless Northern Cheyennes at Pine Ridge seemed determined to rejoin their own people on the Tongue River Reservation in Montana, to prevent it the army sent two troops of cavalry to set up camp west of the agency. At the Cheyenne River Reservation the nonprogressives, outraged over the land sale, had moved their camps eighty miles upriver from the agency. Since they were now within easy striking distance of the families of new settlers who had bought farms in the ceded land, other troops were stationed around them. The presence of troops always made the Sioux nervous, and this was one more irritation.

As most Brulés wallowed in the depths of depression, Billy knew that hunger and most of their other troubles had been caused by the whites. The land sale still rankled both those who had agreed and those who had not, for none of the promises had been kept, and it was clear that the government had forgotten them. The whites may not have caused the drouth, for they also suffered from it, but they had forced the Sioux to rely on crops for food at a time when nothing would grow. Even the grass was withered, and blackleg had killed half their cattle. The Tetons still blamed the land sale for most of their troubles. For all of the commissioners' fine promises and assurances, the whites had duped and cheated them again, taking their land and then cutting their rations until they were starving.

At Rosebud no head chief had ever risen to replace the able Spotted Tail; Crow Dog and others had tried to claim the honor, but all lacked his prestige and ability. Two Strike, who had been Spotted Tail's lieutenant in the old days, was the most prominent by far, but at seventy he was ailing and ineffective. At Pine Ridge there was acrimonious rivalry among non-progressives Red Cloud and Big road, on one side, and progressives Young-Man-Afraid-of-His-Horses and Little Wound on the other. At Standing Rock, Sitting Bull led the diehard faction, while the progressives followed Grass. At Cheyenne River, both Hump and Big Foot still protested the land sale and kept their bands as far from the agency as possible. All of the old-time chiefs were now defying authority, making a last effort to recover the power and influence they had enjoyed before the government tried to eliminate their roles as leaders of their people.

President Harrison had come into office in the spring of 1889 committed to civil service reform, but those who had supported him demanded their rewards. To get around this awkward situation, the administration adopted a policy for the Indian Service it called "home rule." For the Tetons this meant simply that their reservations were turned over to the patronage of South Dakota Senator R. F. Pettigrew and Congressman J. A. Stickler. They began replacing agency personnel with Dakotans of their own party, working slowly up through the ranks toward the agents.

At Pine Ridge the progressive chief Little Wound, whose daughter was dying of hunger and lack of medical care, was foremost among the Ghost Dance leaders until the fanatical Porcupine arrived later that summer after visiting Wovoka. Porcupine started a new Ghost Dance camp on Wounded Knee Creek, where Big Road and other hostiles who had fought under Crazy Horse were settled. The Ghost Dance continued to spread rapidly among the Oglalas, and soon another center was No Water's camp at the mouth of Big White Clay Creek, north of the agency.

It was at No Water's camp, where Jack Red Cloud was one of the dance leaders, that Little Wound's story of his visit to the Spirit Land was first told, but it was soon relayed to all the dance camps.

As Little Wound described it, a great eagle carried him to a village of buffalo-hide tipis in the Spirit Land, where he saw the Messiah. "My son, I'm glad you have come," the Messiah said. "Would you like to see your relatives who have died?" They soon appeared, richly dressed and riding the finest horses Little Wound had ever seen. Before he returned to earth, the Messiah told him that if the medicine men made shirts, put certain symbols on them, and prayed over them, no harm would come to those who wore them. The bullets of whites who wanted to stop the Ghost Dance would fall harmlessly to the ground. He had prepared a hole filled with fire for all white men and non-believers, he said. He told Little Wound to return home and tell his people that if they danced and paid no attention to whites he would soon come to their aid.

As a result of Little Wound's visit and talk with the Messiah, Ghost Shirts first appeared at No Water's camp, but they spread like prairie fire to all the dance camps. Some of these garments were of buckskin, but most were of white cloth, with the sacred designs on them that were supposed to make bullets fall to the ground. Those who wore and believed in the Ghost Shirts now had no fear of the Indian police, and they became defiant. The crop failure and the new cut in rations forced even the nonprogressives to join the Ghost Dancers or to sit quietly at home and watch their children starve. Many chose not to sit at home.

By mid-August the Oglala dance camps were in a frenzy of excitement. Hearing rumors about them, Agent Gallagher became alarmed. On August 22 he sent a squad of Indian police to Torn Belly's camp to break up the dance there. The police returned the next day—the agent's order had been ignored and they had been threatened. They would continue to dance, Torn Belly said, no matter what the agent ordered.

Unable to comprehend the intensity of the Ghost Dancers' emotions, Gallagher angrily decided to take twenty Indian police and break up the dance. Philip Wells, his interpreter, warned him that if he entered the camp with police all would likely be killed. He begged Gallagher to go to the camp with only himself, Red Cloud, and Young-Man-Afraid-of-His-Horses, all unarmed, and try to reach a friendly agreement with the leaders. Gallagher, an Irishman and Civil War veteran, declined. "The camp is full of Ghost Dancers," Wells warned him, "hundreds of them, all armed and itching for a fight." Gallagher shrugged.

"Call up the police," he said.

Special Agent E. B. Reynolds and Young-Man-Afraid-of-His-Horses accompanied them. Before they reached Torn Belly's camp they met an Oglala who warned them there were at least 600 Oglalas there, all in a fighting mood. When they reached the cabin settlement they saw 150 tipis but only a few frightened women and children, and that smelled like trouble to all but Gallagher. He led the way into the deserted dance circle, where an American flag hung limply from the prayer tree in the center, as if in shame for being there.

Wells spotted an old man standing below the creek bank, his rifle leveled toward them. Gallagher ordered Lieutenant Fast Horse to arrest him for threatening them with gun. Wells translated the order, then said, "Don't do it! The agent doesn't know that creek bed is full of Oglalas and we're trapped here." Fast Horse hesitated. "Do as I tell you," Wells said. "I'll take the responsibility." Fast Horse obeyed.

"I know the old man," Wells told Gallagher. "Let me talk him into coming out." He laid his rifle on the ground, and the old man lowered his, but when Gallagher stubbornly insisted on leading the way, the old man snatched up his gun and raised it to his shoulder.

Wells finally persuaded Gallagher to remain with the police while he talked the old man into coming out. When the old man laid down his rifle again and climbed up the bank, hundreds of scowling Ghost Dancers rose into view in the creek bed, all holding rifles ready for use. Gallagher turned pale. "They were," Reynolds reported later, "ready to seal their religious convictions at the mouths of smoking rifles in defense of what they deemed a religious rite."

The police drew their pistols, awaiting an order from Gallagher. Before anyone could fire a shot, Young-Man-Afraid-of-His-Horses rode into the dance circle and the tension immediately eased. Wells quickly explained that the agent hadn't come to interfere with the ceremony but merely to observe it. Torn Belly came out of hiding and invited Gallagher to watch the dance so he could see for himself that there was no harm in it. Gallagher and Reynolds watched, but both were alarmed at what they saw. It was clear that the dancers were in no mood to compromise, and that any attempt to stop them would immediately lead to bloodshed.

Gallagher reluctantly returned to the agency, grimly admitting that the situation was completely out of control. ''Steps should be taken to stop it,'' Reynolds informed the Commissioner, ''but this can be done only by the military unless the weather accomplishes it.'' Gallagher added that the Ghost Dance might have unfortunate consequences ''should there be no restriction placed on it.''

That would be someone else's problem, not Gallagher's. Two weeks earlier he had been informed that he was no longer needed and would soon be replaced by a Republican. So while the Ghost Dance intensified among the Oglalas, Gallagher did nothing to check it, wishing only that his replacement would arrive. He had to wait until October 9.

Chapter Ten

Every issue they faced divided the Tetons, especially the land sale they had all once opposed. The same was true of the Ghost Dance. It was not surprising that the former hostiles and the rest of the nonprogressives were the first to embrace it, for they were the most desperate. At Pine Ridge progressive chiefs American Horse and Young-Man-Afraid-of-His-Horses opposed it from the start. Little Wound, who usually sided with them on every issue, supported the dancers along with Big Road and other nonprogressive leaders. It was the same at Rosebud. At both agencies, however, a growing number of progressives and their families also took up the dance. Teachers at several of the cabin settlements reported that their schools were nearly empty, and they didn't know why. Not all of the missing families were at Ghost Dance camps—many were hanging around Valentine and Fort Niobrara, begging for food.

Surprised to learn that the Brulés were still holding dances after he'd ordered them to cease, Agent Wright sent five Indian police to a dance camp with orders to observe, not interfere. When the men returned they came first to the trading post. They huddled together, staring blankly at Billy when he asked what they wanted. From their sheepish expressions he suspected that they were reluctant to report to the agent.

"What's the dance like?" he asked. They looked at him as if dazed, as if they didn't understand the question. Their mumbled replies were unintelligible. Finally Elk Horn led him aside. Culver joined them, elbow in one hand, the other holding the pipe in his mouth.

"We watched them dancing a long time," Elk Horn said hoarsely, barely above a whisper. "They went round and round in a big circle, going faster and faster, until some of the young women died, the medicine men said. They were stiff like they were dead, but they moaned and said things we couldn't understand. Others, both men and women, also died, but when they came to life again they were happy. The dancers stopped, and the ones who had died told everyone about going to the Spirit Land and talking to dead relatives. They described them so accurately we knew they told the truth. All the spirits told them they would soon come to earth. It was scary, but I think all we have heard is true. There is a Messiah, and he speaks with one tongue."

Billy pondered his words. Maybe I should join the dancers. The Messiah said that only the believers, those who dance, will be saved when the new earth covers the old. I don't want to get buried with the Wasicuns. I wish I knew what to do.

"What do you make of it?" he asked Culver, nodding toward the departing police.

Culver looked thoughtful, and his mustache twitched several times before he replied. "The dancers fast a whole day before they dance; they're already weak from hunger, and it makes them weaker. They're all thinking of the dead relatives they want to see and what they expect them to say. They go round and round in a circle, get all worked up, and finally fall into a trance. That's sort of like being asleep and dreaming with your eyes open. Under those circumstances, most see and hear what they want to see and hear. Being half-conscious, they remember their dead relatives in perfect detail, which explains why their descriptions are so convincing to others who also remember them. There's something hypnotic about the whole process. They get mesmerized."

"Mesmerized?"

Culver paused to light his pipe. "There was an Austrian doctor named Mesmer," he said between puffs, "who discovered a way to put people into hypnotic trances. They called it mesmerizing. The dancers mesmerize themselves. With the help of the medicine men, of course."

"What will happen to the dancers?"

"If no one interferes—tries to force them to stop—in the spring, when the Messiah fails them, the whole thing will die out as quickly as it started. But they're desperate for any reason for hope, and they'll probably be so crushed they'll likely lose their will to live. Some were close to that before they heard of Wovoka. I hate to think what might happen if the government interferes. It would take the army to stop it—the Indian police can't possibly do it—and the army couldn't do it without a big fight." He paused and relit his pipe.

"What Wovoka began as a peaceful religion," he continued, "is no longer peaceful among the Tetons—quite the opposite. From what I hear, those dancers are itching for a fight and are ready to kill anyone who tries to stop them. They figure the whites will disappear soon anyway, so they wouldn't mind sending a few on their way early."

"Short Bull didn't say anything about Wovoka telling them to wear Ghost Shirts. He said we must not fight."

" Correct. I suspect it's only among the Tetons that Ghost Shirts have appeared and the dancers have become militant. After all the bad things that have happened to the Tetons that's not surprising. My wife's folks say the Oglala Little Wound had a vision about the shirts and described the symbols to paint on them. They're supposed to make them stop bullets. They can't, of course, but the shirts caught on and spread to all the dance camps."

"But if they believe the shirts will stop bullets...?"

"That's a big part of the problem. They have no fear of the police, and if soldiers are sent here, God forbid, they'll have no fear of them. That makes for an explosive situation."

"If it's just going to die out in the spring like you say, I'd like to see a dance before that happens. Maybe when Short Bull starts his next dance I'll ride out and watch for a few days. There's got to be something strange about it to get everyone so excited." He said it like he was only considering it, but he'd already decided to go. *I've got to see for myself. I must know before it's too late.*

Culver looked at him sharply. "That's risky," he said. "My advice is to forget it. You just might get hooked on it. Level-headed men like Bull Bear have fallen for it, even some who went to church regularly. I'd hate to see that happen to you. Think about it, but if you must go, keep reminding yourself it's an illusion, not the real thing.''

Billy nodded in agreement, but he wasn't convinced. *Culver's not an Indian; he could be wrong. The Messiah is coming to save the Indians, not the whites.* The dances were held every six weeks, but not at the same time in the different camps. Short Bull's next one would be at White Horse's camp in late September, and that was the one Billy wanted to watch. Short Bull, after all, had talked to Wovoka. He said nothing more to Culver about it, but it was constantly on his mind.

In mid-September the Brulés were at the agency to draw their meager rations when a young man galloped up on a lathered pony. ''Soldiers coming on the reservation!'' he shouted in Lakota.

Before the agent learned what was happening, many Brulé men rushed to get their Winchesters, then mounted their ponies and raced down the road to Valentine and Fort Niobrara. Wright called for the Indian police, and they dashed down the road. When he returned two hours later, he told Culver that when he found the men they were stripped for battle, galloping their ponies back and forth to give them second wind, brandishing their rifles, and shrieking war cries.

''I had a terrible time convincing them it was a false alarm,'' he said. ''I thought at first they'd attack us. I don't understand it, but they looked disappointed, like they were determined to die in battle with soldiers and resented having the opportunity snatched away from them.''

I understand that. It's better to die fighting your enemies face to face than to let them kill you by starvation and disease. I'm not surprised they were disappointed. I would be.

This episode convinced Wright that it was time for a showdown with the Brulés, and he called them together the next morning before they set out for their camps. Billy watched as the young agent, trying to look as stern as General Crook, climbed onto a wagon bed with the glum-looking interpreter following. The stony faced Brulés gathered around to learn what he had to say.

''I have heard from the Great Father,'' he said, pausing for the interpreter. ''The Great Father says the dances must cease. He orders you to stop them at once. Unless you do there will be no more rations issued!''

A growl of protest rose from the lean faces, then the Brulés broke up into groups to talk. Billy heard clicking sounds as some warriors angrily worked the levers of their Winchesters, but no shot was fired. After a half hour the headmen met with Two Strike. The old chief listened impassively, then walked slowly toward the agent, while Billy edged nearer to hear what was said.

The dignified old chief looked Wright in the face as he spoke through the interpreter. "It is a cruel thing for your Great Father to threaten to cut off what little food we receive when we are already hungry," he said. "But we are at your mercy and have no choice. We will do as you say." Then he turned and walked away, still a proud old warrior even in defeat. Billy watched him go, feeling sorrow for him but also for himself. He'd waited too long and missed his chance to see a Ghost Dance.

While the sullen Brulés set out for their camps with their rations, Billy walked to the agency office with Wright. A well-dressed white man arrived in a wagon, and hopped down while the driver waited for orders.

"You're Wright?" he asked. The agent nodded. "I'm J. H. Cisney, Special Agent of the Indian Office. The census shows there are only 5250 Indians at this agency, but you've been receiving rations for 7500. You are hereby suspended while the Commissioner determines what you did with the surplus."

"Surplus? Good God, man! The rations have been so reduced these people are starving. And I even had to threaten some . . . ."

"Don't tell me about it. I'm just following orders. Inspector Reynolds is coming from Pine Ridge to take over while you're suspended. If you can clear yourself, that is."

Shocked, Billy hurried to tell Culver. "What stupidity! Wright's as honest as they come. He's not the problem. It's that ignoramus of a Commissioner and Congress." His hands trembled as he lit his pipe.

"Wright should have no trouble clearing himself, but that may take months, the way they move in Washington. It's one hell of a time for him to be away and for a total stranger to be in charge. Reynolds doesn't know a single Brulé leader, or anything at all about the situation here. I think Wright was starting to get a handle on it, but that's down the creek now.''

A few days later Billy learned that Short Bull had told the Brulés to forget the promise to Wright—he was no longer in charge—and to continue dancing. Billy was relieved. *I'll get to see the Ghost Dance after all!*

Hungry Brulés killed some of the cattle in the tribal breeding herd. When Reynolds heard about it, he sent six Indian police to arrest two of the worst offenders. They returned empty handed. They had arrested the two men, they reported, but a large crowd of armed Ghost Dancers surrounded them. "Let them go or you die, they told us. We let them go.'' Reynolds was angry.

"You seem to know these people as well as anyone,'' he told Culver. "It sounds like Wright let them get out of control.''

"It wasn't Wright's fault. It's the same at the other agencies, except maybe Standing Rock. McLaughlin seems to have kept the lid on so far, but I wouldn't bet that he can continue to.''

"I have orders to stop the dances, and I hear they're still going on,'' Reynolds said. "How would you go about it in my place?''

"There's not much you can do without starting a war. The best thing would be to keep hands off and wait for bad weather to stop it, or for it to die by itself. The next best thing is to have a friendly talk with Short Bull and other dance leaders. Try persuasion, though it's a bit late for that to have much chance. If you can arrange a meeting with them, better use Billy here as an interpreter. Short Bull trusts him.''

With great difficulty, two progressive fullbloods persuaded Short Bull and others to meet Reynolds halfway between White Horse's camp and the agency by promising he wouldn't bring any Indian police. Reynolds and Billy rode alone to the meeting place. Short Bull and two others soon joined them, all three looking determined.

"The Great Father wants you to stop the dancing,'' Reynolds told them through Billy. The three men stared unblinking at the agent.

"We would rather die fighting than starve to death,'' the sharp-faced Short Bull replied. "Threats mean nothing to us, for we're not afraid to die. The day is soon coming when you whites will be gone and all dead Indians will return.''

Reynolds, a little pale, had nothing more to say. Short Bull and the others headed for White Horse's camp. It was almost time for his next dance.

At the trading post Billy bought a Winchester and a box of cartridges while Culver was away. Early the next morning he packed a few scraps of meat and bread in a canvas bag, saddled his pony, and tied his bedroll to the back of his saddle. He hoped he could leave without seeing Culver, for he almost felt guilty. He'd told Culver he wanted only to watch the Ghost Dance. That much was true, but it wasn't the whole story. He wanted to watch, but as a dancer, not a spectator, to learn for himself what caused others to believe. As he thought about it, he realized that he badly wanted to believe. He stared straight ahead as his pony shuffled past the trading post, hoping Culver hadn't gotten there yet. The skin on the back of his neck tingled, and without turning he knew that Culver was standing in the doorway watching him and shaking his head.

After riding at a steady trot for ten miles, Billy fell in with a party of families in wagons, all heading for White Horse's cabin settlement. In one of the wagons was portly Bull Bear, who had criticized Billy for working in his cornfield like a woman. With him were his two wives in long calico dresses. White Faun sat on the folded canvas tipi alongside the tipi poles, which stuck out behind the wagon. Bright Star, her heavier-set older sister sat by Bull Bear. As Billy rode past them, Bull Bear called to him. "You can share our tipi," he said. Both of the young women stared at Billy, then exchanged glances.

Others joined the caravan, until it was so long Billy couldn't see the end. In late afternoon they came to the cabin settlement, and soon the canvas tipis of the newcomers were set up all around it, and hundreds of ponies were grazing on the prairies along the creek. When Bright Star and White Faun set up their tipi, Billy put his rifle and bedroll in it, then unsaddled and hobbled his pony. "We'll fix a bed for you," White Faun told him, dimpling as she spoke. He wondered what it would be like sleeping in a tipi with one man and two pretty women.

After dark everyone gathered around a fire in the center of the big camp. Billy stood at the back of the crowd to watch and listen,

eager to hear what Short Bull would say. *What am I doing here?*
It was like a dream. He remembered Culver's warning: "Keep
reminding yourself it's an illusion." *I don't need to remind myself.*
Nothing seems real, yet everything seems real. Am I already in
a trance?

Recalling Culver's words had set him to wondering. If all non-
believers and Wasicuns are to buried under the new earth, what
will happen to good white men who are married to Tetons? He
didn't care what happened to the rest of the Wasicuns after their
lies and broken promises, but Culver was different. Then he
remembered the Purvis family he'd stayed with summers. Some
Wasicuns were good-hearted people and should be spared. He
wondered if the Messiah was aware of that.

He heard Short Bull's voice and his thoughts returned to the scene
before him. He glanced around the big circle and caught his breath.
Across from him was Pawnee Killer, arms folded, eyes on Short
Bull. So much had happened lately he'd almost forgotten that his
father would surely be at one of the dance camps with other former
hostiles. Without thinking, he felt of his braids—the ends fell to
just below the top of his shoulders.

"Tomorrow we fast," Short Bull said. "The next morning we
must have sweat baths to purify us, as the Messiah orders. Then,
after our faces are painted, we will begin the dance to bring back
our relatives, our land, and our buffalo." Even though most had
heard this before, a murmur of expectation rose from the throng.
Billy's skin tingled as he listened to Short Bull. There was a quality
in his voice, the tone or vibration, that gave it a magical effect.
It sounded different, like it wasn't his own voice but the Messiah's
that came from his mouth. It was awe-inspiring to think of the
Messiah speaking though Short Bull. Billy watched Bull Bear and
his wives return to their tipi, and waited a while before following
them. It was customary for several couples to share a tipi, but single
men usually stayed in a separate lodge. Finally he lifted the flap
and entered, straining his eyes in the light of a small dying flame.
On one side of the tipi were two forms wrapped in blankets, which
he assumed were Bull Bear and one of his wives. On the opposite
side, on a pallet of grass, was another. He couldn't see the bed
promised him, nor his own bedroll. As he groped past the single

figure a hand reached up and grasped his, pulling him gently down. He glanced in the direction of Bull Bear, but could see no movement.

"It's all right," White Faun whispered, her warm lips against his ear. "He's glad you're here, and so am I." She eagerly helped him undress, stroking and fondling his quivering body, then pulled him against her hot skin and wrapped her legs around him. When he collapsed in ecstasy she still clung to him, caressing his body with both hands. After a time he responded by running his hands over her extended nipples and slender thighs, wondering how long it would be before he was ready to go again. It proved sooner than expected. Then, exhausted, he fell asleep. Near morning he dreamed that a strange woman was stroking his body and sending sensations through weary muscles. He awoke to discover it was no dream.

The next day passed slowly. Groups of men and women were scattered about, talking in low tones or sitting silently with eyes closed. Billy walked about the camp hoping to see his father and mother, but gave up and leaned against a tree near the creek. He chewed on a grass stem, trying to forget about eating. *What am I getting into? Culver is probably right—I mustn't lose my head. But what if it's all true?*

As he sat musing, Billy tried to visualize the Messiah. He remembered the pictures of biblical prophets he'd seen at Carlisle. They were all old, with long flowing hair and beards and piercing eyes, and they carried shepherd's staffs. The Messiah must be old like them and have long hair, but since he was the Indian Messiah, he wouldn't have a beard.

In the morning Billy went to one of the sweat lodges to wait his turn. The lodge, like the others, opened toward the east and had a carpet of pungent sage branches. In front of the opening, a buffalo skull on a mound of earth stared blindly at the lodge. Billy and several other men crawled into the low lodge and sat cross-legged on the sage. A medicine man who tended a nearby fire used a forked stick to push several hot stones into a hole in the center, then one of the men sprinkled water on them from a kettle. The water made a hissing sound and filled the lodge with dense steam, while outside the medicine man chanted prayers to the

Wakan Tanka. Billy felt weak when he emerged, but a plunge in the cool stream revived him.

After that he joined others who waited for the medicine men to paint their faces. Billy watched and listened to learn the proper procedure. A dancer went to a medicine man and placed his hands on the man's head. "My father," he said, "I have come to be painted so that I can see my friends. Have pity and paint me." Some of the designs were those that had appeared to dancers in visions. Others were the same as those on the Ghost Shirts. The basic color was red, the color of Wi, the Sun. The designs might be yellow, the color of Inyan, the rock, green, the color of Maka, the Earth, or blue, the symbol of Skan, the sky. It was noon by the time all of the dancers' faces had been painted and they had assembled on the dance ground.

Both men and women wore Ghost Shirts above their buckskin leggings. A few were of buckskin with fringes or feathers, but most were of white cloth. The men's were colored blue around the neck. Painted on them were circles, crescents, and crosses representing the sun, the moon, and the morning star, symbols they had been assured would make bullets fall to earth. As Billy knew, it had been the supernatural powers given their shields rather than the thick buffalo hide that warriors relied on to stop enemy arrows or bullets. They had placed this same reliance on the supernatural powers of the Ghost Shirts. Tying eagle feathers in their hair completed preparations for the dance.

In the center of the dance ground was the prayer tree, a sapling the dancers had cut down and planted there. Near it a young woman raised and lowered her arms toward the west—it was from that direction the new earth would come to cover the old. The dancers crouched tensely in a long line facing Short Bull, Mash-the-Kettle, and the other medicine men. Each carried a rod with a red cloth and a red feather attached to one end. They uttered incantations to the Messiah as they walked along the line hypnotically fluttering the feathers before the dancers' eyes and over their heads. As Short Bull's rod passed over his head Billy felt a strange sensation sweep over his body.

That was like magic, but it was real. He didn't touch me, but I felt it. That was no illusion. Short Bull looked at the sun and uttered a prayer, then the dancers formed a large circle around the tree. Billy felt his pulse quicken as a young woman near the tree raised a red stone pipe toward the sun, while another held four blunted arrows aloft. She shot them into the air one by one, then retrieved them and hung them with the bow on the tree.

Billy's eyes opened wide as he watched the medicine men and those who had already talked with dead relatives in the Spirit Land. Chanting, they marched around the circle of dancers. When they completed the circle they returned to the center and sat on the ground.

"Great Wakan Tanka," Short Bull began, "we are ready to begin the dance you have commanded. Our hearts are now good. We will do all you ask of us, and we beg you to give us back our hunting grounds and our buffalo. Carry us to the Spirit Land that we may see our dead relatives. Show us the good things you have prepared for us and let us return safely to earth."

Then he gave them instructions and taught them the songs they were to sing. Those in the line all faced to the left and placed their hands on the shoulders of the persons in front of them. At a signal from Short Bull they started walking to the left, bending and straightening their knees so their bodies fell and rose. They chanted "Father, I come," over and over until Short Bull held up his hand. "Weep for your sins," he called out. At that the air was filled with piercing wails and shrieks as some of the dancers rolled on the ground, crying out for forgiveness.

When it was quiet again the dancers picked up dust, rubbed it between their palms, then threw it into the air. Raising their eyes to the sky, they stood with hands clasped above their heads, calling on the Messiah to let them see their dead friends. Without thinking, Billy found himself doing whatever the others did.

Finally all sat in place while Short Bull walked around in the center, saying again and again "The Messiah is coming!" Then all rose to their feet, widened the circle, and took the hands of those on either side of them. Across from him Billy saw Pawnee Killer, but Scarlet Robe wasn't with him. The medicine men began singing, and all joined in.

Someone comes to tell us news, tell us news.
There will be a buffalo hunt.
There will be a buffalo hunt.
Make arrows. Make arrows.

Bodies swaying, hands swinging back and forth, they moved slowly to the left. The earth beneath their feet had been pulverized to a thick layer of dust by so many dances in the same place. As they shuffled through it, the dust swirled up around them.

The dancers were young and old, men and women. Some were gaunt from hunger, looking like little more than skeletons, but their movements were as animated as the others'. *What gives them the strength to keep going? Is it the Messiah himself, or their faith in him?* Gradually moving faster, the dancers chanted, "Father, I come. Mother, I come. Brother, I come. Father, give us back our arrows."

This continued for half an hour, when a woman whose hair was flying and whose face turned purple, staggered away from the line and fell. Billy watched her, the skin on his arms tingling, as she lay unconscious, with arms and legs twitching. None of the dancers seemed aware of her, but continued to circle ever faster to the left. Several men and women were stepping high and pawing the air, like they were trying to climb a steep hill. The arms and legs of others twitched and their bodies shook convulsively; some leaped erratically forward and back, wailing and shrieking. When a woman fell in the line of dancers, her husband stood over her as she lay moaning in the dust to prevent others from stepping on her.

At a signal from Short Bull the dancers stopped and sat in place. About a third of them had dropped out, and some still lay where they'd fallen. As those who had died came to life again, they staggered to the center, where they told one of the medicine men what they had seen. The medicine man repeated it loudly so all could hear. The ones who had seemed to be climbing said that they felt the earth rise up and feared it would hit them in the face. One man said that an eagle had flown toward him, but vanished when he held out his hand. When asked what he thought that meant, he scowled. "Big lie," he said.

Billy was surprised that some who had died remembered nothing, while a few didn't believe what they'd seen. But others had talked to dead relatives who assured them they'd soon return to earth.

After resting for a time, the dancers arose, then repeated the entire performance two more times, stopping only to eat at sundown. The medicine men were active the whole time, hopping about, sprinkling sacred powder on the dancers, waving eagle feathers in their faces, and chanting.

When the dance ended, it was already dark, and Billy again waited a quarter of an hour before entering Bull Bear's tipi. There was no fire this time, but he made his way to the pallet he'd slept on before and felt the body of White Faun on it. This time she didn't move as he quickly stripped and slipped under the blanket. Gently he ran his hands over her thick thighs. But White Faun's were slender—it was Bright Star waiting for him, and though she was less demonstrative than her younger sister, she was no less eager.

Each morning as he took a sweat bath to purify himself for the dance, Billy asked himself why he was doing it. *I've seen enough to know what it's like. If Culver is right, it's just make-believe anyway. But I'm not so sure he's right.* So he had his face painted and continued dancing, for he couldn't bring himself to leave. He wanted to know more about the dance, he told himself, but he also wanted more nights with White Faun and Bright Star.

On the fourth afternoon Billy suddenly found that everything seemed to be growing hazy; he felt dazed and not fully aware of what he was doing. Finally his legs gave way and he fell to his knees. Short Bull gently pushed him onto his back and hovered over his upturned face, staring into his eyes and moving his head slightly in a small circle. *His eyes are like a snake's,* Billy thought. Then Short Bull vanished.

In his place was a handsome old Indian with flowing hair who held along staff with a crook at the top. His countenance was serene; his face was bathed in a soft radiance from a circle of light around his head. His eyes glowed brightly, and Billy knew he was a holy man.

"Are you the Messiah?" he asked. The old Indian slowly, majestically, nodded his head.

"Yes, my son. I'm the Messiah of the Indian people. I'm coming soon to save you. Believe in me and you'll be saved." Then a cloud of blue mist encompassed him and he was gone.

Billy opened his eyes, raised his head, and looked around. He was flat on his back, with arms and legs outstretched. Trying to remember where he was, he rolled over onto his knees and arose. He saw prostrate forms around him, some rigid, some twitching and moaning. The dance circle was still moving. He walked unsteadily to the center, where Short Bull greeted him.

"What did you see, my son?"

Billy rubbed his face with both hands. "The Messiah, the Messiah himself. I talked to the Messiah," he said in awed tones.

"What did he tell you?"

"That he's the Messiah of the Indians, and he's coming to save us. He told me to believe and I'll be saved."

"Do you?"

"I do."

Short Bull's sharp face glowed with delight. "You're one of his chosen people," he said. "You're fortunate."

After that Billy remained in the center with others who had also died and come to life again, while the circle of dancers, much reduced in size, continued to move. At one time Billy glanced up to see Pawnee Killer stretched out in the dust. When his father came to life again, Billy listened as Short Bull questioned him.

"Two great eagles carried me to the Spirit Land," he said. "There I saw my son who died ten summers ago when the Wasicuns took him away. He said he will soon be coming."

Billy was stunned. His father had seen him in the Spirit Land, but he wasn't dead. *Does that mean he was only dreaming? And if he was did I only dream I saw the Messiah?* It was a troubling thought. *He was real; I heard his voice. But...I must ask Short Bull what this means.*

He waited until he could speak with Short Bull alone. "Pawnee Killer is my father, but he hasn't seen me since I was small and doesn't recognize me. I couldn't let him see how the Wasicuns made me look; I must wait for my hair to grow long. But how could he see me in the Spirit Land when I'm not really dead?"

Short Bull gazed at the sky and the distant hills while pondering Billy's question. "Your father has longed for the son he knew and believed was dead. When he saw you in the Spirit Land it was the Messiah's way of telling him that you'll soon be with him again, like you were in the old days. Then he will forget what the Wasicuns did to you.''

Billy exhaled deeply. His faith in the Messiah had wavered briefly, but now it was stronger than ever.

Chapter Eleven

In the morning, Billy thanked Bull Bear for sharing his tipi, not to mention his wives. Both smiled shyly at him as he left to walk through the camp, glancing at the women deftly taking down the tipis and loading the wagons. He was in no hurry to return to the trading post, where he would face Culver's questions and disapproval. He saw Short Bull, Mash-the-Kettle, and other medicine men surrounded by a few dozen Ghost Dancers, and stood at the back of the crowd to observe. At twenty-one he was tall enough to have a good view of the dynamic dance leader over the shoulders of others.

Seeing Short Bull made him recall the day he had brought him the letter from his Shoshoni friend to translate. In the interim, the sharp-faced Ghost Dance apostle seemed to have become a different person. His serene countenance, his commanding voice, with its unique and penetrating tone, and his dignified gestures marked him as a man who knew holy things unknown to others. His resonant voice especially was different—just hearing him speak was to believe in him and want to follow him.

As he watched Short Bull, Billy was suddenly aware that another's eyes were on him, and out of the corner of his eye he saw Pawnee Killer staring at him, a puzzled expression on his face. He avoided looking directly at his father, but he involuntarily touched the braids on his back just below his shoulders. They were slowly getting longer, but they were still nowhere near long enough to be respectable. *I wonder if he thinks he recognizes me and can't believe I'm still alive?* He was pondering what to do when Short Bull saw him and pushed his way through the crowd to his side.

Putting his hand on Billy's shoulder, Short Bull led him a few steps away from the others. Billy quivered with excitement. First his father had been looking at him, possibly recognizing him, and now Short Bull wanted to talk to him.

"My son," Short Bull said softly, "I will soon need to send messages to Kicking Bear and leaders at other agencies. Each of us must know what the others are doing and what the Wasicuns are saying. We must get all Tetons dancing so the Messiah won't fail to save us. I'll need you to write the letters and to read those I receive, for we can't let whites or mixed bloods see them. Will you come when I send for you?"

Billy didn't need to think it over before replying. "Gladly," he said. "I'll go anywhere with you."

Short Bull smiled. "Good. I hoped you'd say that." He returned to Mash-the-Kettle and the others. Billy glanced around quickly, and saw his father just leaving. *Maybe at the next dance he'll ask if I'm his son. He saw Short Bull talk to me, and that means I'm not a make-believe Wasicun.*

As he rode toward the agency, Billy's thoughts leaped about like an excited Ghost dancer. He was thrilled that his father might have recognized him, and that Short Bull would soon send for him. Then he remembered Culver's warning to keep reminding himself that it was just an illusion. In the excitement of the dance and his nights in Bull Bear's tipi he'd gradually forgotten that. Now that he remembered, he was sure Culver was wrong. But what will he say when he knows what happened? The more he thought about it, the more he was convinced that Culver mustn't know about his talking to the Messiah or that he expected to join Short Bull. But how to avoid it?

As his pony jogged down the trail, Billy's thoughts leaped to the land sale, and then to General Crook. That reminded him of American Horse talking for days without once referring to the land sale. *That's it. I'll do what American Horse did. The first thing Culver will ask is what I thought about the Ghost Dance. I'll tell him every detail I can remember about it, except what happened to me. Then he'll want to know if I took part in it. I'll have to admit I did. When he asks if I fell into a trance, I'll tell him how close I was to many who did, and that it was almost the same thing.*

"You're back," Culver remarked when they met in the morning. "Tell me about it."

Billy explained in detail the preparations the dancers made each morning, and what Short Bull said and did. He went on and on until Culver stopped him.

"Get to the point," he said. "Did you take part in the dance?" Billy nodded.

"Some," he replied.

"Did you go into a trance?"

"Let me tell you about that. The first afternoon a woman fell and died just a few steps from me. At least she was rigid and looked dead, but she came to life again. There were others too, quite a number of them every day. It's funny, but the young women and girls were always the first to die. I don't know why that is. They all told what had happened to them, so it was almost the same as doing it myself. Some of them couldn't remember anything. I think that's strange, don't you?"

Several mixed bloods came into the post at that moment. While Billy saw to their needs, Culver lit his pipe, watching Billy thoughtfully. Out of the corner of his eye, Billy saw him shaking his head.

At the very moment the Ghost Dance was sweeping the agencies, making the Tetons wild and uncontrollable, Senator Pettigrew and Congressman J. A. Pickler exercised their rights of patronage. On September 1 Pickler replaced the able Charles McChesney at Cheyenne River with Perain P. Palmer, who lacked the experience to be able to cope with the fanatical Ghost Dance followers of Kicking Bear, Hump, and Big Foot. Hump had quit as chief of the Indian police to devote his full attention to the dance.

On instructions from the Commissioner, Palmer dutifully informed the dancers that the Secretary of the Interior was displeased with them. Far from being crushed by the secretary's displeasure, they replied that "the Indian is displeased with the Department *and will dance.*" Then Palmer sent Straight Head, who'd replaced Hump as chief of the Indian police, to break up the dances at Hump's and Big Foot's camps. Snarling Ghost Dancers met the police with leveled Winchesters and dared them to interfere. The police prudently withdrew. Other attempts to stop the dances were no more successful. Their authority gone, one by one the police turned in their badges.

At his camp on Grand River, forty miles south of Standing Rock Agency, Sitting Bull heard about the dances at Cheyenne River. Curious, he requested a pass from McLaughlin, so he could visit the dance camps and see for himself, but the agent refused. Sitting Bull sent a message inviting Kicking Bear to bring word of the Ghost Dance to the Hunkpapas. On October 9, Kicking Bear and five Miniconju dance leaders reached Sitting Bull's cabin settlement. Kicking Bear told the members of Sitting Bull's band of former hostiles of his visit to Wovoka, then taught them the dance rituals and songs.

On learning of this intrusion, McLaughlin sent Crazy Walking and eleven police to eject Kicking Bear and his party. Awed by the Ghost Dance and by the forceful Kicking Bear, the police simply told Sitting Bull that the intruders must leave, then hastily retreated.

Irked, McLaughlin sent reliable Lieutenant Chatka and two men, who boldly rode through the ring of dancers and informed Kicking Bear of the agent's order to leave. Kicking Bear made no objection, and Chatka escorted his party to the southern border of the reservation. By that time it was too late to prevent the Ghost Dance from spreading to Sitting Bull's Hunkpapas, for he now assumed the role of dance leader, and his people danced constantly. John Carignan, who taught at the Grand River school near Sitting Bull's camp, saw the number of his students drop from sixty in September to three in October. When he questioned parents about their children's absence, they replied that their children couldn't attend school because they had to go to church every day.

As the dancers became wilder and more uncontrollable, settlers across the Missouri from Standing Rock reservation became increasingly concerned over the safety of their families. Rumors of a Sioux uprising spread daily, and newspapers elaborated and repeated them. McLaughlin informed the Commissioner that Sitting Bull and several others should be removed, but not until winter, when severe weather would immobilize his followers and prevent them from coming to his rescue.

Secretary of the Interior Noble was unwilling to authorize any action that required calling on the army for assistance. McLaughlin must, he wrote, inform Sitting Bull and the others that the secretary was "greatly displeased with their conduct," and that he would hold Sitting Bull personally responsible for any misconduct or acts of violence. Sitting Bull must immediately make his people "turn their back upon the medicine men who are seeking to divert the Indians from the ways of civilization." What oath McLaughlin uttered when he read this message is not known, but he didn't choose to make himself appear an idiot by delivering it.

He did, however, visit Sitting Bull's camp to see for himself. On November 16 he and interpreter Louis Primeau arrived on the Grand River while a Ghost Dance under Sitting Bull's supervision was in full swing. McLaughlin harangued his old rival in vain, then departed. He was more determined than ever to arrest and remove Sitting Bull, and waited only for severe weather.

"My brothers, you can dance all winter," Sitting Bull told his followers. "The sun will shine warmly and the weather will be fair." He was correct about the weather, but not about dancing all winter.

After returning to the agency McLaughlin wrote the Commissioner on November 19, proposing to isolate the Ghost Dancers from the others, then cut off their rations. By the time his letter reached Washington, it was too late to carry out his proposal.

On October 9, the same day that Kicking Bear reached Sitting Bull's camp, Senator Pettigrew's choice to replace Agent Hugh Gallagher arrived at Pine Ridge, where the Ghost Dance excitement was the greatest. Pettigrew's timing was disastrous and his choice of timid Daniel F. Royer was a calamity. Royer was not only ignorant of Indians—he was terrified of the unruly Oglalas. He had been at his post only a few days when the Oglalas had a new name for him—Young-Man-Afraid-of-Indians. His method of dealing with the Oglalas, teacher Emma Sickels wryly observed, was "Oh please be good and don't make any trouble." Interpreter Philip Wells remarked, "I think he's got an elephant on his hands, as the craze had taken such a hold on the Indians before he took charge."

To make matters worse, the Commissioner ordered Royer to inform the Oglalas that the Ghost Dance would not be permitted on any occasion. When he gingerly relayed the warning, the Oglalas grunted and ignored him. Not knowing what else to do, he repeated it daily with equal effect. On October 12, less than a week after he became agent, Royer wrote the Commissioner that troops might be needed at Pine Ridge. That was the last thing the commissioner wanted to hear. Pompous General Nelson A. Miles, commander of the Division of the Missouri, had loudly criticized the Indian Bureau's management of reservations. Many officers were convinced that the War Department should be given control of the Indians, an opinion they freely expressed. The thought of having to call on the army to control the Sioux made the Commissioner's stomach churn. On October 18 he replied to Royer's suggestion. "I approve your course of using persuasion with the chiefs," he wrote, "and I think you had better continue in that direction."

While Royer dutifully if timidly tried persuasion, the Ghost Dancers were openly defiant. American Horse and Young-Man-Afraid-of-His-Horses supported the agent, but their influence had waned. The Ghost Dancers brazenly helped themselves to the Oglala beef herd; the police, not being inclined to suicide, made no attempt to prevent it.

General Miles arrived at Pine Ridge on October 27 as head of a commission to talk to the Northern Cheyennes about their request to rejoin their own people in Montana. Miles assured Royer that the Ghost Dance craze would die out by itself, but the agent was far from mollified. Miles also held a council with the Oglala chiefs, but they weren't awed by his presence.

"I want to see our people quit trying to act like whites," Little Wound responded. "By continuing this dance they can do that, and they intend to dance as long as they wish. Will you please write this down and show it to the Great Father." Miles was shocked at Little Wound's boldness, and for the first time he was made aware of the Ghost Dancers' confidence in their new religion. He still believed, however, that if the dancers weren't molested, the craze would die out by itself. After Miles left Pine Ridge, Royer again pleaded with the chiefs to stop the dance. They laughed in his face.

Frightened as well as frustrated, on October 30 Royer poured out his feelings in a long letter to the Commissioner. "The only remedy for this matter," he concluded, "is the use of the military. Until this is done you need not expect any progress from these people. On the other hand, you must realize that they are tearing down more in a day than the Government can build in a month."

Unlike Royer, Reynolds appeared calm and unruffled, although the Brulés were every bit as defiant as the more numerous Oglalas. Whatever he may have thought, he didn't bombard his superiors with requests for help from the army. He knew that Short Bull had been ordered to cease holding Ghost Dances before he became interim agent. He learned that after the beef ration was reduced again just as the Brulés' corn was dying the hungry Indians had flocked to the dance camps.

Reynolds sent ten Indian police to Red Leaf's Wazhazha camp on Black Pipe Creek with orders to break up the dancing. The police found the area swarming with half-crazed dancers draped with cartridge belts filled with shells for their Winchesters. Not foolhardy enough to interfere, the police lived to see their families again. Reynolds now informed the Commissioner that for several weeks the Brulés had been buying rifles and ammunition at every opportunity, even trading their ponies and other possessions for arms, and he didn't like the look of it. On top of that, old Two Strike, whose band had been scattered in cabin settlements, had just brought his people together. He had heard, Reynolds added, that Yellow Robe and Crow Dog were urging Two Strike to take his band to join Short Bull's Ghost Dancers. On November 2 Reynolds finally admitted that the situation was out of control. "There appears to be," he wrote the Commissioner, "but one remedy, and that is a sufficient force of troops to prevent an outbreak, which is imminent and which any one of a dozen unforeseen causes may precipitate."

Culver didn't question Billy again about his Ghost Dance experiences, for it was clear he'd learn nothing more. Something had happened, he knew, for even though Billy tried to act as he always had, he couldn't conceal his feeling of expectation. Culver noticed that Billy glanced up whenever anyone entered the post, like he was expecting a caller. He hoped he'd be on hand to dissuade Billy from taking another step in the wrong direction.

In the third week of October, Mash-the-Kettle came to the post to buy tobacco. "Short Bull is at Broken Wing's camp on Black Pipe Creek," he said quietly to Billy in Lakota. "He wants you to come as soon as you can. Bring paper for letters. Big doings." Billy stared after him when he left, and for the rest of the day struggled to hide his excitement. Short Bull had sent for him! Culver watched him thoughtfully that afternoon; several times he semed about to say something, but stopped each time.

Black Pipe Creek was north of the agency and a short distance east of the Rosebud–Pine Ridge boundary, less than a day's ride away. Early the next morning Billy rolled up his belongings, some stationary, and a pencil in his blankets. He put what little food he had in a canvas bag, then saddled his pony. After sticking his Winchester in the rifle scabbard, he mounted and circled the agency to avoid going past the trading post. He found Broken Wing's camp in mid-afternoon. Several Brulé cowboys were holding a small herd of beef cattle in the tall grass, and boys were watching the grazing ponies. Some of the cattle were from the Brulé breeding herd, but others bore the brands of white ranchers whose cattle grazed on or near the reservation.

Short Bull greeted Billy and immediately dictated letters to Kicking Bear, Hump, and Big Foot. "My brothers, I believe the time is near when we should all gather in a few big camps, so we can continue dancing until the earth trembles. If we aren't strong enough to defend ourselves, the Wasicuns will try to stop us. That must not happen. I am going to speak to the Oglalas about it. They say their agent is frightened and talking about calling for bluecoats. That would be bad, but we must not let them keep us from dancing and prevent the new world from coming."

A rider took the letters to Rosebud to mail, and returned with a letter for Short Bull from Kicking Bear. "My brother, your heart will be glad when I tell you I have been to Sitting Bull's camp on the Grand River and taught his people the dance. The agent made us leave the reservation, but the dancing had already taken hold among Sitting Bull's people. He promised to keep it going and not let the agent stop it. Hump's and Big Foot's people are also dancing. Our time comes!''

On the last day of October, Billy accompanied Short Bull, Mash-the-Kettle, and other medicine men south up Black Pipe Creek to Red Leaf's Wazhazha camp. Although the Wazhazhas were Brulés, they preferred to live with the Oglalas, as they had for years, even though they still had to draw rations at Rosebud. As a result, they camped as close to the Pine Ridge boundary as possible, and many Oglalas lived with them.

That afternoon the whole band assembled, and Short Bull stood on a wagon to speak to them, his sharp face radiant, his powerful voice reaching all. ''My brothers,'' he said, ''as you have heard, a new world is coming to cover the old. It will bury the Wasicuns and bring back your dead relatives and the buffalo. I have told you that this will come to pass in two seasons, but since the Wasicuns are interfering so much I will advance the time from what my Father above told me.'' All must dance constantly during the coming Moon of Hairless Calves, he added. ''When the time comes the earth will tremble and the wind will blow, and we will go among our dead relations.'' *It's the Messiah's voice coming from Short Bull's mouth again. I know that is so.*

To prepare for the day of rejoicing, Short Bull continued, believers must gather at the mouth of Pass Creek, on the Oglala reservation a short distance west of the boundary between Rosebud and Pine Ridge, and dance every day. Whites must not be permitted to interfere with this final phase of the Ghost Dance. ''If soldiers surround you pay no attention to them but keep on dancing. If soldiers surround you four deep, three of you on whom I have put holy shirts will walk around them singing a song I have taught you. Some of the soldiers will drop dead and the rest will start to run, but their horses will sink into the earth. The riders will jump off their horses, but they will also sink into the earth. At that time you can do as you desire with them.'' A murmur of happy expectation rose from the warriors. ''You must know this—all the soldiers and that race will be dead. There will be only five thousand of them left on earth. My friends and relations, this is straight and true.''

The Wazhazhas and Oglalas were ecstatic. Billy thought of Short

Bull's promise. If five thousand whites were left on earth, surely good people like Culver and the Purvis family would be spared. He was relieved by that thought, for he didn't want to have to see them destroyed just because they were Wasicuns. Short Bull wouldn't even kill the bluecoats unless they tried to break up the dances, but the aroused Brulés and Oglalas were no longer satisfied merely to defend themselves. Many now talked of a holy war to drive the whites from the country.

For the next three weeks Billy watched as Brulé and Oglala families flocked to the growing camp on Pass Creek near where it entered the White River. Among them was Bull Bear who again shared his tipi. All of the families brought any stray cattle or horses they saw. They had abandoned their cabins and moved to Pass Creek to remain. Kicking Bear and some Miniconjus joined them there, and two of the leading Ghost Dance apostles were now together. Billy wrote letters for them to Sitting Bull, Hump, and Big Foot, telling them about the big gathering at Pass Creek and urging them to join it. Sitting Bull responded by inviting all of the Tetons to assemble in the spring at Bear Butte near the Black Hills to wage an all-out war against the whites. Many of Short Bull's followers were eager to join Sitting Bull in the spring.

Pleas from white settlers in South Dakota and Nebraska, who were certain they and their families would soon be massacred, deluged Washington. Many isolated families abandoned their homesteads and settled temporarily in frontier towns or returned to their former homes elsewhere. Those who remained demanded that they be provided with guns and military protection. On October 31, the same day Short Bull aroused the Wazhashas and Oglalas on Black Pipe Creek, the President ordered the Secretary of War to investigate the situation at the Sioux reservations.

General Miles hadn't returned from his Cheyenne Commission trip, but General Thomas H. Ruger, commander of the Department of Dakota, crossed the Missouri to visit the Standing Rock and Cheyenne River agencies. At the former, he and McLaughlin agreed that the situation was still under control, but that Sitting Bull should be arrested during the winter. Ruger also found that conditions at Cheyenne River were not yet dangerous. He didn't visit Pine Ridge and Rosebud; although both were under his jurisdiction, they were nearer to the Department of the Platte.

Chapter Twelve

Rumors that the Oglala agent had asked for troops reached Short Bull, but he didn't appear concerned about the likelihood that the bluecoats would try to stop the Ghost Dance. As he watched the sharp-faced Short Bull and the tall, rawboned Kicking Bear, Billy was sure the Messiah had spoken to them and promised to protect their people. All they needed to do was to keep on dancing until the earth trembled. He hoped the Messiah would come before the troops arrived.

On November 11, just over a month after he became agent, Royer saw the last shred of his authority vanish. As was usual on ration issue day, Pine Ridge was crowded with people and wagons. At noon the beef issue was made in the customary way—steers were turned loose one at a time while whooping warriors dashed after them on their best ponies and killed them as they had the buffalo in the old days. The Indian Bureau had ordered this ''barbarous custom'' stopped, but Royer was in no position to enforce the order.

An Oglala Ghost Dancer named Little had openly killed cattle in the tribal beef herd, and he brazenly strutted around the agency, as if daring the agent to try to arrest him. When informed of Little's presence, Royer ordered Lt. Thunder Bear to seize him. The police found Little outside the building where the chiefs were holding council. When Thunder Bear told him he was under arrest, Little drew a butcher knife and prepared to resist.

A large crowd of angry Ghost Dancers immediately surrounded

Thunder Bear and his men, brandishing Winchesters and shouting "Kill them!" Hearing the commotion, the chiefs rushed out and saw the crowd recklessly jabbing the police with cocked rifles. Somehow American Horse made himself heard above the tumult. Even though he'd lost prestige by signing the land agreement, his voice was still forceful enough to command attention.

"Stop!" he shouted. "Think what you are doing! Killing these men of our own race? Then what? Kill all the helpless white men and women? What will these brave deeds lead to in the end? How long can you hold out? Our country is surrounded by railroads. Thousands of white soldiers will be here in three days. How many bullets have you? What will you do for food? What will become of your families? Think, think, my brothers. This is a child's madness."

The crowd fell silent and the warriors lowered the hammers on their rifles and released the police. Jack Red Cloud, who had been stirring up the crowd, now rushed up to American Horse and stuck a cocked pistol in his face. "It's you and your kind who brought us to this," he shouted.

American Horse ignored him as not worthy of notice, turned his back, and with head erect walked up the steps to the council room and closed the door behind him. The police could only watch as the Ghost Dancers dispersed, taking the smirking Little with them.

That evening Royer called Dr. Charles Eastman, an eastern Sioux who was the reservation physician, to his office. Already there were Special Agent John Cooper, the chief clerk, and a Sioux Episcopal minister named Cook. "I want your advice," Royer told them. "Do you think I should ask for troops?" Only Eastman and Cook were opposed, for both were confident that the Oglalas had no desire to start a war. The arrival of bluecoats, they knew, could easily change that.

After they left Royer asked chief of police Sword, Thunder Bear, and American Horse the same question. All three, who had been threatened by angry Ghost Dancers, approved. They were sure that troops from Camp Robinson in Nebraska had already been ordered to Pine Ridge, and that the agent had called them in merely to gain their approval of an action he'd already taken.

The next morning an Oglala appeared at Royer's office. "I come from Little," he said through an interpreter.

"Is he ready to surrender?"

"No! He demands that you fire all those police who tried to arrest him. He says if you don't he'll make big trouble for you and American Horse the next ration issue." Royer wiped his moist face with his handkerchief. The Ghost Dancers had openly defied him, and he was powerless to punish them. Now that villain Little was even threatening him. It was too much to bear.

He wired the Indian Bureau that 200 maddened Ghost Dancers had seized control of the agency. The police are powerless and discouraged, he said. "We have no protection. We are at the mercy of the crazy dancers." Troops must be sent immediately to Pine Ridge. He begged for permission to come to Washington so he could explain the situation in person. The Secretary of the Interior showed the message to the President, who remarked that the army was already looking into conditions at the Sioux agencies. For the present, he said, the agents should do nothing more than separate friendly Indians from the Ghost Dancers. They must be careful to avoid any action that might irritate the Indians.

The Indian Commissioner relayed the message to Royer, adding that if conditions were as bad as he claimed it was hardly the proper time for him to leave his post. But because of the flood of pleas and demands for protection from the citizens of Nebraska and South Dakota, on November 13 the Commissioner glumly recommended that Secretary Noble alert the War Department concerning the emergencies at Pine Ridge and Rosebud and request assistance. The President, when informed of the request, directed the Secretary of War "to assume responsibility for suppressing any threatened outbreak, and to take such steps as may be necessary to that end."

At his Chicago headquarters, General Miles ordered his subordinates in Omaha and St. Paul, the commanders of the departments of Platte and Dakota, to prepare to send troops to the Sioux agencies if necessary. Royer's distraught telegram of November 15 convinced authorities in Washington that troops were needed immediately.

"Indians are dancing in the snow and are wild and crazy," Royer stated. "I have fully informed you that the employees and government property at this agency have no protection and are at the mercy of the Ghost Dancers. Why delay by further investigation? *We need protection, and we need it now.* I have submitted to you the result of six weeks' calm, conservative investigation, and nothing short of 1000 soldiers will settle this dancing. The leaders should be arrested and confined in some military post until this matter is quieted, and this should be done at once. Royer, Agt."

Two days later Miles ordered Brigadier General John Brooke, commander of the Department of the Platte, to dispatch troops to the trouble spots—Pine Ridge and Rosebud—to arrive at exactly the same time at each agency. Brooke was to station most of his command along the railroads south of the two agencies and west of the Pine Ridge reservation. "You are to keep pressure on the Indians by your presence only," Miles instructed his field commanders. "Do not come into active contact with them unless it is impossible to avoid doing so." Two trainloads of troops, horses, and equipment were dispatched that night, one to Valentine for Rosebud, the other to Rushville for Pine Ridge.

At daybreak on November 20, round-faced, white-haired General Brooke, accompanied by Royer and Special Agent Cooper who met him at Rushville at his request, rode into Pine Ridge. Following them were three troops of the black Ninth Cavalry, five companies of infantry, and Hotchkiss and Gatling guns. The troops marched through the agency and set up tents in neat rows on high ground overlooking Pine Ridge. The soldiers were armed with single shot Springfield rifles and carbines the army had adopted seventeen years earlier. The Tetons had acquired the most recent model Winchester repeating rifles.

The Oglalas were alarmed and excited by the coming of the bluecoats, but they did nothing to cause trouble and only a few fled. When Brooke sent messages to the cabin settlements for the friendlies to camp at the agency, they began streaming toward Pine Ridge, accompanied by many Ghost Dancers. Soon there were large tipi camps near the agency. Brooke also ordered all white and mixed blood employees—teachers, farmers, and missionaries—to bring their families to Pine Ridge. Several whites were so fearful they didn't stop at the agency but continued on to the safety of towns in northern Nebraska.

The Oglala Ghost Dancers went wild when they learned that troops were at Pine Ridge, and for a time all was confusion. Then Little Wound took charge, and they resumed dancing with greater intensity than ever. Hundreds more joined those on White Clay Creek, all of them determined to fight if troops interfered. When the dances began a few months earlier, no one had been permitted to bring a gun. Now the dancers had cartridge belts draped over their shoulders and carried Winchesters. No one who saw them could doubt that they were ready to kill anyone who tried to stop the dancing.

Little Wound sent a message to Brooke. "We have done nothing wrong," he said. "Our dance is a religious one, and we are going to dance until spring. If we find that the Messiah doesn't appear we will stop dancing. I have been told that you intend to stop our rations. For my part I don't care. The rations we get amount to little. We don't intend to stop dancing for them."

When the bluecoats marched into Rosebud the Brulés panicked, and more than a thousand fled. Most were with old Two Strike, who headed for Pine Ridge. Small bands under Eagle Pipe, Crow Dog, and others rode to the northwest corner of the Rosebud reservation before continuing on to join Short Bull's camp on Pass Creek.

Billy watched for Pawnee Killer whenever new groups arrived, for he was sure his father was still a believer. Finally he asked Short Bull where his father was.

"When Sitting Bull talked about a big war in the spring," Short Bull replied, "your father and some others who'd been with him in Grandmother's Land went to Standing Rock to be with him. I told them not to go, for the Messiah will take care of the Wasicuns in his own way, but they wouldn't listen to me. They'd rather drive the Wasicuns away themselves than let the Messiah do it. They did promise to keep on dancing."

As Eagle Pipe and his people streamed into the camp, Billy was astonished but thrilled to see Mollie Deer-In-Timber in one of the wagons, looking worried and frightened.

"What are you doing here?"

"I had no choice. I was on my way to visit my mother when

they came along, running away from the soldiers. They made me come. I'm afraid.''

"Stay with me and you'll be safe." A young Oglala couple he knew had a small tipi to themselves, and they were happy to share it with Mollie and Billy. "They'll think we're married," Billy told her. "We should be, anyway." She looked at him wide-eyed.

"But we'll just pretend we're married, won't we? We won't...?" Billy frowned but nodded in agreement, for that wasn't what he wanted to hear. Now he had to tell Bull Bear and his wives he was moving out. Mollie waited while he went for his blankets and rifle. Bull Bear was away, but Bright Star and White Faun were in the tipi.

"Our leader, Short Bull, wants me to move," Billy told the women. "I must do as he says. Maybe I can come back later." Both looked shocked and disappointed as he snatched up his belongings and left before they could question him or try to persuade him to stay.

He waited impatiently for night to come, when he and Mollie wrapped up in his blankets. He could hear movements across the tipi, then the young Oglala woman moaned softly, and his heart beat faster. Mollie stiffened when he put his arm around her and pulled her close.

"Remember," she whispered, "Just pretend."

"You're the only one I ever wanted for a wife," he whispered, stroking her legs. She pushed his hand away. "I was so unhappy at Carlisle I never realized how much I loved you," he continued. Running his hand over her legs again, while she half-heartedly pushed it away. "I see your face every night in my dreams. Now, at last, I'm with you, and I'm not dreaming." This time she didn't resist.

In the morning, as the two of them walked through the camp, Billy was aching with love for her. *Somehow I must persuade her to stay with me.* He was suddenly aware they were being watched and turned his head slightly. Out of the corner of his eye he saw Bright Star and White Faun glowering at Mollie as if they'd like to kill her.

At Pine Ridge Red Cloud was nearly blind and unable to maintain his role as head chief, but he urged the Oglalas to remain calm. American Horse and Red Shirt still opposed the Ghost Dance, but other chiefs and many of their people camped at the agency still supported the dancers. Young-Man-Afraid-of-His-Horses and some of his people had gone to visit the Crows. Jack Red Cloud, who'd been one of the most active dancers, now rejected the Ghost Dance and joined the friendlies.

Although the daily sight of bluecoats and the sound of bugles irritated the Oglalas and made them nervous, the troops had been sent to protect the agency and the families there, not to stop the Ghost Dance or provoke a war. Brooke assured the chiefs that the troops would harm no one, not even the Ghost Dancers. That satisfied those at the agency, but not the defiant ones in the dance camps.

The day that troops arrived at Pine Ridge, many Oglala Ghost Dancers had second thoughts about continuing the dance and talked of going to the agency. To dissuade them, the fanatic Porcupine insisted that they let him demonstrate the effectiveness of the Ghost Shirts. While Big Road and No Water and their people watched, Porcupine stood facing Bull Calf, who reluctantly aimed his Winchester at him. "Go ahead and shoot," Porcupine ordered. Bull Calf fired, and Porcupine fell to the ground, badly wounded.

Shocked, Big Road and No Water held council. A few die-hards insisted on continuing the dance, but most had lost faith in the Messiah's coming and agreed to go to the agency. Big Road sent word to Little Wound, then he and No Water took their people to Pine Ridge. Shaken by the news that the Ghost Shirts he had learned about in a trance wouldn't stop bullets, Little Wound rode into Pine Ridge a few days later and informed Brooke that his people were following.

General Miles, who had presidential ambitions, greatly exaggerated the Sioux danger. It was clear that the Tetons would fight only if troops tried to stop the dancing; they had no plan for starting a general war or of attacking white settlers around the reservations. "Since the days of Pontiac, Tecumseh, and Red Jacket," Miles proclaimed, speaking of Sitting Bull, "no Indian has had the power of drawing to him so large a following of his race and molding and wielding it against the authority of the United States."

He was sure that Sitting Bull was plotting a general uprising, and concluded that he should be arrested, but quietly, without starting a fight. Far from attracting a large number of Tetons, Sitting Bull had only about 400 followers, more than half of them women and children. Most of the Hunkpapas opposed him.

General Miles continued to send reinforcements to the trouble spots, while stationing others in a cordon around all the Teton reservations. To Pine Ridge came four companies of the Second Infantry and another troop of the Ninth Cavalry. On November 26 the entire Seventh Cavalry Regiment under Colonel James Forsyth arrived from Fort Riley, Kansas. The Oglalas had good reason to remember Long Hair Custer's regiment, for the Tetons had destroyed half of it when Custer charged their camps on the Greasy Grass. Four companies of the Twenty-first Infantry reached Rosebud from Fort Sidney, Nebraska. Miles now had nearly half of the entire U.S. Army on or near the Teton reservatons. He also authorized Brooke to recruit two companies of Indian scouts, and forty Oglalas and Northern Cheyennes enlisted.

To help preserve the calm at Pine Ridge, on November 27 Brooke ordered Royer to restore the rations to the amount specified in treaties. Their stomachs full for the first time in years, the Oglalas accepted the presence of troops, but hoped they'd soon march away.

Two Strike's people looted abandoned cabins in their path and gathered horses and cattle as they crossed the Pine Ridge reservation to Wounded Knee Creek, about fifteen miles from the agency. There they joined a party of Wazhazhas. After the other Brulé refugees reached Short Bull's camp on Pass Creek, the whole group traveled up the White River until they met the Oglalas camped at the mouth of White Clay Creek, where they resumed the dancing.

On the morning of November 28, Short Bull assembled his people. "Last night," he told them, "four stars came down from the sky and spoke to me. 'Take your people to the Stronghold in the Badlands,' they told me. 'The Messiah is ready to come back to earth, and as soon as your people are dancing at the Stronghold, he will come to you there.' " Short Bull smiled, while the people murmured in pleasure at this good news.

Excited, Billy glanced at Mollie, who stood by his side. Her eyes were open wide, but Billy was sure she didn't believe Short Bull's story. She seemed happy to be with him, but Billy noticed that much of the time she looked sad. "You don't think the Messiah is really coming, do you?" he asked. She shook her head.

"Our minister says it's not true, that all who expect him to come will be disappointed. All this dancing is for nothing." He wanted to tell her that he had seen the Messiah more than once, and each time he'd promised to come, but refrained.

"I want to go home," she said. "Why do these men threaten to kill anyone who leaves?" He didn't answer. He knew that because the fanatics refused to allow anyone to leave, Mollie was still with him. Otherwise she and the large number of nonbelievers would have left as soon as they'd been assured the troops wouldn't attack them. *I can't bear the thought of her leaving. How can I make her want to stay?*

At that moment Mash-the-Kettle beckoned to Billy. "Short Bull needs to send messages and wants you to write them," he said. Billy hurried to Short Bull.

"Tell Two Strike, Big Foot, Hump, and Sitting Bull what the stars told me," he said. "Urge them to come to the Stronghold before the Messiah arrives. Tell Sitting Bull that as the most famous Teton chief, he especially should be there to welcome the Messiah." Billy wrote the letters and Short Bull sent riders off with them. It was no longer safe to send men to the agencies to mail them.

The next day Short Bull and his large following, more than a thousand men, women, and children, moved down the White River to the northeast, while Two Strike's people headed north down Wounded Knee Creek, gathering stray cattle and looting cabins. On December 1 the two parties met on the White River. Now all of the remaining Ghost Dancers from Rosebud and Pine Ridge were together. There were so many warriors among them they had no fear of bluecoats.

As the long procession traveled north under a gray sky and facing an icy wind and light snow, Mollie rode sadly in a wagon. Billy's thoughts were on the new world the Messiah had promised, a world of Indians and buffalo. Mollie's words had raised some doubts in his mind and shaken his faith, but like the other believers, he still pinned all his hopes on the Messiah. He couldn't bear to think about what would happen to the Tetons if the Messiah failed them. In that case he might as well be dead.

They reached the shelter of the high cliffs around the plateau that joined the Stronghold and camped there, sheltered from the gale. When they rolled up in their blankets and he pressed his face against Mollie's, hers was wet with tears. She lay limply by his side, and he knew she wouldn't stop him, but he loved her too much to do more than pat her shoulder. *She won't be happy until she's back with her husband. It doesn't matter if I live or die.*

In the morning they resumed their journey up a trail to the plateau, where there was no shelter from the bitter wind. On to the north they went, shivering in the freezing weather. At the northern end of the plateau they came to a land bridge leading to another high mesa. The bridge was barely wide enough for wagons to cross, and it was the only entrance.

This was the Stronghold the stars had referred to when they came down to talk to Short Bull. Billy held his hand before his face to keep wind-blown snowflakes from stinging his eyes. The Stronghold appeared to be about three miles long and two miles wide; the grass was tall and thick, and two springs provided water enough for people and animals. No soldiers could attack them here, and with all the cattle they'd gathered it would take months to starve them out. By then the Messiah would surely have come, and their troubles would be over. Ghost Dancers and nonbelievers set up their tipis on the open mesa in the blowing snow.

With Short Bull and the tall Kicking Bear were the Brulés who had fought the bluecoats in 1876, most of the Washazhas, Two Strike's band, the people with Eagle Pipe and Crow Dog, and many Oglalas. The majority weren't Ghost Dancers; they had simply panicked at the sight of troops. They badly wanted to return to the agencies, but the fanatics still threatened to kill any who tried to leave.

At Pine Ridge a number of reporters had gathered from far and near to write about the Great Sioux Uprising that General Miles had hinted at. They found the soldiers idle and the Indians calm; there was nothing to report, certainly nothing sensational. As a result they reported every rumor as fact, and reporters from distant cities even manufactured news. The Indians were massing for battle, the situation was explosive, they wrote, and they criticized General Brooke for his inactivity. The firing of one gun, they said, would set off a fight to the finish. The reporters themselves, as if believing their own fabrications, were walking arsenals. Those representing papers in Nebraska and the Dakotas generally told it like it was: everything was quiet and no trouble was anticipated. If fighting began, it would be forced on the Sioux.

Charles Moody of the *Sturgis Weekly Record* pointed out one reason for promoting the threat of an Indian war in South Dakota. "The *Mandan Pioneer* and the local correspondent of that place are entitled to an immense amount of credit for their success in having Ft. Lincoln reoccupied," he wrote. "The Indian scare was a shrewd scheme." A good trade with the fort had been assured for the winter.

Carl Smith of the *Omaha World Herald* blamed Royer's lack of experience for the Indian scare, and accused him of trying to substantiate the fright that caused him to call for troops. "To hold his job, Mr. Royer may succeed in aggravating these Indians into some sort of warlike demonstration, but it will be fighting against their will," he wrote on December 1. Royer refrained from expelling Smith only because the publisher of his paper threatened to seek redress from the Secretary of the Interior if he did. But General Brooke, who had no use for reporters, ordered Smith to leave on the grounds that he obtained his news by listening to the army telegraph operator at Pine Ridge.

On December 1 the Secretary of the Interior ordered all Sioux agents to bring rations up to the amounts guaranteed in treaties. Two days later Congress, which still hadn't acted on the Sioux appropriation bill, debated a measure to provide 100,000 rifles to the citizens of South Dakota, who were believed to be in imminent danger of being massacred. Senator Voorhees suggested, since it was obvious the trouble was caused by hunger among the Sioux, that it might be more sensible to send 100,000 rations to the Indians instead of 100,000 rifles to excited white men near the reservations. Another Senator remarked that the Crook Commission had made many promises to the Sioux, including restoring the beef issue, and that Crook had died of grief over the failure of Congress to honor his commitments. Outraged, Senator Dawes denied that Congress had acted in bad faith. He saw no relief in the present situation, he said, unless bad chiefs like Red Cloud and Sitting Bull were removed, as if they were responsible for the crisis.

Senator Voorhees asked Dawes if General Miles was correct in blaming the Sioux troubles on hunger. Dawes, the spokesman for the Friends of the Indian in Congress, angrily retorted that this was the first time he'd heard of hunger among the Sioux. They'd been away dancing for weeks, and now this talk of hunger. If they stayed on their farms they'd have sufficient food, he was sure. Voorhees asked if he didn't know the Sioux had been starving for two years. Dawes huffily replied that the Sioux were hungry only because they abandoned their farms and left the agencies to dance.

While this was going on, Brooke sent Frank Merrivale, a trader of French descent who was fluent in Lakota, with some Oglala friendlies to try to persuade the Ghost Dancers to abandon the Stronghold and return to Pine Ridge. Merrivale's party returned the next day, for the Ghost Dancers' pickets had turned them back. When he learned of this, Royer rushed to General Brooke.

"It's come!" he exclaimed. "War has come! They wouldn't listen to Merrivale. They shot over his head, killed a lot of cattle, and lit out for the Badlands." Brooke, who had no respect for Indian agents, even able ones, ignored Royer.

George Wright returned to Rosebud as agent on December 1, having been cleared of the charges against him. Special Agent Reynolds stayed on to help. The Brulé headmen welcomed Wright and promised to obey his orders. They blamed their troubles on the Ghost Dance, and begged him not to allow the troops to attack them.

The day after Merrivale returned, December 3, seventy-year-old Father John Jutz of the Holy Rosary Mission four miles north of the agency, offered to try to talk to the Ghost Dancers. Popular with the Oglalas, he had been assured that if there was any fighting his mission would be spared. Jack Red Cloud, now active among the friendlies, accompanied him. The next afternoon scouts met them ten miles from the Stronghold and sent word to Short

Bull that Father Jutz wanted to hold council. By the time the rider returned with Short Bull's approval and Jutz and Jack Red Cloud had covered the ten miles to the Stronghold, it was an hour before midnight.

"Your Ghost Shirts won't protect you," Jutz told them. "A couple of weeks ago Porcupine had someone shoot him to prove his shirt would stop bullets. He is seriously wounded."

Billy remembered Porcupine, one of the most fanatic of Oglala Ghost Dancers. He looked down at his own Ghost Shirt Short Bull had given him, and at the painted symbols that were supposed to cause bullets to fall to the ground. Wovoka had said nothing about Ghost Shirts. He shivered at the thought of bullets tearing through the thin cloth into his body and wondered if the Ghost Dance was, as Culver insisted, an illusion. That was a troubling thought, and he forced it from his mind.

For the rest of the night Jutz sat in council with Short Bull, Kicking Bear, Two Strike, Turning Bear, Crow Dog, Eagle Pipe, and other headmen, while Billy and many other Ghost Dancers listened. The chiefs complained bitterly of the census that had caused rations to be cut again, and about the land agreement and the unkept promises. When Jutz urged them to return to the agency, they wouldn't hear of it. The Wasicuns would arrest them, Short Bull said. They'd rather die fighting than rot in prison. Before morning, however, Two Strike and several others agreed to accompany Jutz to the agency for a council with Brooke. They set out at daybreak in a light snow, although none had slept that night.

Leading the procession was a warrior carrying a white flag, followed by twenty armed warriors who were painted as for war. Their ponies were also painted, and their tails were tied up with ribbons and festooned with eagle feathers. Behind them rode Jack Red Cloud along with Turning Bear, High Pine, and three other headmen in their finest war costumes under their Ghost Shirts. Bringing up the rear were Father Jutz and Two Strike in an old buggy guarded by four Brulé warriors. They stopped for the night at Jutz's mission.

In the morning, fearing arrest, the Ghost Dancers hesitated to continue. Four times they started, but turned back each time as if their ponies refused to carry them to an uncertain fate. Finally

Father Jutz called them around him. "I assure you that you're safe with me," he said, "but if any soldiers threaten you, you may kill me." Shamed, they agreed to continue, but without their paint and feathers.

When the procession neared the agency, the Oglalas in the friendly camp were wild with excitement. Looking straight ahead and showing no sign of fear, the Ghost Dance party rode past the troops to Brooke's headquarters and tied their ponies. There Father Jutz led them into the big tent for the council.

General Brooke was friendly and conciliatory toward the visitors. If they came in, he told them, they would receive increased rations and he would hire some of them as scouts. Turning Bear, a leading Ghost Dancer, spoke for the Indians. There's no need for scouts, he said, because there is no war, but they'd be glad to be paid for scouting. He told Brooke that they would like to come in and camp near the agency, but there were already too many people there and not enough grass for their pony herds. They had many old people in the camps who couldn't ride, and they had no wagons for them. It was true about the grass, but Turning Bear was politely stalling. As to coming to the agency, he concluded, they'd have to talk about that before deciding.

The talks lasted two hours, then the Indians were fed. When they left Brooke gave them boxes of hardtack and other army rations. He was convinced they would soon decide in favor of coming in. Accompanying them on their return to the Stronghold were No Neck and thirty-two young Oglala friendlies as well as Louis Shangreau, a courageous mixed blood.

In the meantime, Short Bull and Kicking Bear had kept those in the camp excited, warning them to have no dealings with the whites, who would try to prevent the new world from coming. Two Strike's party and No Neck's friendlies arrived as a frenzied Ghost Dance was going on; it continued uninte: ʾupted for thirty hours before it was stopped for the council. Short Bull, Two Strike, and Crow Dog spoke for the dancers.

"The agent will forgive you if you come in now," Shangreau told them, "and he will also increase your rations. The only restriction is that you may not dance."

"If the Great Father would allow us to continue the dance, give us more rations, and quit taking away pieces of our reservation," Short Bull replied, "I would favor returning. But if we return he will take our guns and ponies and put some of us in jail for taking cattle and looting cabins. Tell him we're not coming." He then ordered the dance resumed, and the council ended. Although it continued for two days, No Neck, Shangreau, and their party refused to leave. Another council was held on December 10, when Two Strike abruptly announced that he was taking his people to the agency. Crow Dog said he would do the same. Short Bull sprang to his feet.

"At such times as this we should stick together like brothers!" he exclaimed. "These agency men are lying. Louis Shangreau is at the bottom of this! He's a traitor. Kill him! Kill him!"

At that Billy joined other shrieking Ghost Dancers who rushed at Shangreau with clubbed rifles and knives, ready to do Short Bull's bidding. But the young Oglala friendlies surrounded Shangreau, No Neck, Two Strike, and Crow Dog, and fended off the frenzied dancers with their rifles. In the midst of the tumult, Crow Dog sat down and covered his head with his blanket. Seeing him, the Ghost Dancers backed off and fell silent.

Crow Dog threw off his blanket and arose. "Brothers! Stop this! I can't bear to see Tetons shedding the blood of their brothers," he shouted. "I'm going back to the agency. You can kill me if you want to and prevent me from going. I'm not afraid to die. The agent's words are true—it's better to return than to stay here."

Billy felt ashamed that he had impulsively joined in the attack. Crow Dog was right. No Teton should shed the blood of another. Even though Crow Dog himself had killed Spotted Tail, no one reminded him of that.

The camp was immediately astir as women frantically tore down the tipis and loaded the wagons, while the Ghost Dancers ran around shouting "Don't go! Don't go!" In a short time Shangreau, No Neck, and the Oglala friendlies started for the land bridge. Two Strike, Crow Dog, and their people followed. Billy looked for Mollie, and found her in one of the wagons.

"Come with us," she said before he could speak.

"Will you stay with me if I do?"

"I can't. I was married in church. I wish I could."

"I may as well stay then. There's no reason for me to return."
He turned and left her, feeling empty inside.

As the long procession strung out across the mesa toward the land bridge, the Ghost Dancers ran about in confusion. Soon Billy saw some of them strike their tipis and follow, stampeded by the sight of others leaving. When they were gone, only about two hundred die-hards remained in the Stronghold. What was most shocking to Billy was that the tall, rawboned Kicking Bear had deserted Short Bull and gone with the others.

Chapter Thirteen

Once the southern agencies were quiet, and efforts were being made to coax the Ghost Dancers to come in, General Miles turned his attention to Cheyenne River and Standing Rock, where Hump, Big Foot, and Sitting Bull were still considered dangerous. "I concluded that if the so-called Messiah was to appear in that country," Miles remarked, "Sitting Bull had to be out of it. I consider it of first importance to secure his arrest and removal from the country." But an attempt to arrest Sitting Bull could spark the war Miles hoped to avoid. How could it be managed without bloodshed?

In pondering this delicate question, Miles remembered that after he returned from Canada, Sitting Bull had traveled with Buffalo Bill Cody's Wild West Show for a year, and it was said the two had become friends. On November 24 he sent for Cody and questioned him. He and Sitting Bull were indeed old friends, Cody said, and he was sure he could persuade him to come in peacefully. Miles gave him confidential orders, stating, "Col. Cody, you are hereby authorized to secure the person of Sitting Bull and deliver him to the nearest commanding officer of U.S. Troops, taking a receipt and reporting your action." On the back of one of his visiting cards, he wrote, "Commanding officers will please give Col. Cody transportation for himself and party and any protection he may need for a small party," and gave it to Cody. For showman Buffalo Bill, here was a splendid, unexpected opportunity for adventure and especially for publicity. Although his orders were confidential, he was so elated he had to talk to reporters about the Sioux troubles and prepare the way to capitalize later on his anticipated glorious achievement. "Of all the bad Indians," he said of his presumed friend, "Sitting Bull is the worst. If there is no disturbance he will foment one. He is a dangerous Indian."

Boarding the train at Chicago, Cody picked up old friends on the way west—Frank Powell, his Nebraska ranch manager John Keith, and Pony Bob Haslin. At Bismarck, South Dakota, he hired two wagons and men to drive them. He filled one with presents for Sitting Bull, including a generous supply of the Hunkpapa chief's favorite candy. When they boarded the train for the short trip across the Missouri to Mandan, several reporters joined the party, prepared to tell the nation about Buffalo Bill's greatest coup in bringing in the fearsome Sitting Bull.

On November 28 Colonel Drum was surprised to see the famous showman, still dressed in his Wild West Show suit and patent leather shoes, with long hair, mustache, and goatee. Drum's surprise turned to shock when Cody announced the purpose of his visit, and that he was expected to cooperate with him in the madcap adventure. Like most army officers, he heartily disliked meddling civilians, especially publicity seekers. He immediately conferred with white-haired McLaughlin, who was equally disturbed at the new turn of events. Both agreed that Cody was much more likely to get himself and his friends killed or of starting a war than he was of arresting Sitting Bull. Drum promised to stall Cody as long as he could while McLaughlin wired the Secretary of the Interior requesting that Miles' order to Cody be cancelled.

Knowing of Cody's reputation as an unrivaled tippler, that evening Drum invited him to join the officers for a libation. Before long the officers realized that this was a difficult assignment, for they were no match for the long-haired former scout, and they spared themselves the embarrassment of being drunk under the table by several taking turns drinking with him while the others downed cups of black coffee. In the morning, apparently refreshed by army hospitality, Cody informed the bleary officers of the last shift, "I'm off on the most dangerous assignment of my whole career."

Fearing that Cody might set out before a message could arrive revoking his orders, McLaughlin had set in motion an alternate plan for delaying the meeting with Sitting Bull. Early in the morning he sent interpreter Louis Primeau and several others down one of the two roads leading to the Grand River settlement, and another party down the second road, to go twenty miles or more and then return, making a fresh set of tracks toward the agency. Cody met Primeau halfway to the Grand River; the interpreter told him that he had just left Sitting Bull's village and the chief was on his way to the agency by the other road, then showed him the fresh tracks. There was nothing for Cody to do but turn back. When he reached the agency McLaughlin greeted him with a wire from the President rescinding his orders from Miles. Grumbling, Cody left the next day for Chicago.

Early in December a rider reached Sitting Bull with Short Bull's message that the Messiah was soon coming to the Stronghold, and that a prominent chief like Sitting Bull should be there to welcome him. His semi-literate nephew Andrew Fox translated the letter Billy had written for Short Bull. Even though he was a Ghost Dance leader, Sitting Bull wasn't altogether convinced by Wovoka's promises. Besides, going to the Stronghold meant a 200-mile ride in cold weather. He pondered the matter for several days, and on December 11 held a council in his cabin. His old friends agreed that it would be unfortunate indeed if the Messiah came to earth at the Stronghold and the great Sitting Bull wasn't there to greet him. Sitting Bull, who wasn't burdened by modesty or self-doubts, found their logic convincing.

Andrew Fox laboriously wrote a letter from his uncle to the agent. First he told McLaughlin that "I wish no one to come with guns or knives to interfere with my prayers. All we are doing is praying for life and to learn how to do good. When you visited my camp you gave me good words about our prayers but then you took your good words back again. And so I will let you know something. I got to go to Pine Ridge and know this pray so I let you know that. I want answer back soon."

He sent Bull Ghost to Standing Rock with his indirect request for a pass to visit Pine Ridge. A few hours before Bull Ghost arrived, Col. Drum had received orders from Miles to arrest Sitting Bull and to call on the agent for assistance. Drum and McLaughlin read and reread Sitting Bull's letter and concluded that he intended to leave with or without permission. Both were sure he planned to join the Ghost Dancers in the Badlands, and that would be a disaster. They decided to stall Sitting Bull until the next ration day, December 20, when he would be virtually alone in his village. Any attempt to arrest him when all of his people were present would almost surely lead to a bitter fight. They concluded that the Indian police had a much better chance of making the arrest peacefully than the cavalry did.

McLaughlin wrote Lt. Bull Head, chief of the Indian police, to keep a close watch on Sitting Bull and his people. Bull Head's farm was a few miles upriver from Sitting Bull's cabins. White Bird rode through the night with the agent's letter.

While White Bird was making the forty-mile ride to Bull Head's farm, Sitting Bull held another council. His friends decided he should leave for the Stronghold as soon as possible. Since it would take two days to grease the wagon wheels, round up the ponies, and make other preparations for the long journey, Sitting Bull couldn't leave until December 15. Bull Head's police observed preparations being made for a move, and by evening they had managed to learn when Sitting Bull planned to leave.

Bull Head hurried to the school a few miles below the village and asked teacher Jack Carignan to write a letter informing McLaughlin that Sitting Bull would leave on December 15, then sent Hawk Man with it to the agency. At the same time Sitting Bull's spies were riding in the opposite direction with the news that McLaughlin and Col. Drum were preparing to arrest him. Hawk Man reached Standing Rock late in the afternoon of December 14.

McLaughlin and Drum agreed that they had no choice but to make the arrest immediately, regardless of the danger, for the prospect of Sitting Bull joining the Ghost Dancers in the Badlands was frightening. McLaughlin wisely had been sending police to the area around Bull Head's farm in case they were needed. He sent Sergeant Red Tomahawk, a Yanktonai Sioux, racing through the night to Bull Head with orders to make the arrest in the early morning, adding that troops would be at Oak Creek crossing, twenty miles away, in case they were needed. "You must not let him escape under any circumstances," he concluded.

Col. Drum had officers' call sounded at Fort Yates, then ordered

Capt. E. G. Fechet to take Troops F and G, Eighth Cavalry, with a Hotchkiss and a Gatling gun, and to move out at midnight. As they were about to depart, Col. Drum stood by Fechet's horse. "Captain," he said, "after you leave here use your own discretion. You know the object of the movement. Do your best to make it a success." Ninety-nine men, five officers, two Indian scouts, and Louis Primeau, all bundled up in buffalo skin coats, set out at a trot in near-freezing weather. In three and a half hours the cavalry covered the twenty miles to Oak Creek crossing and stopped. A courier from Bull Head was supposed to be waiting for them. There was no courier, and the police cabin there was empty. Fechet, recalling Col. Drum's admonition to use his own discretion, knew that if there was trouble at Grand River in the morning, his troops would be of little use twenty miles away. He gave orders to proceed at a trot, and by daybreak the cavalrymen were only a few miles from the Grand River village.

Red Tomahawk didn't spare his pony that night, for he reached Bull Head's farm in under five hours. During the night additional police arrived, so that on the morning of December 15 Bull Head had thirty men. None of the police were happy about their awesome assignment of arresting Sitting Bull for the whites. Some of them were Yanktonais, but others, like Sitting Bull, were Hunkpapas, and they doubted that what they were doing was right even though Sitting Bull was making trouble for all, and none of them deluded himself into thinking the arrest could be made without bloodshed. All felt sad, but they were determined to do what Whitehair McLaughlin wanted done.

Bull Head gave them their instructions. Before daybreak they would ride to Gray Eagle's cabin, then to a spot south of the river opposite Sitting Bull's cabins. The Ghost Dancers, Bull Head pointed out, would expect any trouble to come from the north, from the agency or Fort Yates. In the early dawn they would cross the river and surround the cabin in which Sitting Bull slept. While Bull Head, Shave Head, and Red Tomahawk made the arrest, Red Bear and White Bird would saddle Sitting Bull's favorite mount, a gray trick horse Buffalo Bill had given him. They would put Sitting Bull on it and leave as quickly as possible, before his people were aware of what was happening.

Gray Eagle, Sitting Bull's brother-in-law, had accepted the fact that clinging to the old ways was foolish and had made a determined effort to adjust. His attempts to convince Sitting Bull to change were in vain. From the moment he arrived at Standing Rock, Sitting Bull had carried on a feud with the agent, refusing to cooperate in any way. He had his doubts about the Ghost Dance, but it provided an opportunity to regain his lost prestige. Another reason he embraced it was that his white-haired foe wanted it stopped. Gray Eagle, like many Hunkpapa progressives, regretfully concluded that for the good of the tribe Sitting Bull should be removed, but for him, too, it was a sad business.

At Gray Eagle's cabin, Eagle Man joined the party with eight more police, bringing the number to thirty-nine. All removed their hats and knelt while Bull Head prayed to the white men's God, asking help in doing what they had to do without bloodshed. Then they remounted their ponies. "Hopo," said Bull Head, and they headed for the river in a misty drizzle that froze on their ponies' manes. In the trees, owls hooted mournfully. Owls were believed to be the ghosts of dead relatives. "They're telling us to be careful," Red Tomahawk remarked. Sensing death hovering about them, the others shivered, wishing they were somewhere else.

They crossed the river in the dim light, and the dogs in the village immediately started barking noisily, alerting the sleeping Hunkpapas to the fact that intruders were coming. The police loosened their reins and galloped to Sitting Bull's cabin and hastily dismounted, eager to get it over with quickly. Bull Head, accompanied by Red Tomahawk and Shave Head, knocked on the door. Red Bear and White Bird ran to the corral to saddle Sitting Bull's horse while the others surrounded the cabin.

"All right, come in," Sitting Bull responded to the knock. The three entered and Shave Head struck a match, located a kerosene lamp, and lighted it. Naked, Sitting Bull sat up, then threw off his blankets and arose. "I come to take you to the agency," Bull Head told him. "You're under arrest."

"All right, let me put on my clothes and I'll go with you." One of his wives brought him his clothes, but he took his time putting them on, while the nervous police tried to hurry him. "Sitting Bull wasn't afraid," Little Soldier admitted later. "We were." When he was nearly dressed Sitting Bull told Crow Foot, his seventeen-year-old son, to saddle his horse.

"We've taken care of that," Bull Head told him.

Bull Head and Shave Head each took Sitting Bull by an arm, while Red Tomahawk walked behind him, pressing his pistol against his back. As they passed through the doorway, one of Sitting Bull's wives began wailing loudly. Red Bear and White Bird hadn't arrived with the horse, so they had to wait. It was still too dark to see more than a short distance.

By now the entire village had been aroused by the dogs and the wailing woman, and everyone ran to Sitting Bull's cabin. Catch-the-Bear, one of Sitting Bull's bodyguards who had sworn to kill Bull Head, looked each policeman in the face, trying to locate his enemy. "Where is Bull Head?" he growled. "Now here you metal breasts are," he continued, referring to their badges, "just as we expected. You think you're going to take him, but you're wrong. You won't get away with him." He turned to the others. "Come on," he shouted, "let's protect our chief."

Sitting Bull's horse was brought from the corral, and the nervous policemen pushed him toward it. From the back of the crowd Crawler shouted, "Kill them! Kill them! Shoot the old metal breasts and the young ones will run."

"Come on," Bull Head told Sitting Bull. "Don't listen to anyone."

"Brother-in-law, do as the agent says," Gray Eagle pleaded. "Go with the metal breasts."

Jumping Bull, an Assiniboine Sitting Bull had adopted years before when he was a boy, also pleaded with him. "Brother, let's break camp and move to the agency. You take your family and I'll take mine. If you're to die, I'll die with you."

Sitting Bull's son Crow Foot came out of the cabin. "You always called yourself a brave chief," he sneered. "Now you're letting the metal breasts take you away." Sitting Bull stiffened at this challenge to his courage. He knew his people were ready to rescue him.

"Then I won't go another step," he said.

As the three police pushed and pulled him toward his horse, his followers shrieked and cursed the police. "You won't take our chief," they shouted.

Catch-the-Bear threw off his blanket, raised his rifle, and shot Bull Head in the right side. As he was falling, Bull Head shot Sitting Bull in the chest with his pistol while Red Tomahawk's bullet struck him in the back of the head. Lone Man leaped on Catch-the-Bear, tore his rifle from his hands, knocked him down with it, then shot him.

Sitting Bull's followers threw themselves at the police with guns, clubs, and knives, and four more police fell. In the midst of the wild melee and flying bullets, Sitting Bull's old trick horse thought it was back in the Wild West Show. It sat on its haunches and bowed its head as if praying. Seeing it the police were frightened, for it seemed that Sitting Bull's spirit had entered his horse. While this was going on Hawk Man mounted his pony and galloped off to find the troops, who were now only a few miles away.

After a few minutes of hand to hand fighting, the police drove the dancers dashing to a line of trees along the river. The police, not wanting more bloodshed, stopped firing at them.

With both police lieutenants out of the fight, Sergeant Red Tomahawk took charge and ordered his companions to carry the badly wounded men into the cabin. Bull Head had been shot three more times as he lay on the ground, and Shave Head was also seriously wounded. One of the police discovered Crow Foot hiding under a pile of blankets. "Uncles, don't kill me!" he begged. "I don't want to die." The policeman asked Bull Head what to do with him.

"Do what you like. He's one of those who caused this trouble." The man knocked Crow Foot through the cabin door, where he sprawled half-conscious on the ground. Two other policemen, with tears streaming down their faces, shot him.

Sitting Bull's followers now began firing from behind the trees and from a knoll at fairly long range. The police sought cover and returned the fire. In the meantime, Hawk Man found the troops and reported to Capt. Fechet that all of the police had been killed, for they had been so badly outnumbered he didn't see how any could survive. While the troopers pulled off their heavy coats and gloves to be ready for action, Fechet wrote a hasty note to Col. Drum. He would, he said, hurry to the relief of any policemen who might still be alive. He handed the note to Hawk Man and sent him on his way, then ordered the troopers to advance at a gallop. Another policeman met the column. The police were cornered in and around the cabin, he said, and they were low on ammunition. Fechet's decision to continue past the Oak Creek crossing saved the police from likely disaster.

In a few minutes the troops crossed a ridge and saw the village half a mile below them. In the early morning light they could see Sitting Bull's cabin shrouded in gun smoke. From the timber and the knoll came the sound of rifle fire. Fechet had a white flag raised as a pre-arranged signal, but the police hadn't seen the troops and failed to respond. Not absolutely sure where the police were, Fechet had the Hotchkiss gunners drop a shell into the open space between the cabin and the timber, where it exploded too close to the police for comfort. Lone Man tore a curtain from the window and ran out, waving it at the approaching soldiers. A few shots into the timber from the "gun that shoots twice," as the Tetons called the Hotchkiss, and Sitting Bull's people fled.

"I saw evidence of a most desperate encounter," Fechet reported later. "In front of the house, and within a radius of fifty yards, were eight dead Indians, including Sitting Bull, and two dead horses. In the house were four dead policemen and three wounded, two mortally. To add to the horror of the scene the squaws of Sitting Bull, who were in a small house nearby, kept up great wailing."

Relatives of policeman Strong Arm who lived at the Grand River village came looking for him. When they saw his body they, too, began to wail. One of them, Holy Medicine, picked up an ox yoke and beat Sitting Bull's corpse with it until trooper Jerry Hart stopped him. "What the hell did you do that for?" he asked. "The man's dead. Leave him alone."

The troops now built fires to cook breakfast. About the time the coffee was ready, the police shouted a warning. Out of the timber about eighty yards away, a warrior on a splendid black horse came toward them at a gallop. He wore a Ghost Shirt and held a long lance as he sang a Ghost Dance song. The police recognized him as Crow Woman, one of the most fanatic of the Hunkpapa Ghost Dancers. While his people watched from hills across the river, he raced toward the soldiers determined to demonstrate the supernatural powers of his shirt.

When the police fired a volley at him, Crow Woman turned his horse and rode back among the trees, only to return again to test their fire. Emerging a third time, he dashed between two soldiers on the picket line. Both fired their single-shot carbines at him but missed. Having proved his point to his satisfaction, Crow Woman rode triumphantly up the valley unharmed. His deed reaffirmed the faith of many Hunkpapas in their Ghost Shirts.

Through Louis Primeau, Capt. Fechet urged Sitting Bull's widows to tell those who had fled that the soldiers were leaving and they could return to their cabins. He sent other Indians up and down the valley to assure any who wanted to go to the agency they could safely accompany the troops. Many took him at his word and came in to follow the cavalry to Standing Rock, and others fell in with them on the way. Still others came to the agency a few days later, but many had fled south to seek refuge with the Miniconjus.

Bull Head, Shave Head, and Middle, the three wounded police, were carried in the army ambulance that had followed the troops. Only one wagon was available, and Red Tomahawk, over the protests of many, ordered the dead policemen piled into it on top of the body of Sitting Bull. The march began after midday, and the column stopped for the night at Oak Creek crossing. At midnight Col. Drum arrived with two companies of infantry. Hawk Man had breathlessly repeated his story that all of the police had been killed, so Drum made a forced march to investigate.

Despite the efforts of the agency and army doctors, Shave Head died the next night and Bull Head succumbed the following day, but Middle survived. The dead police were buried in the cemetery next to the Catholic mission church with military honors, a firing squad, and a bugler playing "Taps." Sitting Bull was interred in the post cemetery at Fort Yates in a grave dug by military prisoners.

Because of the legends that had grown up around Sitting Bull as well as what Miles and Buffalo Bill had said about him, his death was seen as the final act of Indian resistance. The settlers of South Dakota who had fled their homes returned to them, confident now that the dreaded old warrior was no more. Even if they had known that 200 of his followers had fled south to join Hump, they wouldn't have worried. The fierce chief who had once been billed as the "Killer of General Custer" in Buffalo Bill's Wild West Show was lying wrapped in canvas in a rough wooden box under the South Dakota sod.

Surprisingly, the news of Sitting Bull's death aroused mixed feelings outside the reservations. Although many westerners rejoiced, and some Indian reformers felt the last obstacle to progress among the Sioux had been removed, regrettably by violence, others were outraged.

"The land grabbers wanted the Indian land," a New York minister who belonged to Bland's Indian Defense Association proclaimed. "The lying, thieving Indian agents wanted silence touching past thefts and immunity to continue their thieving. The renegades among the Indian police wanted an opportunity to show their power. And so he was murdered."

Newspapers happily joined in the attack, accusing McLaughlin and Drum of conspiring to assassinate Sitting Bull and of having ordered the Indian police to do it. Secretary of the Interior Noble also fell under the glare of adverse publicity, although he had done his best to make it clear that the army had ordered Sitting Bull's arrest. The fact that the deed had been done by the Indian police at the agent's orders caused many to accuse him of having bloodied his hands in the affair. "McLaughlin is so proud of his exploit," Noble wrote Morgan, "that he rather suppressed the source of his action. But it is necessary that it be shown and understood that this was the act of the *Military, without qualification.*"

McLaughlin repeatedly pointed out that he had simply obeyed Miles' instructions as relayed through Gen. Ruger and Col. Drum. The newspapers ignored his statements—the killing was the work of the white-haired agent and his Indian police. Who had ordered it done was irrelevant.

Far from being proud of the tragic event, McLaughlin did resent the public's ingratitude to the policemen who had risked and lost their lives to arrest one of their own race at the bidding of the whites. He immediately began a long and fruitless campaign to secure pensions for the survivors of the dead police.

Although white reactions to the killing of Sitting Bull varied, the news of his death struck terror in the hearts of all Tetons. As they heard it, Sitting Bull had been treacherously murdered by Indian police aided by the army. Their mistrust of whites intensified, and the fear that troops would maneuver them into a defenseless position and then shoot them down gripped many, especially the Ghost Dancers.

Chapter Fourteen

After arranging for Buffalo Bill to bring in Sitting Bull in late November, Miles turned his attention to the other two chiefs he considered dangerous, Hump and Big Foot. In 1877 Hump had served him as a scout against Chief Jospeph and the Nez Perces, and during that time he and Capt. Ezra Ewers had become virtually blood brothers. A few days after contacting Buffalo Bill, Miles sent to Texas for Ewers. When he arrived at Fort Bennett, Miles instructed him to tell Hump that he was now in charge of all the Tetons and that he wanted him and his band to give up the Ghost Dance and move to the Cheyenne River Agency.

Ewers and Lt. Harry Hale rode up the Cheyenne River through blowing snow to Hump's village near the mouth of Cherry Creek on the southern edge of the Miniconju reservation. Hump was away, but when he learned that his friend Ewers had come to see him, he immediately returned. When told what Gen. Miles wanted him to do, he replied, ''All right. If Bearcoat wants me to, I will do as you say.''

Hump had already begun to doubt the coming of the Messiah, and when he and most of his people reached the agency on December 9, he again enlisted as a scout for the army, this time to help persuade the remaining Miniconju Ghost Dancers to give up and come in. Eighty of the most zealous dancers in his own band had refused to leave their cabins, and they continued dancing.

Now, except for Short Bull's people at the Stronghold and Hump's eighty, only Big Foot's people remained away from the agencies. Big Foot's village was twenty miles from Hump's, below the forks of the Cheyenne; it was already under surveillance by a small force of cavalrymen at Camp Cheyenne a few miles to the west. On December 3 Lt. Col. Edwin Sumner arrived from the Black Hills area with more cavalry and infantry, and took command at Camp Cheyenne.

Big Foot, a prominent warrior with a broad forehead, was most respected for his skill in settling quarrels between rival factions. When such disputes came dangerously close to erupting into violence, Big Foot was usually called on to pacify and bring together the contending parties. But to whites he was a diehard nonprogressive who kept his people as far from the agency as possible and whose young men were unruly troublemakers. As one who clung resolutely to the old ways, he had been immediately attracted to the Ghost Dance and the hope it promised for a new world.

All fall his people had danced furiously to prepare for the Messiah's coming. They had made no threatening gestures or even considered molesting whites in nearby Cheyenne City or elsewhere in the ceded lands. Settler George McPherson had been allowed to watch them dance. It reminded him, he said, of a Methodist revival, and he saw no reason to fear it. Big Foot would have been astonished to know that Agent Palmer had repeatedly declared that friendlies around the agency had assured him both Hump's and Big Foot's people wanted to fight and would fight. There was no doubt, they said, that the dancers were preparing for an uprising—Big Foot's men had recently been trading for arms and ammunition. The friendlies didn't add that it was to defend themselves against troops that might try to suppress the dancing, not to take the offensive against whites. It was Palmer's overblown statements that had convinced Miles that both chiefs were menaces and must be eliminated.

Big Foot was badly shaken to learn that Hump had rejected the Ghost Dance and moved his band to the agency. Having doubts himself about the Messiah, Big Foot took no part in the dances thereafter. His people, spurred on by the high-pitched voice of the thin-faced fanatical medicine man Yellow Bird, danced with an intensity born of desperation. Yellow Bird was consumed with hatred for all whites, and he kept his followers dancing until they fell from exhaustion.

Miles knew of no white man who was on as friendly terms with Big Foot as Ewers was with Hump, and who might be able to persuade him to move to the agency. Like Sitting Bull, therefore, he would have to be arrested.

When he learned of Col. Sumner's arrival at Camp Cheyenne with 200 men, Big Foot suspected the whites had become afraid of him. He and his headmen immediately rode through twenty degree weather for a two-day visit with the new commander, to assure him that he and his people would obey orders. He found the bearded Sumner friendly and congenial, a man who understood and sympathized with Indians despite his years as a cavalry commander on the plains. Sumner was equally impressed with the broad-faced Big Foot and his headmen. "Without exception," he reported, "they seemed not only willing but anxious to obey my order to remain quietly at home, and particularly wished me to inform my superiors that they were on the side of the government in the current troubles."

Over the next ten days the two had frequent visits, and Sumner became increasingly convinced that Big Foot was cooperative and trustworthy. His visits to Big Foot's village, however, made him aware that many of the scowling young men were restless and unruly, and he was the more impressed by Big Foot's ability to control them. It was, he knew, far better to leave Big Foot in charge of them than to try to arrest and disarm them, especially without a larger force.

Shortly before mid-December, three Oglalas brought Big Foot an invitation from their chiefs, including Red Cloud, No Water, and Big Road, to come to Pine Ridge to make peace between quarrelling factions. They wanted him to leave at once, and they promised him 100 ponies for his services. Big Foot's headmen urged him to accept, but he said they would go to the agency for rations and to collect their annuities on December 22. After that he would decide.

On December 15, the same day the Indian police killed Sitting Bull on the Grand River, Big Foot informed Sumner that he was taking his people to the agency for rations and annuities. They spent the next day preparing for the ninety-mile journey. On the 17th, the day they set out, a rider from Fort Meade brought Sumner a disturbing wire from Gen. Ruger in St. Paul. "It is desirable that Big Foot be arrested, and if it had been practicable to send Capt. Wells with his two troops, orders would have been given you to try to get him. In case of arrest, he will be sent to Fort Meade and be securely kept prisoner."

Sumner reread the message several times. It was not a direct order to arrest Big Foot, but it was clear that Ruger wanted the arrest made and expected Sumner to make it. Giving Big Foot ample time to be well on his way, Sumner replied to Ruger: "I thought it best to allow him to go to Bennett a free man, and so informed the division commander by telegraph." His wire to Miles had stated that Big Foot was on his way to the agency for annuities. "If he should return I will try to arrest him; if he does not, he can be arrested at Bennett."

Bad news followed, for Sumner's scouts reported that parties of Hunkpapas were descending Cherry Creek, probably to visit the Miniconjus along the Cheyenne River. The scouts suspected that other Hunkpapas were traveling south on trails farther west, dangerously close to white settlements in the Black Hills. They didn't know what had caused the exodus from Standing Rock, but it undoubtedly had to do with the Ghost Dance.

Cursing softly, Sumner pondered his options. If he marched to protect the settlements, he would be held responsible for allowing the Hunkpapas to unite with Big Foot's restless warriors, which might lead to trouble. If he moved to intercept the Hunkpapas on Cherry Creek while others struck the settlements... He shuddered at the thought, and for a day took no action.

Pawnee Killer had joined in the attack on the Standing Rock police and had seen Sitting Bull fall. When the troops drove Sitting Bull's people away, he had ridden a mile to the cabin that he and Scarlet Robe shared with others. Hastily gathering food and blankets, they rode south toward Hump's village, the nearest of the Miniconju settlements, ninety miles away on Cherry Creek. Scattered groups of Hunkpapas were heading in the same direction, some in wagons, some on horseback, others on foot with only the clothes they'd worn that morning. The country was rough and the water was alkaline, but the weather remained fair and the nights barely below freezing.

As he rode, Pawnee Killer wondered which way to turn. Hump's and Big Foot's bands were still dancing, he supposed, and Short Bull and Kicking Bear probably were holding out in the Stronghold. Hump, he knew, had scouted for the army in '77, which made him suspect, but the burly Big Foot was an old friend from the war of '70. If Hump was unwilling to take his people to the Stronghold, perhaps Big Foot and his Ghost Dancers would go there before he suffered the same fate as Sitting Bull.

When Pawnee Killer, Scarlet Robe, and about 200 Hunkpapas reached Hump's village they found it deserted except for the eighty zealous Miniconju dancers, who told a shocking story. Ten days ago, they said, two army officers had appeared, one an old friend of Hump. He had told Hump that Bearcoat Miles wanted him to stop dancing and bring his people to the agency. Hump had immediately agreed, and most of the band had gone with him. For all they knew, Hump might again be helping the army, this time in stopping the Ghost Dance and preventing the new world from coming.

The Hunkpapa refugees were dismayed, but most were too weary to react. Soon, they were sure, Hump would arrive with troops. Most were resigned to whatever fate awaited them.

Big Foot and his people set out for the agency on the 17th and camped that night twenty miles downriver, across from James Cavanaugh's trading post. Early the following morning, two Hunkpapas, one wounded, came to his tipi to tell him about the killing of Sitting Bull. Big Foot came out after a few minutes and told his people there had been a big fight at Grand River and the Indian police and troops had treacherously killed Sitting Bull. His followers had scattered and were fleeing to the Miniconju camps on the Cheyenne. Big Foot's people were confused and terrified. They were on their way to Fort Bennett, but now they hesitated, not trusting the whites or knowing what they might do to them. Instead of moving on, they remained in camp all day, speculating wildly about what might happen next. Yellow Bird kept them agitated by warning them in his high-pitched voice never to trust the Wasicuns.

On the 19th they crossed the river to camp near Cavanaugh's post, where there was more grass for their ponies. The day was clear and warm, so they resumed dancing. All were armed, and to Cavanaugh and his two grown sons they appeared hostile, ready to fight. When several came to the post and told him they were hungry, Cavanaugh nervously gave them a generous supply of provisions. As soon as they left he barred the door, and with his sons headed upriver, where they soon met a cavalry patrol east of Camp Cheyenne. Cavanaugh sent word to Sumner that the Miniconjus had robbed him and that Standing Rock refugees were at Hump's village. Sumner and his entire command marched toward Cherry Creek.

Word of the Sitting Bull fight and the flight of his followers had reached the Cheyenne River Agency. Col. H. C. Merriam, Seventh Infantry, had finally crossed the ice-blocked Missouri, and had been ordered to march up the Cheyenne and unite with Sumner. Merriam considered the order unwise, for Big Foot might consider it a hostile movement. He called on Capt. J. H. Hurst, commander at Fort Bennett, to dispatch an officer to assure Big Foot's people they were in no danger. Hurst sent Lt. Harry Hale along with Hump and some of his men, a policeman, and a guide. They reached Cheyenne City on the evening of the 18th and found it deserted except for old Henry Angell. The previous day, he explained, reports of hostile Hunkpapas approaching had stampeded all of the settlers. Having seen no sign of hostility, the crusty old man believed his eyes rather than his ears, and refused to leave. Hale sent the policeman to Sumner with the news, then ordered the guide to visit Hump's village to learn what he could about the Hunkpapa refugees.

The guide hadn't returned by noon on the 20th, and Hale was preparing to set out after him when Hump saw horsemen approaching—a party of forty-six of Sitting Bull's warriors, among them Pawnee Killer. None showed any sign of hostility, but unfortunately for Hale, he had no interpreter to instruct them to continue on to the agency.

Henry Angell rode up and offered to help, for he knew enough of the sign language to make himself understood. He informed the

Hunkpapas that if they would remain where they were, Hale would hurry to the agency and return with Capt. Hurst and an interpreter. Then Hale had him kill a steer for them, and they agreed to stay. Although he hadn't found Big Foot, Hale feared that the Hunkpapas might join his people. He covered the fifty miles to the agency in under seven hours.

On learning that other Hunkpapa refugees were nearby, Big Foot sent ten men to invite them to his village, where he would give them food and clothing. On the 20th his men found the women huddling miserably around a fire. The men, they said, were across the river waiting for Lt. Hale to return. Big Foot's men crossed the river and found Hump urging the Hunkpapas to surrender.

When Big Foot's emissaries explained their reason for coming, Hump was furious. "You don't have to take them to Big Foot's camp," he roared. "I'll take these people to the agency. If you men want to fight, I'll bring you some infantry to help you," he added sarcastically. At his signal, his men surrounded them with cocked rifles. No shot was fired, for Pawnee Killer and the Hunkpapas informed Hump that if he attacked Big Foot's men he'd have to fight them as well. Hump called off his warriors; Pawnee Killer, Scarlet Robe, and thirty-six Hunkpapas as well as thirty of Hump's Ghost Dancers left to join Big Foot. The remaining 166 Hunkpapas and fifty of the Miniconjus stayed to see what Capt. Hurst proposed. He and Hale, with a sergeant and interpreters, reached Cheyenne City late on the 21st.

After having two steers butchered for the hungry refugees, Hurst urged them to give up their guns and accompany him to Fort Bennett, where their needs would be supplied, although he could make no promise as to their future. But if they joined Big Foot's band, he warned them, they risked serious trouble for themselves and their families. No warrior felt safe among whites without his weapons, but after talking it over, that night they surrendered their guns, and in the morning set out for Bennett with Hurst and Hump.

Col. Sumner and his troops had camped on the ranch of mixed blood Narcisse Narcelle on the southwest corner of the reservation on December 20. That same day Big Foot had sent a message to Sumner saying he was his friend and wanted to see him. In the morning Big Foot and two Hunkpapas rode ahead of the rest to find Sumner, who was riding ahead of his troops, looking for Big Foot.

The two sat down to smoke and talk. Sumner criticized Big Foot for allowing the Standing Rock refugees to join him. "You should have sent them to me at Camp Cheyenne," he said.

"They are relatives and brothers who came to us naked and hungry," Big Foot explained, "and no one with any heart could have done less. How could we refuse to help them?" Sumner had to agree.

"The Standing Rock Indians with Big Foot answered the description perfectly," he said later, "and were, in fact, so pitiable a sight that I at once dropped all thought of their being hostile or even worthy of capture. Still, my orders were to take them and I intended doing so."

The troops and Big Foot's band camped that night at Narcelle's ranch, with units stationed around the Indians. Sumner had a head count made—there were 333 men, women, and children, among them the Standing Rock people, including fourteen warriors. Sumner informed Big Foot they were to continue on to Camp Cheyenne the next day, and his people were not to stop when they passed through their own village. Big Foot agreed.

Having learned of Merriam's approach, Big Foot's people were already nervous, and being surrounded by troops that night didn't calm their fears. In the morning Sumner had them divided into three groups, each accompanied by cavalrymen, for the march to Camp Cheyenne. The Indians were still agitated, and some of the young warriors were ominously painted and carrying their rifles as if they expected trouble.

The first section and its cavalry escort passed through the gate of Narcelle's ranch, but a wagon in the second group caught a wheel on a gate post. The excited women tried to get it loose but got the ponies tangled up in their harness. When an officer rode up and gruffly ordered them to stop blocking the gate, he frightened them even more. At that, Black Fox, Big Foot's surly son-in-law, swung his rifle toward the officer, who backed off.

All of this greatly aroused the warriors, who dashed about in confusion, howling and waving their Winchesters. When the gate was finally cleared they raced through it and along the first section as if they were leaving. The terrified women threw their belongings out of the wagons to lighten them, and prepared to flee. Lt. Duffy, whose troops led the way, spread them out in a skirmish line and forced the warriors back into the column. Big Foot, at Sumner's request, sent his headmen to calm his people; order was restored, but all were on edge, still expecting trouble. That day Big Foot was coming down with influenza, which had spread among the Miniconjus, and he was sick and feverish.

After crossing the river the cavalcade approached Big Foot's village, when the warriors again raced forward. Sumner, fearing a fight was imminent, ordered Duffy to let them pass. Every family now rushed to its own cabin and barred the door. Big Foot hurried to Sumner. "I will go to your camp," he said, "but there will be trouble if you try to force these women and children to leave their cabins. This is their home, where the government ordered them to remain. None of my people has committed a single act that would cause you to remove them by force." Sumner knew he was right; and since Big foot had always kept his word, he felt that he should show that he trusted him.

As he reported later, "I concluded that one of two things must happen. I must either consent to their going to their village or bring on a fight; and if the latter, must be the aggressor, and, if the aggressor, what possible reason could I produce for making an attack on peaceable, quiet Indians on their reservation and in their own homes, perhaps killing many of them and offering, without any justification, the lives of many officers and enlisted men?"

Because Big Foot was needed in his village to control his unruly young men, Sumner allowed him to remain with his people. He asked only that Big Foot come to Camp Cheyenne next day to talk and to bring the Hunkpapas with him. Big Foot agreed, and Sumner withdrew with his troops to his base camp.

After learning that Big Foot intended to take them to Camp Cheyenne the following day, the Hunkpapas held council. "Big Foot promised we would come peacefully," one said. "We must do it."

"No!" said another. "They'll kill us like they did Sitting Bull." They argued while Pawnee Killer listened. Since he wasn't a

Hunkpapa, he knew he could stay with Big Foot. The Hunkpapas finally asked his opinion.

"Big Foot took us in and fed us when we were starving," he told them. "It isn't right for us to abandon him now and make trouble for him. He says he trusts Col. Sumner." The Hunkpapas frowned. "My brothers," Pawnee Killer continued, "I don't know what I would do if he told me I had to surrender to the soldiers. It is something each man must decide for himself. Big Foot is sick, and I intend to stay with him." The Hunkpapas slipped away during the night.

That same night a weary courier from Fort Meade brought Sumner a message from Miles, who was now directing the campaign from Rapid City, South Dakota. "I think you had better push on rapidly with your prisoners to Ft. Meade, and be careful they do not escape, and look out for other Indians." Sumner glumly replied: "Did not succeed in getting Indians to come to my camp on account of want of shelter for women and children. Did not feel authorized to compel them by force to leave their reservation." He added that if Big Foot failed to come to his camp the following day as promised, he would seize him.

He waited anxiously the next morning for Big Foot to appear, and finally sent two scouts to his village to report. By noon neither Big Foot nor the scouts had come, and Sumner was in a quandary. There was still a possibility that hostiles were approaching from the north. And if he arrested Big Foot, as he supposedly had already done, in the ensuing fight most of the Miniconjus might scatter, join the hostiles, and launch an indiscriminate war on whites. His only hope was to persuade Big Foot to take his people to the agency. "All thought of these Indians going south had been abandoned by me," he admitted later, "and I supposed they would either go peaceably to the agency or fight."

While Sumner pondered what to do, a red-bearded rancher named John Dunne, who lived a few miles away in the ceded lands, came to camp with butter and eggs to sell. Redbeard, as the Indians called him, was fluent in Lakota and well acquainted with Big Foot. He reluctantly agreed to visit the Miniconju village along with interpreter Felix Benoit, and to convey Sumner's order to Big Foot to take his band to the agency. He was also to tell him that Sumner would be following to make sure his order was obeyed. Sumner and his cavalry followed at a distance and halted five miles from Big Foot's cabins to bivouac.

At the village, Benoit stopped to question Sumner's scouts about why Big Foot had failed to come, while Dunne went on alone to Big Foot's cabin. The Hunkpapas had left during the night, the scouts told him. Big Foot was sick and also embarrassed to face Sumner.

Dunne delivered Sumner's orders to Big Foot. According to what the Miniconjus said later, he also told him he'd overheard the officers at Camp Cheyenne say they were going to send 1000 soldiers into Big Foot's village at night. They would seize all of them and then send the men far away to the east where they'd be held on an island. The only way to prevent a fight was to flee immediately to Pine Ridge. Big Foot protested, but Dunne insisted. He was telling them this because he was their friend, he said but they must not tell Sumner he had warned them, for he would be angry.

Benoit found a noisy crowd of warriors in front of Big Foot's cabin. The chief quieted them. "I'm ordered to go down to Fort Bennett tomorrow morning," he told them. "We must all go to Bennett; if we don't Redbeard says the soldiers will come tomorrow and make us go or shoot us if they have to." He turned to Benoit. "Does Redbeard tell the truth?" he asked.

"Yes."

As soon as the scouts, Dunne, and Benoit departed, leaving a scout to watch the village, Big Foot and his headmen held a hasty council. "We must go to the agency," some said.

"No! Go to Pine Ridge!" others shouted. Big Foot hesitated. The fact that Sumner was coming from one direction and Merriam from another made Dunne's warning credible. Finally they agreed to move up Deep Creek into the hills and wait to see if soldiers came. If none appeared in three days they could return home. If troops did come after them, they could scatter and flee to the south.

The scout Benoit had left watching the village reported that the Miniconjus were excited and preparing to start for the agency at once. Sumner sent another scout to order Big Foot to remain until morning. He soon returned with the news that the Miniconjus were already on their way south. Sumner sent two scouts to follow them, while he hoped desperately they were headed for the agency. In the meantime, Big Foot's scouts had discovered that Sumner was camped only five miles from the village. They held another hasty council, for they were now convinced that Redbeard spoke with only one tongue. Over Big Foot's objections, the headmen insisted they go to Pine Ridge. He had no choice but to accompany them, although he was almost too sick to travel.

Scout His-Horse-Looking caught up with Big Foot's people traveling south along the Deep Creek Road about midnight. Warriors immediately surrounded him. "Kill him! He works for the soldiers!" they shouted. Big Foot silenced them, then spoke to the scout. "Tell my friend Sumner I'm sorry about what I've done," he apologized. "I wanted to go to Bennett, but my headmen made me go to Pine Ridge." They traveled on, moving as rapidly as possible in the blowing snow of the dark, frigid night. By early morning they had covered thirty miles, and stopped in the shelter of cliffs near the forks of the Bad River, where they rested until dawn.

In the morning of the 24th, His-Horse-Looking rode into Camp Cheyenne with the unwelcome news. Sumner glumly inspected the deserted village. He hadn't heard further reports of hostile Indians in the north, but he couldn't help worrying about them, since everything else was going wrong for him. Still unsure what he should do, and seeing his military career hanging in the balance, he took his troops back to Camp Cheyenne. A rider soon arrived with a message Miles had sent the previous day.

"Report about hostile Indians on Little Missouri not believed," it said. "The attitude of Big Foot has been defiant and hostile, and you are authorized to arrest him or any of his people and take them to Meade or Bennett. There are some 30 young warriors that ran away from Hump's camp without authority, and if an opportunity is given they will undoubtedly join those in the Bad Lands. The Standing Rock Indians also have no right to be there and they should be arrested. The division commander directs, therefore, that you secure Big Foot and the Cheyenne River Indians, and the Standing Rock Indians, and if necessary round up the whole camp and disarm them, and take them to Fort Meade or Bennett."

When he learned that Big Foot had escaped and fled south Miles was outraged at him and at Col. Sumner, and bombarded his field commanders with orders. Unaware of the circumstances surrounding Big Foot's hasty flight, Miles wanted to subject Sumner to a court of inquiry. Sumner was spared that ordeal because he hadn't actually received a direct order to arrest Big Foot until December 24, by which time he was already on his way to Pine Ridge.

Fear of what might happen if Big Foot and his renegades joined the diehard Ghost Dancers in the Stronghold just as efforts were being made to persuade them to surrender generated an all-out campaign to track them down. Col. Eugene Carr of the Sixth Cavalry, a bearded veteran Indian fighter whose base camp was at the mouth of Rapid Creek, appeared to be in the best position to intercept the fugitives. On the morning of the 24th a message from Sumner informed him that Big Foot's band was moving south, and that by a forced march to the east he could cut off their escape. With four troops of cavalry and two Hotchkiss guns, Carr headed east at a trot, dividing his force to cover more territory. By late afternoon they were on the northern rim of the Badlands, where they spent a miserable Christmas Eve in weather so cold the pools of alkaline water froze solid. A wide reconnaissance on Christmas Day convinced Carr that his prey had already passed to the east of his troops; he called in his patrols and returned to his base camp.

Early on the 24th Big Foot's weary people resumed their flight. The sky was clear, but an icy gale blew clouds of choking alkali dust in their faces making travel almost impossible. Even though Big Foot was too weak to ride and had to be carried in a wagon, he kept his people moving. Late in the afternoon they made the difficult descent of the rocky slope from the Badlands to the White River and camped on the south bank. They were only a few miles from one of Carr's patrols before it was ordered back to camp. By now Big Foot was suffering from pneumonia, and they traveled only four miles on the 25th, while Carr scoured the country to the north. Big Foot sent three young men to Pine Ridge to inform the chiefs that he was seriously ill and came in peace.

Major Guy Henry and a force of Ninth Cavalry from Pine Ridge now guarded the eastern trail to the Stronghold, where 500 friendly Oglalas had spent a week pressuring Short Bull's followers to accompany them to the agency. In the evening of the 27th, Henry's scouts reported that the Ghost Dancers had loaded their wagons and started across the plateau, apparently on their way to Pine Ridge.

On learning that Big Foot was south of the White River and heading for the agency, Brooke dispatched four troops of the Seventh Cavalry under Apache fighter Major Samuel Whitside to intercept him. "I do not think there will be any mistake made with Big Foot if we get him," he grimly wired Miles of the 25th. "My orders to Whitside are to dismount him and destroy his arms and hold him."

"Big Foot is cunning and his Indians are very bad," Miles warned him the same day. "I hope you will round up the whole body of them, disarm them and keep them under close guard." Shortly afterward he wired again. "I have no doubt your orders are all right, but I shall be exceedingly anxious until I know they are executed; whoever secures that body of Indians will be entitled to much credit. They deceived Sumner completely, and if they get a chance they will scatter through the entire Sioux camp or slip out individually."

On the night of December 26 Whitside's force camped near Louis Mousseau's trading post, where the Rosebud–Pine Ridge trail crossed Wounded Knee Creek, and he sent out Oglala scouts the next morning. He then had heliographs set up between his camp and Pine Ridge in order to flash messsages quickly to Gen. Brooke. He soon heard from Brooke. "I am directed by the commanding general to say that he thinks Big Foot's party must be in front of you somewhere, and that you must make every effort to find him at once. A solution must be reached at the earliest possible moment. Find his trail, or find his hiding place and capture him. If he fights destroy him."

Big Foot was worse that morning, and travel for him was agonizing. One of his messengers returned from Pine Ridge to inform him that cavalry troops were on Wounded Knee Creek and were looking for him. Another messenger, Bear-Comes-and-Lies, accompanied by an Oglala named Shaggy Feather, rode into camp a short time later. "Short Bull's people are coming in from the Badlands," they told Big Foot. "They will reach the agency in two days. Short Bull and Kicking Bear want you to arrive there the same day." The Pine Ridge chiefs, they said, urged him to make a big swing to the south to evade the troops on Wounded Knee Creek.

Big Foot and his headmen held council and talked most of the morning. The headmen argued in favor of making the detour to the south to get around the troops, but this time Big Foot finally prevailed. "I am too sick for unnecessary travel. We must go straight to Pine Ridge before I die." They set out at noon, and that night continued by moonlight until they reached the abandoned cabins of Little Wound's village. They were now one day's travel from Pine Ridge.

At sunrise, knowing that troops were between them and the agency, they nervously pushed on, expecting at any moment to be attacked. Pawnee Killer and other warriors rode ahead to watch for troops. They had gone only a few miles when a young Brulé wearing a Ghost Shirt overtook them and joined the party. The warriors eyed him suspiciously. In a Ghost Shirt he obviously wasn't an army scout, so they ignored him.

Chapter Fifteen

News of Sitting Bull's death alarmed the former Ghost Dancers at Pine Ridge; even the friendlies were apprehensive, because so many troops were still around them. Past experience had taught them that whenever soldiers had come it was to fight. They wondered if the troops were merely waiting until most of them were disarmed and in one place, where they could easily be attacked, and that troubling thought kept them nervous and magnified every little incident. The rumors that Sitting Bull had been killed through treachery intensified their suspicions.

On December 22 a cavalry patrol intercepted a party of Oglalas and Brulés driving a big pony herd toward the Badlands. The troops fired on them, wounded several, and drove them back to the agency, where their fury and agitation infected others. That same day, while all of the Indians at Pine Ridge were seething and the Ghost Dance believers still hoped for the Messiah to come, a mysterious white man dressed like an Indian and wrapped in a white blanket appeared in Red Cloud's camp. He was an Iowan named Hopkins, but he announced that he was the new Messiah, which greatly increased the excitement.

Hopkins had gained notoriety by proclaiming a new religion called the Star Pansy Banner and by advocating that the pansy be named the national flower. Confused by countless rumors and eager to believe the Messiah was coming at last, some of the Indians accepted him at his word, but the majority rightly regarded him as deranged. Those who believed his tale crowded around him, while many who considered him a dangerous imposter tried to get their hands on him to remove him. There was much shouting and reckless brandishing of cocked rifles, and they were dangerously close to violence. Finally a group of level-headed fullbloods, mixed bloods, and squawmen managed to drag him away before he was torn apart, then took him to Red Cloud.

After questioning Hopkins through an interpreter, Red Cloud concluded he was mentally unbalanced. "You go home," he said. "You're no son of God."

One of the squawmen who'd risked his life to get Hopkins to safety described him more explicitly and with greater feeling. "You're a Goddam son-of-a-bitch!" he said.

When taken to Royer, Hopkins blandly informed him, "I claim to be Christ, the Messiah, in a poetic sense, the same poetic sense in which Hiawatha, Socrates, and General Grant are considered esteemed the world over."

"Prove you're Christ," Royer told him.

"Give me more time among these Indians and I will," Hopkins replied.

Royer frowned. "I'll give you one hour to get off the reservation." He summoned the Indian police. "Keep him out of sight until dark, then take him to Rushville and put him on a train," he instructed them.

The excitement continued to rise that night, and early in the morning many of the Brulés and Oglalas who had been persuaded to leave the Ghost Dance camp panicked. They fled to the Stronghold, Kicking Bear among them.

After Two Strike and the other Brulés and Oglalas had deserted the Ghost Dance camp on the Stronghold, the 200 remaining with Short Bull danced almost continuously in their feverish efforts to bring the Messiah. Billy felt exhausted and dazed, but each day was sure the Messiah would come on the next. Like the others, he still believed the star's promise to Short Bull that if his people went to the Stronghold and danced, the Messiah would soon appear. At first he couldn't even consider the possibility that there was no Indian Messiah, but that suspicion gradually intruded.

He also began to have doubts about Short Bull and Kicking Bear.

Were they really holy men, blessed with certain powers denied to ordinary people? Or were they ordinary men who thought they had, or pretended they had, solved the Great Mystery and set themselves apart from and above other men? It was troubling, and the longer the Messiah failed to appear the greater his doubts about them grew. *It looks like Culver was right all along. It's just an illusion.* He still wore the Ghost Shirt Short Bull had given him, but only from habit. After learning of Porcupine's failed experiment he no longer believed in its supernatural powers.

Less than a week after Two Strike and the others had departed, the scouts reported that 500 Brulés and Oglalas were on their way to the Stronghold. When Brooke had learned that Two Strike's people were coming in he asked Oglala friendlies to join them, return to the Ghost Dance camp, and persuade the remaining dancers to give up. Many of them, eager to have peace restored so the army would leave, wholeheartedly joined the effort to end the dancing.

Billy was surprised one day to see the tall, rawboned Kicking Bear ride into camp with a large number of former Ghost Dancers. Kicking Bear didn't resume the dance, but instead raised a raiding party and headed west on a trail across the plateau toward the Black Hills, to attack white settlers there. The next day they ran into a party of Cheyenne scouts who were guarding approaches to the settlements and who drove them back to the Stronghold.

The 500 friendlies obviously intended to remain until all of the Ghost Dancers agreed to abandon the Stronghold and return to the agency. Billy noticed that each day more men were won over and gave up the dance—only a small group of the most fanatical still danced, and even they appeared to be wavering. Short Bull and Mash-the-Kettle continued to harangue their remaining followers, but Billy could see they were losing ground. *It's only a matter of time, perhaps a few days, before all give up,* he thought. *How will I face Culver now?*

The Hunkpapas who'd deserted Big Foot arrived unexpectedly, and repeated the story of Sitting Bull's death. Although the Ghost Dance diehards had learned of it from the Pine Ridge Indians, hearing the details by participants aroused them to a frenzy, for they saw the same thing happening to themselves if they surrendered.

Knowing his father had been with Sitting Bull and fearing he might have been killed, Billy approached Black Badger, one of the Hunkpapas. "Do you know where Pawnee Killer is?" he asked anxiously. "He's still alive, isn't he?"

Black Badger nodded. "He came south with us. When Big Foot promised to turn us over to the soldiers, we slipped away. Big Foot is sick, and Pawnee Killer refused to leave him. The last we heard they started for Pine Ridge the next day and should be across the White River by now."

Billy pondered that. It was clear the Ghost Dance would soon end and that the Indian Messiah would never appear. Now all that mattered was for his father to recognize him as his son. That yearning had been almost forgotten from time to time in the excitement of the Ghost Dance, but it had never been far from his thoughts. If the Messiah had come, as promised, he and his father would have been quickly reunited, but that was not to be. I must find him, he thought, before it's too late. After that I don't care what happens.

He rolled up his blankets, packed enough cooked beef to last a few days, and caught his thin pony. As he rode out of the big camp Short Bull saw him.

"Where are you going?" the sharp-faced medicine man asked. "You're not deserting me like the others?"

"I've got to find my father. That's the only thing that matters to me now." Short Bull frowned but said nothing more as Billy headed for the land bridge and left the Stronghold.

After searching for a half day he found where Big Foot's wagons had come down the slope, and at dark stopped where his people had camped several days earlier. He hurried along their trail in the morning, passing two other camps not far apart, and he was greatly relieved to see they were traveling slowly. At dark, when he rolled up in his blankets not far from Little Wound's village, he smelled the smoke from their fires and was elated to know he would overtake them in the morning.

At dawn Billy arose and followed the wagon tracks into Little Wound's village. His heart beat faster as he saw thin spirals of smoke still rising from the chimneys of the abandoned cabins. Still wearing his Ghost Shirt, he trotted after the Miniconjus, and in few miles caught up with the rear wagons escorted by sullen warriors who saw his Ghost Shirt and let him pass. He continued riding past the wagons until he saw his mother in one.

Scarlet Robe gazed at him sorrowfully. "My son, soldiers are looking for us and must soon find us. I have a bad feeling that something terrible will happen, and I'm afraid for your father. Protect him from harm if you can." He nodded and rode on, wondering what terrible thing was in store for them. Perhaps the soldiers would attack them on sight and refuse to allow them to surrender. He looked for his father, but Pawnee Killer was with the scouts riding ahead of the wagons.

In the lead wagon he saw Big Foot, his burly form wrapped in blankets, his nose bleeding, his face contorted with pain caused by the jolting wagon. The column moved steadily on despite Big Foot's discomfort, and before noon crossed the divide between American Horse Creek and Porcupine Tail Creek. As they were descending Pawnee Killer and other warriors rode up to Big Foot's wagon with four captives—the famous mixed blood scout Little Bat, Old Hand, and two other Oglalas, the scouts Major Whitside had sent out that morning from his camp on Wounded Knee Creek. While his people stopped to eat at Porcupine Tail Creek, Big Foot sent Old Hand and another Oglala to tell Whitside he was bringing his people to the soldiers' camp.

When interpreter John Shangreau relayed Old Hand's message to him, Major Whitside ordered his bugler to sound "Boots and Saddles." "But Major," Shangreau interposed, "Big Foot told them he was coming to the camp, and we may as well wait for him here."

Whitside reminded him that Major Henry's column was searching for Big Foot somewhere to the north, and there was danger the two might clash. "And don't forget," he added, "that Big Foot told Colonel Sumner the same thing before he struck out. We can't take any more chances."

The sun was directly overhead in the cloudless sky when Whitside set out with his four cavalry troops, two Hotchkiss guns, and an army ambulance, moving at a trot. In two hours they reached Pine Creek, which made its way between pine-covered hills below

Porcupine Butte. Over the next divide was Porcupine Tail Creek, where Old Hand had left the Miniconjus. Two horsemen suddenly topped the distant ridge and galloped down the slope toward the troops—Little Bat and the other Oglala, who'd been released. As their ponies slid to a halt in front of Whitside, several Miniconjus crossed the ridge toward them nearly two miles away. Others soon followed.

"How does it look with those Indians?" Shangreau asked Little Bat.

"They look plenty tough," was the reply. "We're liable to catch it today."

The troops continued until they were nearly halfway to the advancing Indians before halting. Whitside ordered his troopers to dismount and form a skirmish line, while the horse-holders led the mounts to the rear. Then he signalled the gunners to move the Hotchkiss guns in front of the troops. The Miniconjus continued to advance, spread out in a long line, most of them carrying rifles. Several had tied up their ponies' tails as they did in the old days when preparing for battle. A few raced back and forth, holding their Winchesters aloft. A white flag hung limply from a pole attached to Big Foot's wagon. When a hundred yards away the warriors stopped, then two headmen dismounted and walked toward the troops.

Shangreau met them and accompanied them to Big Foot's wagon, which was moving through the line of warriors toward Whitside. Big Foot lay heavily wrapped in blankets, with blood dripping from his nose and freezing on the wagon bed. The nervous warriors rode around in small circles, a few of them menacingly working the levers of their Winchesters. Dewey Horn Cloud rode quietly up to the troopers, but made no threatening gesture. Instead, he leaned over and thrust two fingers into the muzzle of one of the Hotchkiss guns. When asked later why he did that, he replied, "I wanted to die right then."

Billy watched Whitside reach down to shake hands with Big Foot as the warriors crowded around the wagon. Pawnee Killer, he noticed, kept his distance from the troops, eyeing them suspiciously. Through Shangreau, Whitside informed Big Foot that he must bring his people to the army camp on Wounded Knee Creek.

"All right," Big Foot weakly replied. "I'm going there." He added that he was on his way to Pine Ridge to settle a quarrel and receive 100 ponies.

Turning to Shangreau, Whitside said, "Tell him I want their horses and guns."

Billy was shocked and Shangreau looked alarmed. "Look here, Major," he exclaimed, "if you do that there'll most likely be a fight, and if there is you'll kill all those women and children and the men will get away."

Whitside frowned. "But General Brooke's orders are to disarm and dismount them."

"That may be, major, but you'd better get them in camp and then take their guns and ponies." Whitside glanced at the scowling, well-armed warriors and knew what Shangreau said was true. "Very well," he said, "tell Big Foot to move down to the camp." Shangreau spoke to Big Foot in Lakota.

"All right," Big Foot replied. "I'm going down to the camp. I was going there anyway." He weakly shook hands again with Whitside.

Seeing that the ailing Big Foot was jolted mercilessly in the springless farm wagon, Whitside signaled for the ambulance. Troopers took hold of Big Foot's blankets, carefully lifted him out of the wagon, and then gently lowered him into the ambulance while his warriors' keen eyes watched for any sign of treachery. The blue-clad cavalrymen mounted their horses and took their positions around the Miniconjus. Two troops led the way, followed by the ambulance; then came the Indians. The other two troops and the Hotchkiss guns brought up the rear.

On the way, Whitside sent a courier ahead with a message to be flashed to Brooke, the good news that Big Foot's band, 120 men and 250 women and children, had surrendered. He also requested that Col. Forsyth bring the rest of the Seventh Cavalry to Wounded Knee Creek to help in disarming the warriors. "My object," he remarked later, "was that, by their presence, we could overawe the Indians so they would submit quickly to being disarmed. I was convinced from a hostile demonstration at the time of surrender that otherwise, trouble might ensue."

Brooke smiled in relief when he received the news of Big Foot's surrender and ordered Col. James Forsyth to prepare to march at once with the four troops of the Seventh Cavalry's First Squadron and two Hotchkiss guns. Forsyth, a popular Civil War veteran with a square chin, piercing eyes, and bushy eyebrows, had no previous experience with Indians. While he made hasty preparations, Brooke wired the welcome news to Miles, suggesting that once the Indians were disarmed they should be taken immediately to the railroad station at Gordon, Nebraska, and put on a train to Omaha.

"All right," Miles replied. "Use force enough. Congratulations."

As Forsyth's column prepared to move out late in the afternoon, Brooke issued him orders. "Disarm Big Foot's band; take every precaution to prevent the escape of any; if they fight, destroy them. After they are disarmed, Major Whitside is to hold them with the Second Squadron on Wounded Knee Creek until ordered to march them to the railroad, while you and the First Squadron return to Pine Ridge." The four troops, a company of Oglala scouts, and two Hotchkiss guns under Captain Allyn Capron, a huge man with a voice like a bull and courage enough for a hundred men, set out for Wounded Knee Creek at a trot.

Near sundown, Major Whitside and his prisoners reached the campground in the valley of Wounded Knee Creek. On the western side of the valley were two ridges separated by a dry ravine. The column passed midway between Mosseau's trading post and the ravine, where the cavalry tents were already standing in neat rows. It continued to the north edge of the ravine, where the Indians were told to set up their tipis. Whitside ordered the two guns placed on a low hill overlooking the Indian camp, and had sentinels positioned around Big Foot's people.

At the south side of the cavalry camp was a large tent for the Indian scouts and another for Miniconjus who had no shelter. Near them a wall tent with a stove to warm it was set up for Big Foot. Assistant Surgeon James Glennan immediately did what he could for the ailing chief.

Col. Forsyth and the First Squadron arrived quietly after dark, and Whitside turned over command to his superior. Capron's two Hotchkiss guns were also stationed on the hill and aimed at the Indian camp, and he assumed command of the four-gun battery.

Then the officers relaxed briefly to celebrate the taking of the wily Big Foot. Trader James Asay had followed the troops in his wagon and had thoughtfully brought a small keg of whiskey.

There was no celebrating in the Indian camp that night and not much sleep. Forsyth had tried to slip into camp unnoticed, but Oglala scouts had called to their Miniconju friends that the rest of Long Hair Custer's old regiment had arrived. Big Foot and some of the older warriors had helped wipe out half of that regiment in '76, and they couldn't help wonder if the Seventh's troopers still thirsted for vengeance. They slept fitfully, and they weren't eager for day to come.

At reveille on that chilly morning of December 29, Forsyth's command numbered 438 officers and men, not counting the twenty artillerymen and two officers who manned the rapid-fire Hotchkiss guns. Six troop commanders were veterans who had served under Custer. Few of the soldiers, on the other hand, had ever heard a gun fired in anger, and nearly one-fifth were recent recruits whose only knowledge of Indians was from tales they'd heard of treachery and massacre. Also present were Father Francis Craft and three reporters from Nebraska newspapers. The weather was fair, although two days earlier Yellow Bird had predicted a blizzard within three days.

Because the 120 warriors were so badly outnumbered that any resistance would be suicidal, Forsyth and his officers were confident the Indians would quietly submit to being disarmed. After reveille the troops distributed bacon and hardtack among the Indians, and soon the aroma of frying bacon floated over their camp. Billy ate halfheartedly, for he knew the Miniconjus were to be disarmed, and he couldn't dispel the feeling of impending disaster his mother predicted. Pawnee Killer was talking with the older warriors, while Scarlet Robe squatted near a fire with other women. Billy approached her. "Does my father know I'm his son?" he asked.

"He may, but I'm not sure."

"Tell him, then. I have a strange feeling, and I want him to know as soon as possible." She nodded.

At seven the bugler sounded "Officers Call," and Forsyth gave each troop commander his orders. The warriors were to assemble in front of Big Foot's tent, where they would be surrounded by a square of dismounted troops. Farther back, prepared to cut off any attempt to escape, would be the mounted troops. While the soldiers moved into position, Shangreau walked to the Indian camp, and soon Wounded Hand, the camp crier, was passing among the tipis calling the men to a council with Forsyth. Knowing that many more troopers of the Seventh had arrived during the night, the Miniconjus were apprehensive. Most were anxious to hear what the soldier chief had to say so they could be on the trail to Pine Ridge. As they headed for the square, their children played among the tipis, while the women appeared relieved the flight was finally over.

Lt. Harry Hawthorne, who was near the artillery on the hill overlooking the Indian camp, watched the troops form a square in front of Big Foot's tent below and was puzzled. If a fight broke out, the troopers on opposite sides of the square would have to shoot directly at each other if they opened fire on the Indians between them. "Isn't that a rather strange formation of troops in case there's trouble?" he asked Capt. Ilsley.

The captain laughed. "There's no possibility of trouble that I can see. Big Foot wants to go to the agency, and we're a guard of honor to escort him."

The warriors, many wearing Ghost Shirts under their blankets, began gathering in the square as ordered, but some of them nervously paced back and forth between Big Foot's tent and their own tipis. Finally Forsyth ordered Shangreau to tell them to sit down and listen. Billy squatted nervously among the others, then noticed that Pawnee Killer was staring at him. *I wonder if at last he knows I'm his son and is ready to accept me.*

Through Shangreau, Forsyth explained in a friendly manner that to avoid the possibility of trouble it was necessary to ask them for their guns. Billy sensed a wave of shock and resentment that immediately spread through the young warriors. Forsyth assured them that without their guns they would be perfectly safe in the hands of their friends the soldiers, and that hunger and their other troubles were now happily over. The warriors glanced at one another, their expressionless faces concealing their anger. None had anticipated having to surrender his weapons. In every warrior's head was the vision of soldiers taking their guns and then shooting them down as they tried to flee.

The headmen and leading warriors now began talking rapidly about what they must do. Finally two of them entered Big Foot's tent to explain what the soldier chief demanded and to ask his advice. Shangreau accompanied them and heard Big Foot tell them to give up their bad guns and keep the good ones. Because of the rumor that Sitting Bull had been slain through treachery, he didn't trust the troops enough to allow his people to surrender their weapons. Still, he had no wish for a fight.

"Better give up all your guns," Shangreau advised Big Foot. "You can always buy more guns, but if you lose a man you can't replace him."

"No," Big Foot replied. "We will keep the good guns." Shangreau shook his head, while the two men left to tell the others what Big Foot advised.

When the two had entered the tent, the medicine man Yellow Bird began capering around in a circle in front of the warriors, chanting incantations. The young men glanced at him occasionally, but most of the time their eyes were fixed on the line of soldiers facing them with carbines in their hands. They watched every move the soldiers made, like they were expecting them to open fire.

Forsyth now sent twenty men from the left side of the line to the Indian camp to bring their rifles. While they were gone the others nervously milled about, while Yellow Bird continued his gyrations. The twenty men finally returned and threw down two useless carbines, insisting they had no others. Whitside was angry.

"We'll never get them this way, that's clear," he told Forsyth. "When we met them yesterday they had plenty of new Winchesters. Let's bring out Big Foot and order him to tell them to cooperate." A hospital orderly and an Indian carried Big Foot outside the tent and stretched him out on his back facing his warriors. As he lay there weakly, his brothers-in-law Horned Cloud and Iron Eyes came forward and sat behind him. Regimental Surgeon Dr. Hoff was also beside him.

When the young warriors began milling about again, Big Foot asked to be raised so he could calm them, but his voice was too weak for them to hear. To prevent the warriors from wandering back and forth to the Indian camp and frightening the women, Forsyth had troops line up behind them. Then he had interpreter Philip Wells instruct Big Foot to order his men to hand over their weapons.

"They have no guns," Big Foot replied. "The soldiers at Cheyenne River seized all of them."

"You tell Big Foot," Whitside ordered Wells, "that yesterday, when they surrendered, they were well armed. I know he's deceiving us."

"They have no guns," Big Foot insisted. "I gathered up all my guns at the agency and gave them to the soldiers. They burned them."

Whitside and Crawford conferred again. "We'll have to send details to search their camp," Whitside said. Forsyth sent two officers and fifteen men to begin searching the tipis at the east end of the camp and others to start at the west end. To avoid frightening the women unnecessarily, only the officers entered the tipis, while the soldiers searched the wagons. Shangreau accompanied one group and Little Bat went with the other. As they began the search under Whitside's supervision, he ordered the troops in the square to move a few paces closer to the Indians, which made them even more apprehensive.

It was a difficult search, for the women had skillfully concealed the guns; some were sitting on them and had to be lifted to one side. Gradually, however, the officers and men built up a pile of guns, hatchets, and knives—anything that could serve as a weapon. When they saw the guns carried away, the women wailed.

While the slow search went on, the Miniconju men became even more agitated, and the troops were as nervous as the Indians. Yellow Bird was still dancing and chanting in front of the warriors, but he finally stopped and began shrilly haranguing them. "Don't be afraid," he said. "Let your hearts be strong to face what is before you. There are many soldiers around you and they have lots of bullets, but I have been assured their bullets can't penetrate your shirts."

"Hau!" the warriors responded. Although the air was chilly Billy wiped sweat from his face, for he knew the Ghost Shirts couldn't stop bullets. Porcupine had proved that.

Yellow Bird began dancing and muttering again and blowing on his eagle-bone whistle as Whitside returned from the Indian camp. "Major, that man is making mischief," Wells warned him, nodding at Yellow Bird.

"Tell the colonel," Whitside replied.

Through Wells, Forsyth ordered Yellow Bird to sit down and remain quiet. "He'll sit down when he gets around the circle," Horned Cloud told Wells. Yellow Bird completed the circle and took his place among the squatting warriors. Billy glanced at his thin face and shuddered. Yellow Bird's eyes blazed with hatred, and he looked eager to fight.

After an hour the search details returned with 38 rifles, but only a few of them were good Winchesters. Billy knew that one of them was his, for he hadn't hidden it. Whitside grimly shook his head. They still had many rifles. There was only one place they could be—under their blankets. He looked over the sullen warriors, wondering how they could conceal rifles even while squatting. Searching them would be a ticklish business, for they would bitterly resent it. But would they resent it enough to fight against such over-whelming odds? He shrugged and looked at Forsyth. "They've got them under their blankets, colonel," he said. "It means we've got to search every last one of them, and if anything can touch off a fight, that's it." Forsyth nodded and gazed at the Miniconjus with piercing eyes, his bushy eyebrows twitching. "My orders are to disarm them," he said in a flat voice. "I think we should wait till they're at Pine Ridge and let the Oglala friendlies disarm them, but we can't do that." He nodded to Wells.

"Tell them I don't want to subject every man to a personal search," he said, "but they must submit to inspection. Tell them to come forward like men and remove their blankets, then throw their guns on the ground." Wells translated the order.

"Hau!" the older warriors responded. Twenty of them arose and walked toward Whitside and Forsyth, who stood in front of Big Foot's tent. While the young men remained sullenly in place, the others removed their blankets in front of the two officers. Not one of them had a gun. To Billy, the young men looked like cougars tensed to spring, their eyes on the soldiers.

At that moment Yellow Bird arose and stretched his arms westward toward the Messiah, begging him to make the Ghost Shirts strong. Then he began haranguing them again, urging them not to give up their guns. "Your Ghost Shirts will protect you," he reminded them. "Bullets can't harm you." Billy trembled, for it was clear they believed him. Hearing this the scouts shouted to the young men not to make a false move and to give up their weapons.

Whitside and Capt. Charles Varnum stood facing each other a yard apart and motioned for the young men to pass between them. From the first three they removed two rifles and emptied their cartridge belts. Yellow Bird continued haranguing the young warriors, his voice shriller than before, the young men even more agitated. "Look out!" he said. "Something bad is about to happen. I have lived long enough. It's a good day to die!" That was, Billy knew, what men said when going into battle. Wells urged Horned Cloud to silence Yellow Bird and reassure the young men they were in no danger, but the medicine man ignored him.

The rising tension, like the electric air around a lightning bolt, seemed to envelop white and Indian alike. When many of the Indians began singing their death chants, the frightened Oglala scouts drew back, for they knew what was coming.

Lt. Charles Mann glanced over the crowd. "I had a peculiar feeling come over me," he recalled later, "a presentiment of trouble." Billy heard him quietly warn his troopers. "Be ready," he said, "there's going to be trouble." He ordered them to fall back fifteen paces.

A Miniconju named Black Coyote, "a crazy man, a young man of very bad influence, in fact a nobody," in the words of scout Turning Hawk, took his new Winchester from under his blanket and waved it over his head. "This gun is mine!" he shouted. "It cost me much money! No one takes it without paying me for it!" Two troopers walked up behind him and grabbed him. As he brought his rifle down it fired in the air.

At that moment Yellow Bird snatched up a handful of dirt and threw it in the air, then blew on his eagle-bone whistle—the old-time signal for battle. Six young men on one end of the line leaped to their feet, threw off their blankets, and leveled their rifles at the troops facing them. Lt. W. W. Robinson, who was between the two lines, spurred his horse out of the way. "Look out, men!" he shouted. "They're going to shoot!"

Capt. Varnum spun and saw the men with rifles at their shoulders. "My God! They've broken!" he exclaimed. It seemed, Lt. Mann remembered, that the warriors appeared to hesitate for an endless moment. "I thought, the pity of it! What can they be thinking?" Revolver in hand, he moved to the front of Troop K as the Indians fired a volley and the square exploded into gunfire. "Fire! Fire!" he shouted.

B and K troops fired at the same time as the Indians. The warriors fired their repeating rifles as rapidly as they could work the levers and pull the triggers, while the soldiers replied as fast as they could reload their single-shot carbines. In seconds a cloud of smoke and dust obscured both sides; the firing was so constant it sounded as to some men like the tearing of heavy canvas.

Some of the troops were between the Indians and their camp, and when the warriors missed their targets their bullets sped toward the women and children, who screamed and ran. When some of the warriors ran among the tipis and continued shooting, the Hotchkiss guns, which were aimed at the Indian camp, opened fire. Exploding shells burst among the tipis, setting some on fire and striking down the terrified women and children.

At the first sound of gunfire, Big Foot pulled himself into a sitting position, then fell back against Horned Cloud with a bullet hole in his forehead. His daughter screamed and ran toward him, only to fall across his body with a bullet in her back.

The shrieking women and children fled in all directions, many of them up the ravine to the west. The hand to hand fighting between Indians and soldiers was over in little more than a minute as the surviving warriors broke through line of troops between them and the ravine, clubbing soldiers with their rifles as they tried to reload their carbines. Terrified, and deafened by the roar of gunfire, Billy raced after the warriors to the mouth of the ravine. When a warrior fell in front of him, Billy snatched up the Winchester he dropped. He was shaking so he feared his legs would fail him.

Suddenly Billy realized he was running alongside Pawnee Killer. They dashed up the ravine and around a bend, where they were shielded from the sight of the pursuing troops. Billy gasped. Blood was spreading rapidly down the side of Pawnee Killer's white Ghost Shirt. His father slowed down, then stopped. "Save yourself, my son. I can go no farther. I'll hold them off as long as I can."

Billy whirled and ran a few steps up the ravine, then stopped, his thoughts racing. *He called me his son. That's what I've waited for. I'm no longer a man on two ponies.* He turned back and knelt by his father, filling the rifle chamber with cartridges from his pouch. "You told me once it is better to die young fighting your enemies than to grow old and weak," he said. "Like Yellow Bird said, it's a good day to die." He cocked his rifle. The shouts of the soldiers came closer.

Pawnee Killer weakly turned his head and looked at Billy. "You're a real Brulé, my son," he said.

Epilogue

"If he fights, destroy him," General Brooke had ordered Forsyth when he marched to Wounded Knee to help disarm Big Foot's band. The Soldiers of the Seventh Cavalry, shocked into a blind fury by seeing their comrades fall in what they considered a treacherous attack, did their best to carry out Brooke's command. Once the battle had started, they shot at any Indian that moved. The officers shouted again and again at the pursuing troops not to kill the women, but when men and women were together and the warriors continued firing at them, the soldiers returned the fire indiscriminately. Bodies of slain women and children were found three miles away.

Near the smoke-shrouded square, Yellow Bird darted into the Oglala scouts' tent and cut a slit in it. He had shot several soldiers before others spotted his smoking rifle barrel. "I'll get the son-of-a-bitch!" a private of Troop K shouted as he ran toward the tent with knife in hand.

"Don't! Come back!" Lt. Mann bellowed, but the private cut a slash in the tent, only to catch Yellow Bird's bullet.

"My God! He's shot me! I'm killed! I'm killed!" he exclaimed, staggering a few paces toward Lt. Mann before falling. His infuriated comrades riddled the tent with bullets and set it on fire. As the tent burned to the ground they saw the charred corpse of Yellow Bird still clutching his rifle, his scorched face contorted with undying hate.

The firing into and out of the ravine finally stopped, and Wells called to the Indians: "All of you still alive come over here; you won't be shot at any more." A wounded old man farther up the ravine painfully raised himself as a mounted unit that was sweeping the ravine from the upper end appeared. Seeing the old man move, the troopers riddled him with bullets.

Forsyth, who was trying desperately to stop the killing, screamed "For God's sake stop shooting them!" One by one the wounded Indians crawled out and were carried off to the hospital area.

Wells went next to the square, where at least fifty men lay dead or wounded, and called for those still alive to raise their heads. A dozen responded. One of them, a warrior named Frog, pointed to the body of Yellow Bird. "Who is that man?" he asked. Wells told him. Frog pointed his closed fist at the grisly corpse and shot his fingers out toward it. This was the Teton's deadliest insult, meaning I could kill you and still be dissatisfied because I could do no more to you. "If I could be taken to you, I'd stab you," he growled, then turned to Wells. "He is our murderer," he said. "But for him inciting the young men we'd all be alive."

At Pine Ridge that morning the keen ears of the Indians heard the dull booming of the Hotchkiss guns fifteen miles to the east and, knowing that Big Foot's people were under attack, went wild with rage. Two Strike's warriors were aroused to action; 150 of them hastily painted their faces, mounted their ponies, and raced toward the sound of the guns. They met two cavalry troops that had gathered some Miniconju women and children and drove them off, killing one trooper. The Brulés took the women and children and rode away.

The remaining Brulés at Pine Ridge and many Oglalas struck their tipis, loaded their wagons, and despite the efforts of Brooke and Royer to calm them, fled north. Shortly after noon, the Brulé war party returned with the rescued women and children, and their tale of the killings aroused the others even more. The Brulés especially were eager to fight. A large number of them rode over a ridge southwest of the agency, which was protected by only a few companies of infantry and the Indian police, and fired at them out of rifle range.

General Brooke wisely ordered the infantry and the police not to return the fire, and thereby prevented a serious attack on the poorly defended agency. He knew that all were excited, but he was convinced that not many were actually hostile. The Brulé war party left before dark, forcing old Red Cloud to accompany them.

The Indians were kept agitated by the rumor that Big Foot's men had been disarmed and then callously attacked. The whites heard that the Miniconjus had attacked the troops and had the cavalry cut off, and they huddled in the agency buildings in terror.

Two Strike's people and the Oglalas under Little Wound, Big Road, and No Water fled down White Clay Creek and camped about fifteen miles from Pine Ridge. On the way they met Short Bull, Kicking Bear, and their followers, who were cautiously moving toward the agency, and who immediately joined them. Together they numbered about 4000, a fourth or fewer of them warriors. During the night a number of wounded men and women who had escaped from Wounded Knee straggled into the camp, and the doleful wailing of the women and the death chants of the men mingled with the howling of coyotes. Short Bull and Kicking Bear ordered that no one was to leave the camp—they would fight and die together. The aroused Brulé warriors enforced the order.

On December 29 Major Henry's black troopers of the Ninth Cavalry made a fifty-mile scout for Big Foot's band, then returned to their base camp after dark. At nine that night two Oglala scouts arrived with orders from Brooke to Henry to make a forced march to Pine Ridge to defend the agency against an expected attack. The weary troopers struck their tents, loaded the wagons, and, wrapped in their buffalo hide coats, rode the fifty miles to Pine Ridge in a light snow. They arrived at reveille and found that Forsyth and half of the Seventh Cavalry had reached the agency the previous afternoon.

At noon the same day, Forsyth and the First Squadron rode out to check on burning buildings in the vicinity of the Drexel Mission. Warriors lured them into low ground and other hostiles in the surrounding hills cut them off. In the skirmishing, Lt. Mann was fatally wounded. A courier raced to Major Henry, whose black troopers were soon in the saddle again, although their jaded mounts could barely trot. They drove the hostiles from the hills and rescued the beleagured troopers of the Seventh, who embraced their deliverers.

On December 31, Gen. Miles arrived at Pine Ridge and took charge. He immediately ordered Forsyth relieved of his command because of the Wounded Knee debacle. Despite Miles' heavy handed pressure, a court of inquiry exonerated Forsyth of culpability for the killing of women and children.

The huge hostile camp was cut off from the Stronghold by a concentration of troops to the north and west of them. Miles sent conciliatory letters to the chiefs, gently reminding them they were surrounded by a great many soldiers. Not a shot would be fired or a hand raised against them, he assured them, if they did as he directed.

The chiefs were willing to trust Bearcoat Miles, for he had never lied to them, but the Brulé followers of Short Bull and Kicking Bear refused to surrender or to allow others to leave. Day after day they quarreled bitterly in council. Finally Big Road, He Dog, Little Hawk, and Jack Red Cloud slipped away at night, and others left when they had the chance.

Two companies of Cheyenne scouts kept the hostile camp under close surveillance day and night. One company was under Lt. Edward Casey, a promising young officer who was genuinely concerned for the welfare of the Indians. His scouts frequently met and talked with men from the camp. On June 6, several of them visited Casey in his camp and encouraged him to talk to the leaders, most of whom were eager to return to Pine Ridge.

The next day Casey and two Cheyenne scouts rode up the valley and met several men from the camp. One returned, carrying a message to Red Cloud that Casey wanted to talk to him. Red Cloud replied that Casey must leave at once, for the fanatics in the camp would kill him on sight. Just as Casey received the message, two Brulés rode up and stopped to talk, a warrior named Broken Arm and Plenty Horses, a youthful Carlisle graduate. As Casey turned to ride back down the valley, Plenty Horses shot him in the back of the head.

When the influential Young-Man-Afraid-of-His-Horses returned to Pine Ridge from his long visit to the Crows, Miles sent him to the hostile camp to persuade the Indians to come to the agency. With difficulty, he induced the reluctant, tempestuous Brulés to move the camp a few miles nearer the agency. The troops to the north, now commanded by Gen. Brooke, immediately followed, which made the Brulés hesitant to move again. Miles, well aware that it was a delicate, explosive situation, ordered the troops to make no threatening gestures, but their mere presence a few miles away kept the hostiles nervous. On January 11 they finally reached the Drexel Mission, after several more short moves. They were now five miles from the agency, with the troops not far behind them. Short Bull, Kicking Bear, and most of the Brulés still preferred to die fighting rather than surrender. They continued to quarrel furiously every day.

On January 12 the Oglalas in the camp, over the threats of Brulé fanatics, moved two miles closer to the agency. The Brulés, seeing themselves alone and exposed to the nearby troops, soon struck their tipis and hurried after the others. They had hardly departed before troops bivouacked at the mission. White Tail, a Brulé chief, rode back to the soldier camp and begged Brooke not to follow them so closely. Finally, on January 15, they entered the agency and surrendered.

When asked for their guns they handed over 200 rifles without protest. Miles knew they had many more but he judiciously refrained from pressing the matter. More guns were voluntarily surrendered once the fear of a treacherous attack subsided. Symbolizing the end of the Ghost Dance affair was a meeting between Kicking Bear and Miles. The two warriors stared at each other for a few moments, then the tall Ghost Dance leader leaned over and laid his rifle at Miles' feet.

Brig. Gen. L. W. Colby of the Nebraska National Guard, who'd been at Pine Ridge as an observer, remarked: "This Indian war might be regarded as the result of a mistaken conception or misunderstanding of the Indian character and of the real situation and conditions on the reservations. The general condition of things, however, which made such misunderstanding possible, was the result of the Indian policy of the government."

Those who'd had a heavy hand in designing that ill-begotten

policy, the Friends of the Indian, met at Riggs House in Washington on January 8. News of the Wounded Knee fiasco made them angry and resentful, eager to pillory someone for wrecking their pious plans for remaking the Sioux. They sniffed at the possibility that someone might be misguided or depraved enough to charge them with being responsible for the sufferings of the Sioux. It was, they concluded, their usual whipping boys—Red Cloud and other stubborn old chiefs, and the sinister nonprogressives in general who were to blame. They ignored the fact that it was the desperate young men who'd caused the bloodshed. Roundly damning their scapegoats, Congress and the administration, lifted their spirits, and they were quickly able to look on the bright side of the tragic affair.

The Messiah craze, they happily agreed, was the last stand of the evil nonprogressives. The Sioux, they assured themselves, having learned the penalty for heeding wicked leaders, were now ready to make the instant transformation into imitation white farmers. Commissioner Morgan wholeheartedly agreed with the brethren. There was, he said, no reason to be any more despondent over Wounded Knee than over the Haymarket affair. He cheerfully quoted carefully selected and doctored Indian Office figures to show a bright future for all tribes.

On January 21, the troops at Pine Ridge held a final parade before departing the following day. While Miles watched infantry and cavalry pass in review, a blinding, suffocating sandstorm swept over the parade ground, concealing the marching columns from the Indians who nervously watched from the hills. Still not fully trusting the bluecoats, they'd taken the precaution of rounding up their ponies in case flight was necessary.

Miles departed on January 26, accompanied by twenty-five Ghost Dance leaders who were to be confined at Fort Sheridan, Illinois, until the echoes of Wounded Knee had died away and the Indian Messiah was forgotten. Buffalo Bill was preparing to take his Wild West Show on a year-long European tour, and he requested permission to take the Indians. The army was pleased at the prospect of having the troublemakers out of the country for a year, but Commissioner Morgan had a low regard for circus life and denied the request. Cody secured the help of the Nebraska congressional delegation in persuading Secretary Noble to overrule Morgan and allow the Indians to go.

Before leaving Pine Ridge, Miles arranged to have a delegation of chiefs and headmen, both progressives and nonprogressives from all the agencies, taken to Washington to present their grievances to the Secretary of the Interior and other officials. He proposed having an army officer of his choice escort them, but his arrogance and unconcealed contempt for Indian Bureau officials made them seethe with fury. Morgan persuaded the President to order the Indians escorted by civilians.

Thirty chiefs and headmen reached Washington on February 4 on a visit Miles had designed for the purpose of putting them in a happy and cooperative frame of mind. They expected leisurely discussions and opportunities to talk freely and at length, but Washington officials had more pressing concerns and their time was limited. The Indians chose Grass, American Horse, Young-Man-Afraid-of-His-Horses, Hump, and several others to speak for them, but the Secretary insisted their talks be brief. Young-Man-Afraid-of-His-Horses was able to ask some embarrassing questions, but he received no satisfactory answers. To Miles' outrage, the chiefs were sent home more discontented than before.

Miles, who regarded himself the leading expert on the Sioux and who was nearly correct, pushed his own program for them. It was far more reasonable and practical than the Indian Bureau's plans. First the government must win their confidence, and it could start by belatedly making good on the promises of the Crook Commission. On January 19, in fact, the President had already signed the hastily passed bill that had been before the House for nearly a year without action.

It was, Miles continued, patently wrong to teach Indians to support themselves by starving them. Rations should be maintained at an adequate level until the Indians could provide for their own sustenance. Since the climate and soil of Dakota prevented them from ever supporting themselves by agriculture, the farming program so dear to the Friends of the Indian and certain officials should be jettisoned in favor of stock raising. "I do not think any one thing would please those Indians more than to give each family, as far as possible, the Angus or Galloway cattle, which come nearer to their dream of the restoration of the buffalo than anything else.''

The young Brulé Plenty Horses, who killed Lt. Casey, was arrested on February 18 and taken to Fort Meade. He had no money to hire a lawyer even if he'd been inclined to raise a hand in his own defense, and the Indian Bureau had no funds for such purposes. His plight aroused the sympathy of officers like Col. Sumner, who informed the Indian Rights Association about him, and it engaged an attorney to plead his case. To the federal grand jury in Deadwood that same month, Plenty Horses explained the reason for his fatal action.

"I am an Indian,'' he said. "Five years I attended Carlisle and was educated in the ways of the white men.'' As a result, he said, both whites and Indians despised him. "I was lonely. I shot the lieutenant so I might make a place for myself among my people. Now I am one of them. I shall be hanged and the Indians will bury me as a warrior. They will be proud of me. I am satisfied.''

Since Plenty Horses had freely admitted his guilt, the grand jury had no choice but to indict him. In April he was tried in the federal district court at Sioux Falls, but the jury was unable to reach an agreement on whether the charge should be murder or manslaughter.

He was tried again in June. The judge now ruled that Plenty Horses acted as a combatant in time of war and therefore couldn't be held liable under criminal law. The jury returned a verdict of not guilty, and Plenty Horses returned to Rosebud a free man.

The Ghost Dance affair had cost the government $1,200,000. At Wounded Knee, twenty-five officers and men were killed and many more wounded. The Indian losses can never be known, for an unknown number escaped only to die of their wounds later. When the burial party reached the battlefield, the grisly scene was shrouded in a light blanket of snow brought by the storm Yellow Bird had predicted. A huge trench was dug where the Hotchkiss guns had stood, and 146 bodies—84 men and boys,

44 women, and 18 children—were interred in it. The site was known thereafter as Cemetery Hill. As anthropologist James Mooney remarked, the cost in lives and money was a significant commentary on the bad policy of breaking faith with the Indians.